Death at
Buckingham Palace

When Jane Bee decided to leave her home on Prince
Edward Island, Canada, to spend a year in Europe, she had
no idea she would find herself working as a housemaid for
the Queen of England! But life at Buckingham Palace is
certainly never dull . . . .

One morning, while tackling the sticky problem of
pink chewing gum on the Axminster carpet, Jane hears
some disturbing news. The night before, her friend Robin
Tukes, a Palace footman, was found unconscious in the
Page's Vestibule – by none other than the Queen herself.
Robin, it seems, had taken an overdose of pills and is now
recovering in hospital.

Why would fun-loving Robin try to commit suicide –
and only hours after the announcement of his engagement to housemaid Angela Cheatle? An announcement, it
has to be said, that came as a shock to everyone, particularly Robin's gay lover Karim. And just what was Robin
doing in the Page's Vestibule, only one hundred feet from
Her Majesty's bedroom, so late in the evening?

Days pass and life soon returns to normal. Until the
Queen once again stumbles on Robin's prostrate figure –
only this time he is very dead.

Jane believes he has been murdered – and so does a
Very Important Person, who asks Jane to help her
investigate . . . .

C. C. Benison

Death at Buckingham Palace

Her Majesty Investigates . . .

MACMILLAN

First published in the United Kingdom 1996 by Macmillan

an imprint of Macmillan General Books
25 Eccleston Place, London, SW1W 9NF
and Basingstoke

Associated companies throughout the world

ISBN 0 333 65666 0

1 3 5 7 9 8 6 4 2

A CIP catalogue record for this book is available from
the British Library

Phototypeset by Intype London Ltd
Printed by Mackays of Chatham PLC, Chatham, Kent

Author's Note

The treatment of the characters – both real and imaginary – in *Death at Buckingham Palace* is fictional and not in any way based on fact. The novel was researched entirely from secondary sources, of which there is an astonishing quantity and array. I know no one among the Household and Staff at Buckingham Palace – so I can truly say, as the old disclaimer goes, that any resemblance to any person living or dead is entirely coincidental.

Nan, you would have had a laugh.

Introduction

This is me (although I guess it would be more grammatical to say, 'This is I'). Maybe the best way to start would be to say, 'This is one.' That's the way the Queen talks. 'One likes to think one has done one's duty,' is the kind of thing she will say.

This is one: one's name is Jane Bee. One is twenty years old and a housemaid at Buckingham Palace.

Oh, enough of this 'one' business!

I didn't set out to become a housemaid at Buckingham Palace, or anywhere, for that matter. It just sort of happened.

I was born and raised in Canada, in Charlottetown, Prince Edward Island. My father is a staff sergeant with the Royal Canadian Mounted Police and my mother is the editor of the Charlottetown *Guardian*, the Island's morning newspaper. They met in the sixties after my father completed his police training and my mother became the first woman the newspaper ever hired as a reporter. They had three daughters. I'm the youngest. My oldest sister, Jennifer, is in her first year of residency at Grace Maternity Hospital in Halifax, Nova

Scotia. Julie, the middle one, married a potato farmer on the Island and is, as I write this, expecting my parents' first grandchild. My sisters are both settled as hell.

I'm not. After high school I spent a year working about five McJobs – store clerking, waitressing, that kind of thing – and then I spent a year in arts at the university. Being back in school was okay but I had met people with master's degrees who were doing – guess what? – store clerking and waitressing. That's the economy these days for people my age. So I decided there was no point in rushing through school, not if there were no decent jobs at the other end. I didn't have Jennifer's mind for science, anyway. Going into something technological wasn't for me. And I would never marry a potato farmer and get tied down with a bunch of kids, at least not for now.

I decided instead to spend the next year travelling around Europe. I still had money left over from my year-of-five-jobs, and I had been living at home and still working part-time while going to university. Of course, Steve and Ann – the aged parents – were not exactly chuffed about my plan. Steve, particularly. I got the usual cop view of the world in his lecture, Europe being full of murderers, rapists, terrorists, con artists, and men *with one thing on their minds* (my father's so quaint). My mother did her usual parental solidarity bit on matters concerning us children, but in private she wasn't completely unsupportive. After all, feminism had come to us with mother's milk. Mum slipped me some cash before I left.

So, in September, off I headed to Europe. Five

months later, I was broke. Who would have thought Europe was so expensive? I'd had a great time, though, and I didn't want to go back. And it was January. January in Canada is no treat. Greece in January *is* a treat – it's PartyWorld – but I couldn't even afford that and Greece is cheap! Comparatively. I had just enough money to get back to England, to my Great-Aunt Grace, who had offered to put me up. Or put up with me, as my father said when I made a collect call home from Athens.

Aunt Grace is my father's father's youngest sister, a Bee just like me. She lives in the village of Long Marsham in Buckinghamshire, in a cottage that's cosy in September but fairly freezing in January, thanks to her great penchant for fresh air.

It was she who got me working in Buckingham Palace. One day, when I was moaning about money and about having to go back home, my aunt suggested I get a job. I admit this notion had been rattling around in my mind, but I had been too wrapped up in blankets in a big overstuffed chair in the sitting room actually to get up and do anything about it.

Aunt Grace looked through the various daily papers and read aloud the situations vacant. I was underqualified for most of them. The ones I was qualified for were – guess what? – store clerking and waitressing. But the pay for these jobs was so low and the cost of renting a room in London so high that it hardly made it worthwhile unless you were sharing, and I didn't really know anybody in London. Meanwhile the idea of commuting from Long Marsham seemed ridiculous for that kind of job – the village was beyond the reach of the Metropolitan line and train fares would have to be afforded daily, not to mention the time involved. We wrote off to a few adverts with box numbers that held the promise of live-in domestic work – I figured I could do that – and the first reply to arrive, much to my astonishment, bore the seal of the Lord Chamberlain's office in Buckingham Palace.

'Perhaps you're getting an MBE,' I said to Aunt Grace, confused at first by the creamy-looking stationery. As I said, Grace is my grandfather's youngest sister. For her generation, this meant staying at home taking care of ageing parents and never marrying. If she ever had any regrets, she never said. She is a brisk sort of woman, full of common sense, good humour and a great interest in everything around her. I liked her enormously. Since her life seemed to be one of constant service to the community in one way or another, whether it was organizing Meals on Wheels or volunteering in a hospice, she seemed a natural for royal recognition.

She dismissed the notion. 'Quite unlikely. The New Year's Honours List came out a fortnight ago and I think I would have heard from someone if I had been on it. Besides, isn't the letter addressed to you?'

It was indeed. 'Jane Bee, c/o Grace Bee.' Imagine my further astonishment when the letter requested my presence for an interview for the position of Housemaid at Buckingham Palace a few days hence.

The interview was easy. The official seemed half-asleep and asked the most routine questions. There was no problem with my citizenship. My grandfather was British-born and that allowed me to work in the United

Kingdom without obstacle. The pay was terrible but I didn't care. It was a live-in position. I got to be right in the heart of London, a city I had grown to love when I had been there in the late summer. And it was a lark. I figured living and working in Buckingham Palace was something I could tell my grandchildren. The interviewer more or less indicated that few stayed long at these jobs anyway. I'm sure he didn't expect me to stay long either, and he didn't care that I was between years at university and so seemed an unlikely candidate for long-term work. But by September I was still at the Palace, having chucked another potential year of university, not to mention the rest of my open airline ticket as well. My parents went berserk. But then they had decided to separate that summer – I knew it was coming – and so they were more than a little volatile and insecure. Fortunately, they were also six thousand miles away in Charlottetown, Prince Edward Island.

And that's how one found oneself at Buckingham Palace.

Chapter One

It all began on a Friday in late October. The Queen had returned a few weeks earlier from summer vacation at Balmoral in Scotland. And Buckingham Palace had become its old self again, rather like a big hotel with one very exacting guest and her husband.

It was about eight o'clock in the morning and I was hoovering all by myself in the awesomely elegant Green Drawing Room, which overlooks the Quadrangle, or inner courtyard, of the Palace. Normally we work in teams of two, but my regular team-mate had taken leave to care for her mother, who was convalescing from an accident. It had taken me ages to get halfway across that football field of an Axminster carpet, and I was stabbing with my toe at a crusty wad that appeared for all the world to be dried chewing gum, when Nikki Claypole darted through the central door from the Picture Gallery and switched off my vacuum before I had time to be startled.

Nikki rooms right next to me in the housemaids' quarters on the attic floor of the Palace and we sometimes have breakfast together, but I had missed her that morning in Servants' Hall. Having partied intensely the evening before, Nikki had remained in bed until the very last minute while I had had my coffee by myself and started work before she had even got up. I know this sounds almost nauseatingly virtuous, but lately I seemed to be growing out of my old sleep-long-and-late habits. I think it was turning twenty.

'Do you have any idea how to get gum out of a carpet?' I inquired over the dying whine of the hoover.

'Bloody tourists,' she said, referring to the hordes that had tramped through in the summer.

'Couldn't be tourists. This is the original rug. They've put it back for the State Visit.'

Nikki gave a dismissive wave of her duster. Something else was clearly on her mind – I could tell from the look of wicked glee on her freckled face. So I ignored the gum and awaited enlightenment.

It seems that late the previous evening, Thursday, Her Majesty, who had been at some reception or other somewhere in London, had arrived back at the Palace and stepped off her private lift on the principal (or second) floor en route to her bedroom. HM had just started to pass the Page's Vestibule when Robin Tukes, one of the footmen, fell out of the doorway flat on to his face. Too late, the Queen suddenly found herself sprawled on top of him.

Nikki went into a fit of giggles at that point, and her mirth was so infectious I started laughing, too. I know that sounds mean – Her Majesty is, after all, a senior citizen – but the very idea of the Queen of England (no less) tripping over someone was, well, killing.

Nikki takes a dim view of the reverence that all Members and Officials of the Royal Household (the upper two crusts of the Palace hierarchy) and most members of the Staff (the lower crust) have for royalty, and she occasionally expresses it with awful impersonations of Her Majesty. Between snorts, as she tried to catch her breath, she mimed HM clutching at her handbag, frowning that famously frumpy frown and squeaking with annoyance.

' "Rise, Mr Tukes. Rise, I say. I am the Queen of England!" '

Nikki collapsed into one of the gilt and green brocade chairs and was wiping away the tears with her duster when a sharp command pierced the air.

'Nikki Claypole, get off that chair!' snapped a familiar figure with a familiar clipboard. 'You are not assigned to this room. And get back to work, Jane.'

Nikki's features fought for composure as she rose with a deliberate lack of hurry from the chair. But as soon as Mrs Harbottle, the Deputy Housekeeper, retreated from the room my friend thrust out her tongue.

'Old bat,' she said under her breath. 'We're stuck doing the Grand Hall this morning. All those bloody stairs! So,' she added, brightening, 'can you believe it? Robin and Her Maj. in a heap on the floor?'

'But what happened to Robin?' I asked as she headed towards the door leading to the sky-lit Picture Gallery, which is more of a grand art-laden hallway connecting many of the State Rooms. 'What did he say to *her*?'

'Oh, nothing,' Nikki replied, stopping to fiddle with her braid of ginger hair in the door's mirrored surface. 'Least, not as far as I know. Robin was right out of it. Paralytic. Well, it *was* his birthday party, wasn't it? Sorry, forgot. You weren't there.'

No, I hadn't been there. I had started going out with one of the members of the film crew that had been haunting Buck House on and off while they were finishing a documentary on the inner workings of the Palace. I was sorry to miss the birthday party – it was for Robin's twenty-first – but this film guy had potential.

'By the way,' said Nikki, disappearing into the Picture Gallery, 'something else *really* interesting happened at the party last night.'

'What?'

Her voice floated back. 'Sorry, the Grand Hall beckons. You'll find out soon enough.'

Gossip is the lubricant of Buck House, to be sure. But I began to wonder how this story about the Queen falling over Robin had got about so fast. Robin had obviously been blotto at the time. And HM was unlikely to broadcast something so damaging to her dignity as a tumble over a footman. So had her minder, her ever-present bodyguard from the Royalty and Diplomatic Protection Department, blabbed? Not if he didn't want to walk a beat in Brixton. Who, then?

It may seem an odd point. Who cares? Buckingham Palace is over-run with servants – more than three hundred, last count – and it could have been anyone. But those around the Queen's private apartments late in the evening are an elite few. And they are assigned. They're *supposed* to be there. They're discreet. Robin was not one of them. If he was stumbling about in a drunken stupor in the Page's Vestibule, a mere hundred feet from Her Majesty's bedroom, why did no one pull him out of the way? Where was everyone?

I spent the rest of the morning hoovering the crimson and gold Axminster with its pattern of Tudor roses and running a cloth over the grand piano and the eighteenth-century cabinets and the huge gilt candelabrum held up by three kitschy goddess-figures. And I managed not to shatter the pot-pourri vase that once belonged to Madame de Pompadour, even if it was shaped like a ship and looked like it should set sail for someone's attic. We were all doubling up our usual workload. A State Banquet was scheduled the following week for the RamaLamaDingDong, the king of some South-East Asian nation whose real name no one could pronounce. The banquet was to be the centrepiece of the documentary film, and all the extra tidying-up and so forth of the State Rooms had started well in advance of the occasion. Most of the time we housemaids spend our time skivvying – sweeping, dusting, bedmaking – in remote corners of the Palace that even the Queen never sees (Buck House has over four hundred rooms and three miles of corridors), but the forthcoming Banquet had brought a more interesting change to our rota. We got to spend more time in the great big rooms amid all the expensive stuff. And we had the dubious thrill of occasionally walking into a bank of lights and sound equipment as Cyril Wentworth-Desborough, the very intense film director, waved his walking stick about and bellowed orders.

Thus it wasn't until some while later, when I was

heading down to the Linen Room in the basement, that Freddie, one of the underbutlers, told me something that put the question of who had witnessed the royal pratfall out of my mind: Robin Tukes had gone to hospital. He had been taken to the Devonshire Hospital and was expected to be there for at least a day or two.

'They pumped his stomach,' Freddie announced, seeming to relish the notion. 'He must have been *really* sozzled.'

By lunchtime, when I joined Nikki and one of the other footmen, David Pye, in Servants' Hall, the story had begun to get stranger still. It wasn't just booze. It was pills. The rumour was that last night Robin had been trying to commit suicide.

'But that's crazy,' I said, separating out the disgusting kidneys in the steak and kidney pie and putting them in their own pile. 'To begin with, if someone was going to kill himself why try to do it in the Page's Vestibule, of all places?'

'Well, Robin does have a certain theatrical touch, doesn't he?' Davey said. 'Maybe he did it deliberately so Her Majesty would discover him.' He struck a pose. 'Can't you just picture it? Mother bending over him, her pearls flapping, his face pale, his eyes fluttering open. "Oh, Your Majesty, you love me, you really love me." You know, unrequited love can affect a man terribly.'

'Ha, you should know that well enough,' Nikki said.

'You wound me.'

'Come on, you two,' I said. 'This sounds serious.'

'Well, I don't know,' Davey said, more solemnly. 'If it is true, then the Page's Vestibule does seem like a rather weird place to . . . well, you know.'

'Kill himself?'

'Quite. Though Robin has been acting a little strangely lately, don't you think? I mean, I've always thought of him as having a sort of manic edge. You know: lots of high energy, the outrageous behaviour, then suddenly falling into depression. Especially depression, lately. He didn't have much to do with any of us up at Balmoral this summer. He was no fun and Balmoral can be *such* fun if you put your mind to it! And then last night, announcing—'

'But I would hardly describe him as suicidal!' I interjected. I just couldn't believe it. Since returning from Scotland, Robin had had a definite case of the glums. I noticed the difference particularly since, being low on the totem pole, I hadn't had the privilege of joining other members of Staff at Balmoral, the Royal Family's summer home. But a suicide attempt was too much.

'Oh, I don't know,' Nikki said. 'What do you expect? He's bent. He's all, you know, conflicted . . .'

Davey rolled his eyes extravagantly. ' "Conflicted"? How you do mangle the language. It's that rubbish you keep reading in women's magazines.'

'Get knotted. I don't read *women's magazines.*' Nikki glared while Davey lifted a spoonful of trifle to his lips. 'You know what I'm talking about.'

'No, you don't know what *you're* talking about,' he mumbled through his mouthful of food. 'For heaven's sake, I'm gay. Practically all the footmen are gay. And consider the senior members of the Staff – there's more than one queen in this hive, as you well know. Being gay doesn't make you suicidal.'

Nikki grimaced and took a sip of her tea. 'I know

that, you twit. You didn't let me finish. I mean Robin's gay and here he is engaged to marry that silly cow Angela Cheatle. I call that "conflicted".'

She dropped her teacup noisily in its saucer and crossed her arms victoriously across her breasts. Davey, defeated, pursed his lips, sending a crease across each plump and rosy cheek. My jaw was gathering dust on the floor.

'Engaged? Robin engaged?'

'You didn't know?' Davey glanced at Nikki. 'What uncharacteristic restraint on your part, my dear . . . Yes, Robin announced it last night at his party. Oh, I *am* enjoying your reaction, Jane. You look like we did last night, rather like small animals caught in headlights. You could have heard the proverbial pin drop when he finished. At first we thought it was a joke, but Robin looked awfully fierce – Angie, too – so we all went along with it, didn't we, Nikki? Then he got drunk, wandered off, and the next thing you know he's in hospital.'

'Engaged to be married?'

'It's knocked you for six, hasn't it?'

'Well . . . yes. I mean . . .' Actually, I was a bit miffed. I had fancied Robin myself when I first met him.

'Perhaps he's been "bi" all along, then,' Davey mused, stirring his tea with his finger. 'I don't know. I'm not really sure there is such a thing as bisexuality. It's most certainly never happened to me.'

'And not likely to either,' Nikki added.

Davey made a face at her before sticking his finger in his mouth.

My brain was still buzzing with the news. 'I didn't even know they had much to do with each other,' I said. 'I mean . . . Robin. And Angie? Engaged? To be married?'

'Yes, it is odd, isn't it?' Davey pushed his dessert plate aside and tipped back in his chair. 'I think the only time I've ever really seen them together was at Balmoral, the night of the last Ghillies' Ball. I . . . yes, Jane? Your brow is furrowed.'

'*Whose* Ball?'

'Ghillies'. Oh, some old Gaelic word for us servant types. You'll usually find a ghillie standing behind a great laird as he shoots a poor wee beastie for sport. Anyway,' he continued, dropping the Scottish accent like it was cold haggis, 'the Ball is for the estate workers and neighbours and, well, for us, of course. Too bad you weren't there, Jane. You could have danced with the Prince of Wales. I even had a twirl with Mother. Light on her feet, she is—'

'But what about Robin and Angie?' Nikki interjected.

'Oh, yes. Love's sweet duo. As I was saying, the night of the Ghillies' Ball I popped back to Staff quarters at one point for something or other, and there they were, both of them soaked through, looking quite peculiar . . .'

'Probably because some of you sods had just thrown them in the Dee.'

'Untrue, Nikki dear. Everyone was being good. We had already thrown the Prime Minister's senior adviser in that day and Mother was not amused. She never minds if we throw *her* senior advisers in the river, but she minds very much if they're someone else's. Besides, by tradition we always strip them naked first.'

14

'So you think Robin and Angie had had a romantic moonlight swim?'

'I said, "soaked through", Nikki. They were wearing their clothes. Angie claimed they had been larking about on the banks and fell in. Could be true, I suppose . . .'

'I can't imagine Angie "larking about",' I said.

'Nor I.'

There was a moment's silence as Nikki and Davey digested their meals and I digested the news.

'Well,' I said, finally, sighing over my uneaten and coagulating steak and kidney pie, 'I guess it's no secret by now that Angie's pregnant.'

Angela had remained tight-lipped, but rumours of morning sickness and a slight but noticeable weight gain had suggested to us girls that one of us was going to be making a lifestyle change before very long.

'No secret at all,' Davey agreed. 'They announced it the same time as they announced their engagement. And a son, no less.'

'How do they know that?'

'One of those tests, I expect.'

'Really? Yuck.' Visions of unpleasant-looking needles danced in my head.

'But that doesn't mean Robin's the father.'

'Then why would he marry her?'

'Well, I'm sure I don't know, do I?'

'And why, after announcing something that's supposed to be joyous, would he go off and try and kill himself – which, by the way, I don't believe for a minute.'

'Robin hasn't looked well lately, you know. Maybe it

was what they call "a cry for help",' Davey said. 'If only he'd had Di's lemon slicer handy.'

'Oh, please . . .'

'But the question is: why is *she* marrying *him* – that's what I want to know.' Nikki was clearly on her own train of thought.

'True. She will have to give up her fabulous career. Can't have a married housemaid in Buck House. Rules, you know.'

'I know that . . .'

'. . . although I wonder if you could be an unmarried-mother-housemaid? Hmmm, now, that would be a step into the twentieth century. They could set up a day nursery. We never see any kiddies around here, not since those little York princesses' mummy went and bolted.'

'What I want to say, Davey, *if* you'll let me get a word in edgeways, is that a footman wouldn't be good enough for the likes of Angie Cheatle. Angie's got her sights on something higher, I'll tell you.'

'Oh, do tell, then,' Davey said. 'Who?'

'Well, I don't know, do I?' Nikki said darkly. 'But the airs she puts on sometimes . . . I've seen her give the eye to more than one nob around here when she's had the chance. And have you noticed some of the things she's been wearing? How can she afford them on our pay?'

'Nikki, love, I don't spend much time assessing female pulchritude. Although, now that you mention it, Angie has had some fetching frocks lately. I'd ask to borrow one for the next Alexis vs. Krystle competition at Toodle's, but, alas, I'm not her size.'

'Maybe it's impending motherhood.' I felt the need

to divert the conversational flow from Davey's interest in drag. 'Her baby needs a father and she's found someone to fill the role, whether he's the biological father or not.'

They both looked at me glumly.

'Why would Robin do that?' Nikki asked.

'Well, I don't know.'

'If anyone should be suicidal, it should be Karim,' Davey mused. 'Although . . .'

'What?'

'Well, I was going to say that Robin's engagement to Angie had to have been a shock to Karim, but now I'm wondering if he knew beforehand. Maybe that's why Robin and Karim haven't spoken to each other in weeks.'

'Couldn't prise them apart with a bargepole most times before,' Nikki remarked.

'I know. Odd. I can see the attraction from Karim's point of view. But for Robin? Karim is so – I don't now – what is it about Karim? He's so *moody*. Whatever you say to him he looks put out. He doesn't do a thing for me.'

'Well, we all know who you fancy, don't we?' Nikki said slyly.

Davey lifted his teacup and simpered. '*He* gave me a wink the other day, you know. I'm sure of it.'

'You're mad.'

It was a joke among some of the staff that Davey was attracted to a Very High Personage in the Palace whose name Aunt Grace says I should refrain from writing down. I'll have to think about it.

*

Maybe I should explain here about Robin, since he is the centre of the story. Robin Tukes, a fellow Canadian, had already been at the Palace about six months when I arrived, achieving his position as footman the same way I got mine as a housemaid – by answering a newspaper advert. It was easy to see, once you knew some of the ins and outs of Palace life, why he had been hired, and it wasn't because he just happened to fit one of the available uniforms, which is at least half the reason for hiring anyone to be a footman. Robin was almost classically good-looking – tall, lean, dark, chiselled features: the type you might find in an American soap opera.

The allusion makes him sound shallow, though. He wasn't. If both of us were thirteen years old, I would have said Robin was 'deep'. It's the kind of word you'd use to describe a boy with a terribly attractive ability to brood. But the difference between a thirteen-year-old and a twenty-one-year-old, on the whole, is that the latter probably has more serious stuff to brood about.

Our friendship was sparked by something simple – mutual delight at finding another Canadian in a stack of Brits. Not long afterwards, you could have found Robin and me in the Bag O'Nails pub down Buckingham Palace Road rubbishing the English in an affectionate way – at least on my part. From Robin, the joking occasionally possessed a sharper edge. It turned out he had been in a nasty relationship with someone who gave whole new meaning to the expression 'English sang-froid'. The affair was the last straw in a life that had turned into one of those lost-weekend things you read about in novels, which normally sound dead romantic but in this case seemed somewhat 'dissolute' – a word Aunt Grace once contributed to a discussion about Robin, and which seemed to fill the bill.

Robin had been sent to England by his family to have a 'proper education'. (He relayed this mockingly with nose in air.) But he took the tuition money, forsook Cambridge and moved to London. It was like being sprung from a cage. I know the feeling. When my plane from Canada touched down in London, I was all come over with this 'yippee, yahoo' sensation. But where I dipped into new-found freedom, Robin plunged. I can only set it against what little he told me of his home life back in London, Ontario – a place, Robin once said, where there's more life in the cemeteries. His father had been deceased some few years, his mother shattered by her husband's death, and the roost was ruled by a bossy-boots sister nearly fifteen years Robin's senior. There was money in the family, evidently. Robin had been packed off to all the best private schools, the last of which was Upper Canada College in Toronto. But he had hated it, or said he did. His adolescence seemed gloomy.

But, in London (Eng.), it was PartyWorld big-time. Robin's particular bent was theatre. He liked acting, or at least the idea of acting, which, I'm sure, any psychiatrist worth his fee would say was a typical response to a repressed childhood. He got involved with various fringe acting groups, but the acting scene intersected with the gay scene, which intersected with the drugs scene, which interesected with this scene and that scene (there's a travel brochure opportunity here:

London: City of Scenes) such that Robin woke up one morning all scened-out. Out of funds, too.

That's how he ended up at Buckingham Palace. He needed money. He needed a job. He had the same immigration status as me – in fact, *both* his grandfathers were English-born.

But he needed something more – a place of escape, a place to straighten out, to lick wounds, to decide what to do with the rest of his life. And, in an odd way, famous as Buck House is, big as it is, it's an ideal retreat for the world-weary. It's like a little village. There are social clubs and sports teams, a post office, a bank and a cafeteria, and you get a room of your own. You could practically live and die there without ever going out the gate. If you chose to.

Over the spring and early summer, Robin and I cemented our friendship by visiting London's tourist sites together. Nobody else wanted to, not even Karim. The other Palace denizens, being locals, figured they had a lifetime to see the Tower of London, much like New Yorkers who reach the Day of Reckoning without ever having once stood atop the Empire State Building. So, when Robin had an urge to escape the village atmosphere of Buck House, I would accompany him. I loved going to St Paul's Cathedral and the British Museum and Westminster Abbey, or even as far up the Thames as Hampton Court or as far down as Greenwich. But I soon realized that Robin was interested less in history and pageantry and more in being places – tourist haunts being a prime example – where he was unlikely to bump into any of his old mates from pre-Buck House days. He once hustled me out of the Tate Gallery sharpish because he had glimpsed near one of the Cubist paintings a certain someone he preferred to avoid. Though he made light of the episode, as he was inclined to do, I could tell he was upset. And I felt bad because I was the one who had insisted on the Tate, a place to which Londoners are as likely to flock as foreigners.

All this makes Robin seem as though he were a handsome recluse. And it's true that he wasn't all that keen on going out to pubs or wine-bars or the like, other than the reliable Bag O'Nails. But inside Buck House it was a different story. As Davey said, there as a manic edge about Robin, a kind of recklessness that led to bursts of outrageous behaviour.

Back in the spring, a bunch of the footmen were watching a delayed broadcast of the Academy Awards on telly in the footmen's lounge when an old clip from the seventies, a decade that had become fashionable lately, popped up. It featured a naked guy racing across the stage behind some old actor. Someone recalled reading about this fad called 'streaking', so Robin dared them to do the same. They were all half-corked anyway, so they all got barebuff and raced around the Palace, even past the Royal Apartments. The Master of the Household, way at the top of the Palace hierarchy, heard about it and went ballistic. Apparently HM, hearing the commotion, had put her head out of her Sitting Room and glimpsed an undraped buttock. She was not amused, at least officially.

We were, I must say. Unofficially.

And then there was another time, a party just after Trooping the Colour, on the Queen's official birthday in June, when HM's personal troops, the Guards, march before the sovereign on Horse Guards Parade in their scarlet tunics and bearskin hats. We of the lower orders were all having a blast when suddenly the Queen arrived. Only she had grown about a foot in height. It was Robin, in drag. It was a terrific performance. Some costumer Davey knew had outfitted him in the sort of posh gear HM wears to open Parliament – a white gown with a blue sash and the Order of the Garter pinned to the bosom. The wig was perfect, greying hair teased and spongy-looking; there was a ton of pancake on his face, and he had all the proper accessories – the tiara, the owly eyeglasses, the handbag. But it was the acting that really carried it off. Robin was so good at being politely inquisitive in inane conversation, and utterly frosty towards impertinent remarks, that before long he had everyone calling him 'Ma'am' and curtseying. What was so amazing was that the performance was almost *respectful*. He never slipped from character.

It was a great turn – Davey was green with envy – and it did get him into trouble. (He took the rap and got a right dressing-down from the footmen's boss, the Travelling Yeoman.) It was also, I think, a glimpse of Robin more as he was in pre-Palace days – impetuous, extravagant, bold. It made me wonder if it was these attributes that lay behind this strange business of his engagement to Angie. Was it an impulsive act, as in the old days? Or one calculated to help restore the order he seemed to be seeking in his life?

At that point I had no answer.

But one thing I did know: the Robin who had returned from Scotland in October was not the Robin who had gone up in August. In the past few weeks he had seemed to withdraw from everyone. He looked so damned serious, as if the weight of the world were on his shoulders. It was his glumness, in fact, that had initially prompted the idea of a birthday celebration. Everyone thought it might cheer him up.

I intended to go to the hospital to see Robin, but I didn't get a chance to slip away. On Friday the Queen goes to Windsor for the weekend and work at Buckingham Palace just seems to go slack as soon as she leaves, but that particular Friday Mrs Harbottle was acting like a slave driver. I was looking forward to spending part of my weekend in Long Marsham, and I had told Aunt Grace I would try to get there early Friday evening. It left no time for a hospital visit that day.

On my way out of the Palace through the Side Gate on to Buckingham Palace Road I brushed past Karim Agarwal in his black tailcoat and white shirt – everyday apparel for a footman. He didn't acknowledge me at first, and so I called out to him. He turned and looked at me uneasily.

'Yes?' he said.

'Robin. Have you seen him? How is he?'

Karim looked away.

'There's some weird talk of a suicide attempt,' I babbled on. His non-reply was making me awkward. 'That can't be true, can it?'

I couldn't seem to catch his eye. Karim appeared to be transfixed by the usual scene in front of him – the policeman at the sentry box, the high gates, the traffic –

while I, fumbling for something to do, buttoned my jacket against the late October damp.

'Sorry, maybe I shouldn't have asked . . .'

'Look, I don't know what happened,' Karim said defensively, turning to me at last, his dark eyes glowing. 'I haven't seen him. I might go up this weekend, maybe.'

'Well, say hello for me, then. That's if you're going,' I replied, shrugging. 'Tell Robin I'll visit Sunday afternoon.'

I let him go. Conversation with Karim was like pulling gum from a Buck House rug.

Like Davey, I couldn't quite figure out the attraction between Karim Agarwal and Robin Tukes, other than the enticement of Karim's dark good looks. But he didn't really fit in with the other footmen. It was partly because he wasn't English – that is, English in the sense of being Anglo-Saxon, although he had lived in England since he was a baby, his parents having been kicked out of Uganda during Idi Amin's rule. Some of the Staff made the rudest comments about Karim behind his back. Some made them to his face. He was the first footman of Indian parentage the Palace had hired, as far as I knew, and it wasn't taken happily in some quarters. It's unbelievable how off-handedly racist the English can be at times.

Anyway, Karim also didn't fit in because he wasn't quite the hellraiser the other footmen were. He rarely joined in the different pranks and jokes – he wasn't one of the lads. The Queen never spotted *his* little bare buttocks running past the Royal Apartments. I guess the others thought of him as a bit wet. I think he was just conscientious about his work in ways the others weren't. You could sense he had other ambitions. In Buck House, ambitious people were regarded with suspicion and resentment. But Robin tended to stand up for him with the others, even though he, Robin, was often the orchestrator of, or participant in, the various shenanigans. I think, for Robin, Karim was a kind of anchor, someone comparatively steady when all around were a lot of raving loony Englishpersons.

On that Sunday I left Aunt Grace's in the early afternoon, got off the train at Marylebone Station, hiked up Baker Street past Madame Tussaud's really boring wax museum and headed for the Devonshire Hospital, which is only a few blocks away. By three o'clock I was in the ward. To my surprise, Karim was there too. When I entered I could see him leaning forward on a chair next to Robin's bed in what appeared to be intense, whispered conversation. The conversation broke off abruptly the moment I appeared bedside.

It's hard to describe the look in Robin's eyes: sort of dazed, I guess. In fact, it seemed to take a moment for him to register my presence. When he did he smiled quickly, greeted me and then looked sharply at Karim. It was some kind of signal. Without acknowledging me, Karim gathered up a plastic Selfridge's bag he had dropped on the bed, tidily transferred an orange plastic jack o'lantern brimming with candy to a side table – I had forgotten it was Hallowe'en – and hurried out.

I felt suddenly awkward, as though I had been introduced to Robin for the first time. It had been all that talk of suicide, I think. An uncomfortable subject. However well you think you know a person (and I thought I knew

Robin as well as anyone at Buck House, except maybe Karim) there are moments when that person can seem to you an utter stranger. This was one of those moments. It struck me that I didn't really know Robin that well after all. He was awfully self-contained, no matter how personable. He had a charming way of deflecting your questions, if he didn't want to answer them, with a blazing smile or some needling humour. There were times after our jaunts through tourist London when I realized I had been rabbiting on about my hopes and dreams and troubles and he had disclosed very little. Now, as I stood by his bed, I realized there were whole areas of Robin's personality, of his life, that had eluded me. I thought of the things he wouldn't talk much about (his family) or didn't talk much about (unhappiness).

I suddenly remembered a girl in my grade nine class who had killed herself. She had seemed normal and cheerful. And then she had been found by her mother in the bathroom with her wrists slit. We grade niners had been intensely absorbed in this tragedy when it happened. But we never really satisfied ourselves as to the motives for her death.

Anyway, I thought Robin didn't look bad for someone who had recently had his stomach pumped and had been lying in hospital for a few days. In fact, he looked rather good. He was a bit pale, but it seemed to set off a day's growth of beard. That, with his black hair and dark eyes, made him look sort of swashbucklerish, if that's a word (and it probably isn't). He was just missing the ear-ring he normally wore when he wasn't on duty at the Palace.

I started to unwrap one of the candies from the jack o'lantern, and asked the usual dumb hospital questions. How are you feeling? *Fine.* When are you getting out? *Soon, I hope.* Sweet? *No, thanks.* I wondered whether Karim had been whispering to him simply because the ward had no privacy. There were ten other beds with men in them. I too found myself starting to whisper. But there was something extremely distracted in Robin's manner. He was practically monosyllabic. Finally the small talk petered out. I made up my mind and got straight to the point.

'There's this talk of a suicide attempt, you know,' I said, my teeth sinking into a second gooey caramel.

'Yeah, I know,' he replied evenly.

'Is it true?'

He shrugged and looked down at a blue envelope he had been holding between his thumb and forefinger. 'I've been feeling a little bit low lately,' he said, reaching over and placing the letter next to the jack o'lantern.

'I'm told you were a little bit high Thursday night.'

He snorted softly. 'What the hell! It was my twenty-first birthday. Might be my last.'

'Robin! Don't say that.'

'Okay, I won't.' The irritation in his voice was followed instantly by a look of apology. 'Sorry,' he said. 'It's a bitch lying around here doing nothing. So, anyway, where were you that night?'

It was my turn to be apologetic. I told him about being out with Neil, the camera assistant on the film crew. 'I didn't think you'd miss me,' I said. 'Besides, I haven't exactly had a lot of dates since I starting working at Buck House.'

'Nice guy?'

'Yeah, he's okay. I've told you about him before.'

But Robin's attention was drifting. He was staring glumly at the ceiling.

'Robin, what's the matter? *Is* something the matter?'

He didn't answer.

'Is it this thing with Angie? Nikki told me about your engagement. You're not really going to marry Angie, are you? I know that sounds kind of nosey but . . .'

A smile began to form at the corners of his mouth. He said, 'Jane, darling, Angie's the love of my life.'

'Oh, cut it out. She is not.'

'Is too.'

Suddenly he grinned in the old familiar Robin way – lots of teeth, dazzling. The sun was out. It was distracting. I sighed inwardly. Gay. What a waste. That's if he *was* gay, strictly speaking. Which brought me back to the subject of his impending marriage.

'What,' I demanded, 'are you up to with Angela?'

'Love and marriage. Horse and carriage. Hmm, sounds like rap. What do you think?' He started shifting around in bed to some imagined rap tune.

'Am I going to get a straight answer out of you?'

'A *straight* answer?'

'Tell me this, smart boy,' I persisted, 'did you know that none other than the Queen of England tripped over you and fell flat on her face?'

'I heard.'

'The question is: what were you doing in that part of the Palace at that time of night?'

'We decided to have a scavenger hunt at the party. I

had to find a member of the Royal Family, put him – or her – in a sack and bring him back to the starting point.'

'Aha! So you didn't know she was out for the evening.'

'Oh, I knew. I had read the Court Circular in *The Times* earlier in the day.'

'In other words, you planned it. You *wanted* to be in that part of the Palace at that time of the evening.'

'Clever Jane.'

Something began to dawn on me. 'Let me see if I have this correctly. You planned to be in that part of the Palace at that time of the evening because . . . because what? Because you suddenly had an urge to see the Queen up close?'

To my surprise, Robin's expression turned sombre. He was silent for a long time, as if making his mind up about something. 'I did want to see her about something,' he admitted. 'Privately.'

'You're not serious?'

'Never more.'

'*You* wanted to see the Queen? The very Queen of England? Privately? Are you nuts?'

My voice must have carried, for suddenly the man in the next bed swivelled his head towards us. His stare was more censorious than astonished, so I assumed he was more alarmed at the volume of our conversation than at its content.

'Jane,' Robin said, lowering his voice and reaching out to grasp my wrist. 'This is serious. I shouldn't have even told you that. And I don't want you telling anyone. Do you understand me? No one.'

'But . . .'

'I just had to see her. That's all.'

Suddenly I felt strangely confused and frightened. The Queen was a remote figure to most of us in the lower orders, someone glimpsed only infrequently from a window when she was leaving the Palace through the Queen's Entrance on the north side, or from a doorway when she passed by on her way to one of the State Rooms. Some housemaids would even dart into an adjoining room to avoid her if they heard the warning sound of yapping corgis. So what would drive someone to seek a private audience with HM? And how possible could it be for someone of our position? Despite the security lapses over the years which had reached the press, and despite those which hadn't, communicating with the Queen away from her close attendants had always struck me as pretty difficult.

'Wouldn't you have to go through someone to get an appointment?' I asked.

'Her Private Secretary.'

'Him, then.'

'I couldn't do that.'

'Why not?'

'I can't say.'

'Well,' I said, frustrated, 'what on earth would you want to talk with her *about*?'

'I wanted to know what she keeps in her handbag.'

'Robin!' I snatched my hand away.

'Look, Jane, I can't tell you any more. And please, don't say anything about this. I'm serious.'

'Then why tell me at all?'

'Because I want *one* person to know I wasn't playing the fool.'

'So this was no suicide attempt then, was it?'

His mouth formed a grim line. He replied: 'Apparently I was unconscious, I was rushed to this hospital and I had my stomach pumped.'

He said this like he was reading a hospital admission form. Yet he didn't answer my question.

That was really the end of our conversation. There was so much more I wanted to ask, but his manner indicated that my visit had worn itself out. I asked when he expected to be back at work and he said probably Monday or Tuesday. He didn't know why the hospital was keeping him so long anyway. I reminded him that Cyril Wentworth-Desborough and his film crew would be returning to the Palace to film more pre-banquet footage on the *Backstage at Buckingham Palace* documentary (*Housesluts and Footpigs* we called it, since we liked to think it was mostly about us 'downstairs' types) and that we housemaids and footmen could expect to trip over electrical cables once again as we went about our business. I also reminded him of his prominent spot in a 'set-up' shot – Breakfast in Servants' Hall – scheduled for early in the week. 'Looks and charm will out,' I told him coaxingly. 'Well, it's a *part*,' I said finally. I thought this might cheer him up a bit, since he was interested in acting, but he just frowned and then grew distant. I left the hospital feeling little better than when I had gone in.

Chapter Two

A busy Monday went by. I didn't see Robin back at the Palace. The following morning I found myself dusting and polishing the White Drawing Room which, as it happens, is very close to Her Majesty's private rooms on the first floor of Buckingham Palace. It was after nine o'clock and, as I was finishing, I could just catch the strains of the bagpipes which are played each morning outside on the terrace below the Queen's private dining room. Being a housemaid is fairly routine work and so my mind began to wander a bit as I flicked a duster over a gilt-edged eighteenth-century rolltop desk, the kind of exquisite piece of furniture I might have savoured on a better day.

I was worried about Robin. I said before that most of the time he was quite charming, the type who really *should* be an actor. But Davey was right about one thing. Robin was a bit manic. There were the highs. I've mentioned some of those. And then there were the lows. There were one or two occasions during the time I had known him when his energy just seemed to evaporate. He would barely participate in conversation, or he would stare past you with a kind of numb pain registered on his handsome features. Each time this happened I thought I had offended him and when, after a few days of being ignored, I confronted him, he told me that he was prone to occasional bouts of depression. It ran in his family, he said. He was always able to snap out of it. And he did.

Except that he didn't snap out of the depression he brought back to London with him from Balmoral. And then he went out and confounded us all by getting engaged to Angela Cheatle, of all people.

I suppose Angie would be considered a prize in some people's books. Some *men's* books, that is. She's blonde and she's well-upholstered in all the right places and she's got huge eyes and pouty lips and the whole bit. When she's out of the boring white uniforms we wear and takes her hair out of the prim braids and knots that Mrs Harbottle demands of us, she looks quite smashing. She spends a lot of time poring over *Elle* and *Marie Claire*, and when she talks it's mostly about what famous and titled people are up to. She can't get enough of the Princess of Wales.

Was I envious? I suppose, if I really examined my feelings, I was a little in love with Robin. A *little*, I say. But I'm smart enough to know when something is hopeless. *Robin and Me* was hopeless, except as good friends. But *Robin and Angie* printed on all those wedding napkins? I couldn't see it. No, I wasn't jealous because I still didn't believe it. And it wasn't the sexual-orientation problem. It was because Angie Cheatle just wasn't Robin's type as a human being. She wasn't much fun, as far as I could see; she was just decorative. I was the one who went out exploring London with Robin. I was the one with whom he'd had a few laughs. He was a great person to be with. He knew things. So do I. Maybe Canadian educations are better than British ones. Angie just seemed dim to me. What she knew of public affairs or the world at large seemed to come from *Hello!* magazine.

On the other hand, there was something a bit calculating about her. Half the time she never appeared to be actually listening to what you were saying. She seemed to be sizing you up instead, as if she was trying to slot you into some category. Don't get me wrong, I didn't *not* get along with her. I just think my being Canadian confounded her because I didn't have the tell-tale accent and the other baggage that make the English so 'slottable' to each other.

I was brooding about all this, staring out of the window spattered with patchy November rain towards the artificial lake in the garden, when I heard a soft thud out in the hallway, followed by a fevered yapping of dogs. My ears pricked up immediately. Compared to the crash of a crockery-laden tray hitting the floor – a not uncommon occurrence at the Palace, given the amount of drinking done by the staff – that thud was an uncommon sound. And then immediately afterwards, above the noisy dogs, came this very familiar voice – the one from all those Christmas broadcasts on CBC that my staunch monarchist Grannie insisted we hold up dinner for every year in Charlottetown. This very familiar voice issued two words in a very vexed voice, two words I thought I would never hear part those lips.

'Bloody hell!'

Without thinking I dashed into the Picture Gallery, through the Ante Room and into the corridor, running past the Private Apartments as fast as I could to find the Queen draped atop the supine figure of a man in tailcoat and trousers, who was lying face down on the rug. At the same time Humphrey Cranston, the Page of the Backstairs (a sort of personal footman to the sovereign), a broomstick of a man with a face perennially as long as a wet weekend, appeared at the door of the private dining room. For once Humphrey's expression was different. The wretched man looked aghast. We must have both been so stunned that we just stood there for a few seconds – a few seconds longer than was decent. But the sight of Her Most Excellent Majesty by the Grace of God, of the United Kingdom of Great Britain and Northern Ireland and of Her other Realms and Territories Queen, Head of the Commonwealth, Defender of the Faith and so on and so on, this dignified figure remembered from old films about the coronation and early morning broadcasts of royal weddings, struggling on her hands and knees amid a posse of yapping corgis was unquestionably astonishing.

She was pointed in my direction and I could see she had that severe frown on her face – you know, the famous one she uses to express extreme disapproval. Honestly, it could, as my Dad would say on a wintry Charlottetown morning, freeze the you-know-whats off a you-know-what. A newspaper she must have been carrying had fallen forward and I hastily scooped it up. But half because the Queen frightened me a little, and half because I remembered our protocol training saying that touching the Queen's person was taboo, I hesitated to go to her aid.

'Well, give me a hand, girl,' the Queen said in a irritated tone, noting my presence.

'Yes, Your Majesty,' I said, and nearly dipped into a curtsey.

I gave the Queen my free hand – hers felt quite tiny and very dry – and she rose slowly, and with more dignity than I could ever muster, from the carpet.

The figure on the floor flew from my mind, for there I was, face to face with the Queen of England.

I can't tell you what an odd sensation it was. I recall a dream I once had as a little girl. In the dream, the Queen is coming to tea and my mother and my two sisters are fussing about getting things ready, tidying the house and themselves, worried and nervous. There is a tremendous sense of expectation, curiously, almost of doom, although for some reason I'm detached from it. I am on a high stool by the door – stable-type door, with the bottom closed and the top open. In the background, outside our house, the sounds of crowds and horses and marching bands grow louder and louder as though she were travelling to our home in a coach with a great entourage. Though her arrival is imminent my mother and sisters remain in the kitchen putting the last touches on the cakes and breads, a groaning tea-table of foods that I somehow know the Queen will not eat. Suddenly the noise stops and a face pokes its head in through the door. It is the Queen. There is light about her head but it does not obscure her face. She looks over the room, looks at me for a moment, smiles suddenly and then withdraws. The clamour starts again and the odd sense of doom vanishes. That is the end of it.

What is strange is that I should remember this

dream. And it is her face I remember most clearly because my perspective is like that of a baby held so close that large worlds appear in small things. It is the particles of powder that fascinate me. They gather in the creases that fan from her eyes and cling to tiny soft hairs that run from feathery eyebrows down along the edges of her cheeks to her neck, where three strands of fat pearls imitate with their opalescence the powdered milkiness of her skin. There are, of course, the familiar teardrop nose, the brilliant blue eyes and the Hanoverian hairdo (now greyed), but it is the soft powdery cheeks which preoccupy me – the same ones, only tinged with the pink of exertion, that held my attention as I stood nearly open-mouthed before her. We are the same height – that is, short, about five foot three without heels – and so I couldn't help but get a good look.

I must have been staring longer than is polite because lines of disapproval began to gather around the Queen's mouth. Finally, I had the sense to ask: 'Are you all right, Ma'am?'

'Yes, I am, thank you,' she replied evenly and turned to look at Humphrey, who was standing indecisively at the private dining room door.

'Humphrey, would you go and fetch Mr Dowse and tell him I wish to speak with him immediately. And I think perhaps Dr Elcott as well.'

'Yes, Ma'am,' said Humphrey, and darted off down the hall to get the Palace Steward, HM's senior domestic servant, and the Palace Physician.

HM regarded the unmoving figure on the carpet for a moment, a faintly puzzled expression on her face, then turned to me.

'What is your name?' she asked.

'Jane Bee, Ma'am.'

'Jane, would you see if this young man can be aroused?'

I bent down and, as I did so, a peculiar feeling came over me. I saw what I hadn't noted before – that the young man in question was Robin. But it wasn't his identity which made me feel queer. It was the pallor of his face, the rigidity of his features and a smell that I had never smelt before. I looked up at the Queen and I could tell from the expression on her face that she, too, was disturbed. There was an absolute hush in the hall. Even the corgis had fallen into uncertain silence. My heart racing, I put my fingers to Robin's neck, searching for the pulse spot. There was warmth along the skin. But I could find no pulse.

'Oh, Ma'am,' I gasped. 'Ma'am, I think he's dead!'

I don't know how much time passed between my tearful declaration and the Queen entering her study. Perhaps it was only five minutes, or fifteen. I can barely remember how I got there, though I assume HM herself ushered me in and then went to await the arrival of the Palace Steward and the doctor. The only thing I do remember is hearing the Queen's very nervous minder apologizing profusely for his absence, blaming some tummy-rattling vindaloo he had eaten the night before. I wondered why there had been no one sitting in attendance when I raced past.

The Queen sat at her desk, a thoughtful expression on her face, and indicated for me to move to a chair

opposite. Her desk was surprisingly cluttered, overflowing with papers and books and framed photographs
fighting for space with an ornate silver inkstand, an
antiquated-looking brass lamp and a blue vase with a
spray of pink carnations. Soft light filtered through
sheer silk curtains on the casement window overlooking Constitution Hill. It framed her head and made it
look for all the world as though an aura surrounded her
– a real aura, not the mystical one my Grannie thinks
hovers around her. The Queen's presence, which I'm
sure would have unnerved me in other circumstances,
now seemed strangely comforting.

'Are you feeling better, Jane?' she asked as she
adjusted her glasses. I could hear a couple of corgis sigh
as they settled down at her feet.

'Yes, Ma'am,' I said miserably, an unfamiliar
handkerchief balled tightly in my hand. 'It was the
shock. Is he really . . .?'

'Yes, I'm afraid so.'

'Ohh.'

'A particular friend of yours, was he?'

'Well, Ma'am, we're both Canadians, so we had that
in common. Strangers in a strange land, I think the
expression is.'

'Not so strange, surely?'

I think she was trying to cheer me up. I braved a
smile. 'No, not so strange . . . I guess.'

There was a moment's silence. The Queen glanced
at a small table adjoining her desk. On it were piled
three brass-handled boxes bound in red leather. They
were, I realized through the fog of my misery, the
famous dispatch boxes containing government

documents delivered daily for HM's inspection from 10 Downing Street and the government offices in Whitehall. When people said the Queen was 'doing her Boxes', these were the boxes they were talking about.

'This was the boy sent to hospital last week, I believe,' the Queen continued.

'Yes, Ma'am. Robin was taken there after you trip—' I bit my tongue. The tiniest hint of exasperation showed on her face – 'after he was taken ill,' I mumbled, looking away. I could feel my face burn.

'I was told he had been depressed.'

'Well, Ma'am, it runs in his family. Or so he told me. It's true, he has seemed a little low over the last few weeks, but . . .'

'Unhappy enough to consider suicide?'

She had been briefed very quickly, I thought. My mind went back to my conversation with Robin in the hospital.

'No, Ma'am, I don't believe that Robin wanted to kill himself. He had even got engaged to be married last week. And, if I may say so, it strikes me as very odd that anyone in the Palace considering suicide would choose to do it outside your door.'

'And twice in one week, too,' the Queen added, the look on her face letting me know that she knew that I knew about the previous incident. 'Perhaps he wanted to make a spectacle of his suicide. Perhaps he wanted to shock me.'

'Oh, no. He wasn't like that – well, not really.' The streaking incident crossed my mind but I dismissed it. 'Robin was outside your door for a reason. He had been trying to see you privately.'

A frown settled on the Queen's face. 'See one privately?' she said. 'That would be most unusual. If the young man had a problem he should have discussed it with Mr Dowse, or perhaps with one of the assistant Masters of the Household. All my appointments are handled by my Private Secretary.'

'I think he felt it was extremely important. You see, Ma'am, my sense is that he felt he couldn't trust anyone – not even, if you don't mind my saying . . .' I gulped, 'your Private Secretary, Sir Julian Dench.'

Was I wrong, or did a certain alertness come over her face?

'And you don't know what he wanted to see me about?' she asked.

'No, I don't.'

'Then we shall have to tell the police about this.'

'Oh, Ma'am,' I blurted, 'please don't. I know Robin was in his right mind. He had a real reason to want to talk to you privately. I'm sure of it.'

Her Majesty regarded me gravely. Then her eyes swept for a moment the mementoes on her desk. She seemed to gaze at one photograph in particular, but as its back was to me its subject was hidden.

'You realize what you're implying, Jane, do you?'

I hadn't until that point. I guess I had been too upset. But when she said that, a kind of horror swept over me. The look of it must have shown on my face, for HM nodded.

'Yes,' she said, removing her glasses and focusing her blue eyes on me.

'Ma'am . . .!' I was rendered speechless.

The two of us sat in silence. And then the Queen,

perhaps to distract me, perhaps to reassure herself, began to ask me about myself, as though I were one of those people she might meet during a walkabout. I told her about my father being with the Royal Canadian Mounted Police and my mother a journalist and my sisters and my aunt and why I was in England and all that. Perhaps it comes from years of listening politely to other people rambling on, but she actually seemed to be interested in everything I was saying. She watched me intently as I spoke: I almost felt like I was being laser-scanned. Finally, she glanced at the clock on her desk. She appeared to have made up her mind about something.

'You seem like a sensible girl, Jane Bee. You're Canadian. Canadians *are* rather sensible people. Now, I want you to tell no one about this conversation. No one whatsoever. One is aware of the extent of gossip in this place, and one can understand its temptation, but I want you to resist. And I want you to keep your eyes and ears open. Do you understand me?'

'Yes, Ma'am,' I said, although I wasn't entirely sure what she meant.

'Thank you, Jane.'

It was the signal for dismissal. I rose from my chair and made an awkward curtsey.

As I turned towards the door the Queen put on another, smaller pair of reading spectacles and reached for one of the two telephones on the desk.

'Ma'am,' I said turning back. A question had come suddenly to mind. 'If I may . . .?'

HM look up inquiringly over the half-frames.

'Who told Your Majesty that Robin was suicidal?'

'Sir Julian.'

'And, Ma'am, if I may, when did Sir Julian tell you this?'

'On Friday. Before I went to Windsor.'

A look passed between us.

'Remember my warning,' the Queen said. As I closed the door behind me, I could hear her telephone dial start to click.

Chapter Three

I stood in the corridor outside the Queen's sitting room feeling dazed. So much had happened in such a short time. Robin Tukes was dead and I'd had a private conversation with the Queen of England. And yet if Robin's death had caused any disturbance in the normal running of the Palace, as I was sure it had, it was not the least bit evident. The old institutional hum had returned. Off in the distance was the muffled whir of a hoover. From the Page's Vestibule across from the Queen's sitting room came the low drone of conversation, while a corgi's bark could be heard from the dogs' room adjacent. The corridor itself was devoid of evidence of a recent death. Robin's corpse must have been whisked away in moments.

I walked to the spot where he had lain. I felt terribly sad. But I could also feel a kind of anger rising in me. Robin killing himself just did not make sense, even if he was troubled, even if he didn't contradict the idea that he was suicidal, even though doing something bizarre like having his dead body found outside the Queen's door wasn't completely beyond his sense of theatre, macabre as it might have been.

Murder at least brought with it the certainty that

someone else was to blame for his death, and that thought, for some perverse reason, seemed to temper my spurt of anger. And yet murder seemed even more out of the question than suicide. Who would want to kill a nice guy like Robin Tukes? It could only be someone working within the Palace, I decided. While it was true that half the time security was more form than substance (vindaloo, indeed!) breaching it would still be pretty difficult for a stranger – even though it had been done in the past, notably that time years ago when some disturbed individual had found his way into the Queen's bedroom. But who in the Palace would have it in for Robin?

I thought about my conversation with Her Majesty. It was she who had introduced the idea of murder, although she hadn't actually used that word. And yet, if she believed murder were possible, wouldn't she say so to Palace security? Wasn't it her duty to report any such suspicion? The idea of 'duty' was one of her big things. Still, I was sure that she, like me, couldn't conceive that something like murder could be committed in the confines of Buckingham Palace. Raising suspicions would surely trigger a terrible fuss which would soon get out of the Palace and into the press, particularly into the tabloids which felt few constraints when it came to reporting on the doings of the Royal Family. It was a rumour I'm sure she didn't want to get out if it proved baseless, particularly during an impending State Visit. 'Keep your eyes and ears open,' she'd said to me. Did she want me to investigate on my own?

I thought it curious that Sir Julian's name seemed to have an effect on her. It had become an article of faith

around the Palace that the Queen didn't much like her
Private Secretary, although how these things become
known I'll never know.

Sir Julian Dench was a relatively new appointment.
He had arrived at the Palace over the head of a deputy
Private Secretary who had expected to inherit the job.
Sir Julian had preceded me at the Palace by about a
month, so he had only been there a little less than
a year. He was in his early fifties, good-looking for a
man of his age, with a full head of curly, silver hair and
a large, handsome face with wolfish eyes that gave him
a kind of ruthless – but undeniably sexy – appearance.
He certainly wasn't one of the reedy, tweedy, eunuch
types like some of the occupants of the high-level
Palace sinecures. Neither was he an old-guard courtier,
discreet and cultivated. Like most of his predecessors in
the job, Julian Dench had held a commission in the
armed forces. But then, unlike the others, he had gone
on to be an extremely successful businessman. Sir
Julian had made a great deal of money in the grocery
business, it was said, and then sold that to take up a
particular cause of his, efficient management theory
and practice. He was well-connected politically, of
course. You had to be. And he had married the daughter
of a peer, which didn't hurt.

Sir Julian Dench, KCB, KCVO, looked to me like a
man who was used to having his own way, and I could
see why people would think HM didn't care for him. He
just wasn't really her type, even if he had married into
the aristocracy. But there wasn't a whole lot the Queen
could do about it. Private secretaries to the monarch are
vetted by the government, and it was rumoured that Sir

Julian's appointment came on the heels of the Queen's *annus horribilis*. After so many cock-ups it was felt that a take-charge kind of guy was needed to put the monarchy back on track. So HM was stuck with him, and his position in the Household was powerful. Sir Julian was responsible for organizing and managing her daily schedule: no one could see Her Majesty without his permission. Which is why Robin's attempt to bypass him to see the Queen was so remarkable.

It was all so strange. But it planted a certain resolve in me. I turned away from the spot where Robin had lain and made my way back to the White Drawing Room, where I had left my cleaning stuff on one of the gilded wood chairs. There was a chance that Robin's death would be declared to be murder, and if that happened there would be nothing the Queen or I could do about it. But until then I *would* investigate on my own. It suddenly seemed the natural thing to do. Was I not the daughter of a police detective? We had had our disagreements, my father and I. I've already mentioned how grumpy he was about my interrupting college to go to Europe. But I guess something of him was in me after all.

What to do?

Check Robin's bedroom, I decided. As good a place as any to start. I had my cleaning schedule and I was supposed to be working in the Music Room, next door to the White Drawing Room. Mrs Harbottle would be sore as a boil if she came in and didn't find me there but, I decided, to heck with it. I would take the consequences later.

I made my way up to the third floor of the Palace, to

the west wing where the housemaids' and footmen's quarters are. No one stopped to talk to me along the way. Activity seemed to be heightened. With another State Banquet approaching, extra effort was being put into cleaning and polishing, and of course there was the film crew intruding here and there as we worked towards the big day.

The attic floor, on the other hand, was quiet – everybody was at work elsewhere in the Palace – and at first I felt some trepidation being there. Entering Robin's bedroom uninvited seemed like an invasion of privacy. I stood at the door, looked up and down the corridor, and slowly turned the knob. I don't know what I expected to see once I got inside, but for some reason my heart began to beat faster.

The door was unlocked. Many of the locks on the attic floor were broken, or else their keys had been lost and never replaced.

I slipped in and closed the door behind me, grateful that the hinges did not squeak. Once inside, I felt less apprehensive. What had I expected to find anyway? Another dead body?

I had been in Robin's room before, of course, but I had never paid much attention to its detail. It was too similar to mine to be remarkable: narrow and high-ceilinged, with fussy wallpaper (cabbage roses in his case, violet sprigs in mine) and an equally fussy floral rug. It was not unlike the room in which I had spent my very first night in London, in a cheap hotel in Earl's Court with an ancient fusty smell and stained walls. The furnishings were similarly sparse and mismatched – a bed, a wardrobe, a washbasin, a chest of drawers, an easy chair and a small table with an old goose-neck reading lamp. Robin had tried to relieve the drabness with a couple of posters on the wall, one of a production of a play at the National Theatre called *The Duchess of Malfi*, which I had heard of but never read, and another of a play I'd gone to the Lyric Theatre with him to see, *Entertaining Mr Sloan*, which we both thought kind of corny and dated (though the poster was colourful). Still, the place had the look of a bedsit, which, I suppose, was what it really was in a way.

The bed looked like it hadn't been slept in. This was surprising. Or had Robin returned from the hospital that very morning? It seemed unlikely. There were some clothes strewn on the floor, casual clothes, but that suggested little. Although Robin was always meticulous in his appearance, he was just another man who never picked up after himself.

The wardrobe was next to the door, so I opened it. Inside I found nothing but clothes: the scarlet tailcoat worn for semi-State occasions such as Royal Ascot week, and the full scarlet livery with the gold braid worn for special State occasions like the forthcoming banquet. There were breeches, a pair of black buckled shoes and two soft white shirts with turn-down collars that were part of a normal daily dress. And then there were the clothes that my Dad would call 'civvies', the kind of thing you wore when you weren't on duty, away from the Palace – or away from Mountie headquarters in my father's case. Nothing in Robin's wardrobe looked remarkable – not that I'm adept at figuring out men's clothes. And nothing, as far as I could tell, was missing. There was even an expensive Burberry – which only

American tourists can afford these days – that looked somehow out of place next to jeans.

On top of the bureau, in disarray, were a hairdryer, brushes and combs, two cans of mousse, a mirror, a Walkman, an assortment of cassette tapes, a travel alarm clock, an electric shaver, a saucer with Palace insignia containing 83p in loose change, a couple of ear-rings and a dog-eared *London A–Z* guide that Robin had borrowed from me ages ago and never returned.

I stuck the guide in the pocket of my uniform and opened the first drawer of the chest. Three-quarters of the space was filled with neatly folded underwear and socks. The rest was miscellaneous stuff in a separate box: a clear plastic container of aspirins (nearly full), cold drops, a bottle of vitamins (empty, judging from the way it rolled about soundlessly) and some little packets of antacid. There was a brown plastic bottle with a white plastic lid – the unmistakable kind that contains prescription drugs.

It appeared to be empty, with only a fine dusting of white powder visible on the inside surface of the plastic. Looking at the bottle gave me an eerie feeling. Might the contents have accounted for Robin's death?

The label was turned well to the side and impossible to read. I reached for the bottle, then hesitated. If Robin's death was murder, as I thought it might be, and if pills were the means, then I was about to get my fingerprints all over what might be an important piece of evidence. I knew my Dad wore latex gloves when he was at a murder scene (the few times there ever was a murder on Prince Edward Island), but latex gloves weren't exactly the sort of thing I carried with me on a day-to-day basis. So I took my duster, gave it a little shake, and used it to cover my fingers as I carefully lifted the bottle from its berth.

The label contained the usual information. The prescription had been made up at A. Tate, Dispensing Chemist, at an address not far away in Grosvenor Gardens near Victoria Station. Robin's name was typed on, as was that of a doctor whose name was unknown to me. It wasn't Dr Elcott, the Palace Physician, nor any other member of the Medical Household that I knew of. 'Take two at bedtime,' the label said, with the warning: 'Do not consume with alcohol.' I looked at the name of the drug. 'Trichlorosertrapam' was one of the words. 'Zolinane' was the other. Neither meant a thing to me.

Reluctantly I returned the bottle to its place, hoping that I would be able to remember the drugs' names – at least the last one – should it be necessary. I continued my search through the remaining two drawers but found only clothes – the stiff white shirts worn with some of the liveries, and casual clothes such as sweaters.

I looked over at the table where a number of books and magazines were stacked untidily. The lamp was still on – something I hadn't noticed when I entered the room. With a few brave rays of sunshine washing the room from a high-perched window, the light that the lamp cast on the surface of the table was feeble. But had Robin been reading earlier this morning, when it was still dark? Suddenly it all seemed so poignant, thinking of him sitting there reading before starting work.

The books themselves suggested little. I could see paperback copies of works about Olivier and Gielgud and an autobiography by Kenneth Branagh. There were some plays and novels, a few Stephen Kings and similar works which we both liked to read. And there were some histories about different aspects of London. They were the kinds of things I bought, too, and Robin and I traded them back and forth. Currently, I was going through one of his – essentially a well-annotated tour of playwrights' London. And he was going through one of mine, a history of Jack the Ripper that he had borrowed just after returning from Balmoral. That seemed to be the one he was reading most recently because it was nearest the chair. A bookmark poked out from between the pages.

I had just picked up the book and was about to put it in my pocket when I suddenly became aware that I was no longer alone in the room. Someone was standing behind me, near the door. I clutched the book to my chest, my heart beating wildly, and wheeled around.

It was Karim, and the expression on his face appeared to be one of shock combined with something approaching rancour.

'What are you doing here?' he demanded brusquely, after a strained moment in which we gaped at each other in silence.

'I might ask you the same question,' I replied, which wasn't really very clever. Or appropriate. It was obvious that Karim had just learned of Robin's death and was fighting for some kind of control over his emotions – the male way, by getting angry.

'I was looking for a jumper Robin had borrowed.'

'Oh,' I said, 'I was just looking for . . . some books he had borrowed, too.'

Neither of us was very believable. *Why was he here?* But I knew that, if I probed him any further, Karim could immediately ask me the same question. Stalemated, I said the only thing I could think of at that moment.

'I guess you know about Robin.'

'Yes,' he said hollowly.

'I'm sorry,' I said, not knowing what else to say. I added: 'I guess I'm surprised.'

Karim looked at me suspiciously. 'At what?'

'I mean, I guess I'm surprised that Robin would kill himself.'

His eyes moved away.

'Do *you* think he killed himself?' I persisted.

'Does it matter?' he retorted.

A whole lot, I thought, but said nothing. Instead I asked him if he'd had a chance to see Robin earlier in the morning, before the tragedy. He had. Apparently Robin had been released from hospital late on Monday. Cyril Wentworth-Desborough had contrived to get some of them in an informal breakfast situation in Servants' Hall for his filming, so this morning Robin, Angela, Karim and Nikki had been shot at a buffet table, at a tea urn and at a dining table, all pretending it was just the start of another working day at Buck House, even though housemaids tend to eat breakfast earlier than most of the footmen. All this was after I had left for the White Drawing Room.

I wondered what W-Dez (as we called the director behind his back) would do with that bit of footage now.

I wondered what he would do with the whole damn film. The death of a footman was a story in itself – but there wasn't much chance of it being told, given that the Palace had final approval of the documentary. Still, this information of Karim's gave me an idea that I tucked away for later.

'Robin really seemed depressed after you guys got back from Balmoral,' I told him. 'Did something happen up there?'

'How would I know?' he snapped. Then he hesitated, seeming to change his mind about something. 'No, nothing happened. At least not that I know of.'

'So something *did* happen?'

'Look, I don't know what happened. I really didn't see much of him aside from work, that's all.'

'But why? You guys have always been close.'

'I don't know.'

'Angie?' I ventured.

'No!' He was vehement.

'Okay, okay! Well then, when exactly did Robin seem to change? His other depressions have usually been triggered by something.'

A look of irritation crossed his swarthy face, but he answered anyway: 'I don't know. Early on, I guess. He went off to Aberdeen a couple of times on his own. It was around then. He started to keep to himself. At least as much as you could up there.'

Balmoral, where the Royal Family spends its holidays from mid-August to October, is rather like summer camp. At least it is for the Staff, who, they tell me, get up to all kinds of things they wouldn't normally get away with at Buck House.

'But how about when you got back here? How were things then? When I visited Robin in hospital on Sunday afternoon, you guys looked like you were having a pretty intense conversation.'

At this point Karim's handsome face suddenly lost its fierceness and, to my discomfort, a tear rolled out of each of his eyes and down his cheeks, leaving two moist little paths that glistened against his skin. He didn't raise his hands to wipe his eyes but instead held himself stiffly, arms at his sides, as if struggling to repress any further expression of grief. You don't see men cry very often outside of films, so when they do it's always a bit of a shock. At any rate, I wasn't sure how to respond – whether to make some comforting gesture or pretend it wasn't happening. But it didn't matter, because in the second I was deliberating Karim turned abruptly and tore out of the door. Without the jumper, of course. But then, I wasn't there looking for my borrowed books either.

Thinking about the books made me realize I was still clutching one of them in my hand. *Jack the Ripper, 100 Years of Investigation* was the title. I had bought it after going on one of those Jack the Ripper walking tours where they take you to the places in the East End where he killed all those women, and I had found it really unputdownable.

As I quickly thumbed the pages, the protruding bookmark leaped out and twirled to the floor. Bending to pick it up, I noticed it wasn't a bookmark at all – not a proper one. It was a business card. On it was the name, an odd name, of a firm of solicitors in Lincoln's Inn

Fields, Chancery Lane, in the City of London. 'Chol-mondeley & Featherstonehaugh', the card read.

What, I wondered, would a twenty-one-year-old Buck House footman want with a solicitor?

Chapter Four

I didn't get a chance to find out until later, of course. I had to beetle back to the White Drawing Room in case I had been missed, and, no surprise, I had been. Mrs Harbottle, the old prune, was standing there, tapping her sensible-shoed foot, her eyebrows so elevated with annoyance they looked like they had been tacked to the top of her forehead. The shock of Robin's death cut no ice with her. I got the usual harangue about slackness and responsibility and then went back to work, though my mind was scarcely on what I was doing.

Mealtimes that day were strangely subdued. It was as if the idea of suicide had cast a pall over everyone. Nikki wasn't around at supper – she probably had a date with one of her boyfriends. Angela Cheatle wasn't anywhere to be seen, although it could be fairly said that she had a reason to be in seclusion, given that her fiancé had just died. (Fiancé – it still sounded odd in relation to Robin.) When I ran into Davey later, coming out of the Staff lounge, even he was monosyllabic – which was really peculiar given his general volubility no matter what the subject.

I went to bed early, quite exhausted. I guess it was the shock and – though I didn't like to admit it – the excitement that the day had brought. I didn't even hear Nikki come in next door.

In the olden days, when I was a teenager and obliged to face another boring 8.30 maths class, I hated getting out of bed in the mornings. But I was up well before the sun the next day, practically spontaneously, which probably goes to show that if you do have something to get up for, you get up. If my father could have seen me he would have been enormously pleased, considering how often he'd threatened to pour cold water over my head to rouse me. Anyway, I dressed quietly, put a down shell jacket on over my uniform, and slipped out into the passage.

I knew the film crew was going to be doing a sequence near the Side Gate where produce deliveries were made early each morning. But when I arrived filming was already in progress, and looked as if it had been for some time. Neil Gorringe, the camera assistant who had caused me to miss Robin's birthday party, glimpsed me as I popped out of the door. He rolled his eyes to let me know that old Cyril was driving them nuts.

Basically, Neil and the rest of the film crew weren't too keen on Wentworth-Desborough. It wasn't just that W-Dez had to be pushy to get things done. That was expected of a film director. According to Neil, it was because W-Dez's temper too often went over the edge; he was arbitrary in his decisions and condescending to just about everybody who wasn't his status or higher. I had had a little taste of him myself. He had filmed me pushing a hoover down the Picture Gallery and then had me do it again, and then again, each time calling me 'girl' and barking instructions as if I didn't know how to vacuum a carpet, for God's sake.

I thought I knew what his victims felt like that morning. One beefy, red-faced man stood ready, holding a huge metal churn, while another held a giant wooden box – milk and cheese, presumably, taken from a nearby truck marked 'Express Dairies'. Both men looked completely pissed off; they had probably gone through the delivery routine umpteen times. So much for the spontaneity of documentary film.

Suddenly there was a halt in the muttered conversation and on some indiscernible cue the two men, grunting, their breath curling in the cold air, made their way through the entrance while the Senior Storeman appeared to check something off on a clipboard. Another van rolled up, this one marked 'J. Lyons & Co.', but something must have gone wrong for Cyril W-Dez leaped in the air, waved his silly walking stick – an affectation; the man was perfectly fit – and shouted, 'No, no, *no*, gentlemen' in tones of great exasperation, then darted over to a thin, nervous-looking guy holding a very large lamp.

Neil sidled up to me and gave me a big smile.

'Hello, there,' he said in a subdued voice, rubbing his hands against the cold. 'What brings you out here this time of the morning?'

'I thought I'd like a word with your boss.'

Neil regarded me as if I had lost all hold on reality.

'Really? *Der Führer*? Well, you'll probably have your opportunity soon. Nothing's gone right and now it's too bright and he's got to let us go for a tea break in a minute. This was supposed to be shot at sunrise, not

C. C. BENISON

when the sun is blazing at noon, which is what it will be
if he keeps going on at this rate.'

'What's the problem?'

'Oh, he's just being really stupid and fussy about
everything. This bit will probably be less than thirty
seconds in the final cut. It's not worth the bother. And
those two over there are going to break the *Führer*'s
neck if they have to carry those crates and things one
more time . . . So,' he went on, changing the subject,
'when do I see you again?'

'I'll bet you have some bird waiting around everywhere you shoot.'

Neil grinned. Nature had been generous with his
mouth and eyes so that his expressions had a disarming
frankness, which made me wonder how he would ever
succeed in the film business.

'Not true. How about tonight, then? When do you
get off from dusting Her Majesty's china?'

'Not tonight, Neil. Busy.'

His face fell. 'Oh, well, then,' he said with exagger-
ated suffering, 'I guess I'll carry on somehow.'

'Sorry.'

The grin returned. 'It's all right. Cyril has plans for
us anyway.' He sighed. 'I'm considering writing a piece
called *The Documentary Film Crew: A Study in Feudal-
ism*. Sometimes I think my job isn't much different from
yours, Janet – being at someone else's beck and call all
the time.'

It was his standard rant. I said nothing.

'So, then,' he continued, detecting my boredom,
'why do you want to talk to Cyril?'

'Well . . .' I hesitated. Neil was a great guy and lots of

60

fun. He had shown me things about London's rave culture I mightn't have experienced otherwise. And, of course, I had introduced him to the Maple Leaf pub near Covent Garden for a taste of the world's best beer – Canadian. But I didn't know him super-thoroughly. I suspected the London film community was as gossipy as the Palace. And I remembered HM's warning from the day before.

So I said, 'I was just wondering about the filming you did yesterday in Servants' Hall with a couple of the footpigs and housesluts. Did you know one of them died?'

Neil frowned. 'I heard. Suicide, poor bugger. What is it you were wondering about?'

'Just if I could take a look at it – the bit in Servants' Hall.'

'Good bloody luck. I can't see Cyril letting you do that. He's been particularly on edge the last few days. His wife's really been up his backside about something or other. She's even shown up here a couple of times.' He shrugged. 'Not that Cyril would let you look at his precious footage any other time. But why . . .?'

I touched my mouth with my hand and tried to look all cute and innocent.

'A secret, then,' he said. 'All right. Looks like you'll have your chance in a minute.'

We both looked at the crew, the delivery men and the Palace Storemen, each group huddled in its own knot. While we were talking they had been practically motionless, muttering, their breath rising in white puffs, the shadows of their bodies blending into the shadows of the great plane trees in the courtyard.

As we waited, I tried to recall what Neil had told me about W-Dez. He had started his career in the late sixties as a tea-boy during the filming of *Royal Family*, a film that showed the Queen, her husband and the kids as normal folks who liked to barbecue and eat dinner in front of the telly. (All before my time, of course.) He'd had a career at the BBC but had later become an independent film-maker, specializing in pieces about the arts and culture and architecture and the swell lives of rich people in the marvellous 1980s. At any rate, W-Dez must have made the right connections over the years because he had been entrusted to make this documentary about the daily workings of Buckingham Palace. Neil said it was because he had done a film about the operation of one of the great London hotels and what was the difference anyway, but I think he was just being cynical.

My musings were broken by a shout that sent a few pigeons flapping.

'Gorringe!'

The tableau before me dissolved. The delivery men began hauling their wares through the door in earnest, the Senior Storeman disappeared before them, and one of the five-man film crew fiddled with the lamp while beckoning to Neil. Wentworth-Desborough stood with his hand to his mouth, worrying a fingernail, a look of concentrated disgust on his face.

'Well, that's it. I'd better go,' Neil said, adding with a meaningful look, 'and best of luck.' And off he darted to do his master's bidding.

Unpleasant though he was, Cyril W-Dez didn't seem to me to be a complete ogre. But then, of course, I didn't have to work for him on a daily basis. The director was short – well, short for a man – thin, although that morning he was swaddled in a green anorak and great grey muffler wrapped several times around his neck, and he looked to be somewhere in his forties. His black hair was salt-flecked and contrasted sharply with his face, which was perpetually flushed, as though he had high blood pressure or spent too much time under a tanning lamp. It wasn't standard English pallor.

'Mr Wentworth-Desborough,' I said, approaching him, thinking even as I said it that hyphenated surnames always sound silly on the tongue. 'Mr Wentworth-Desborough? Excuse me?'

It took a moment for him to register my presence. When he did, his expression changed from disgust to crinkly-browed impatience.

'Yes. What?'

'You know the sequence you shot yesterday morning in Servants' Hall with Robin Tukes and Angela Cheatle and the other—'

'Yes, yes.'

'Well, I wonder if I could take a look at it.'

'Of course you can't look at it.' He regarded me with utter disdain.

'Why not?'

He cast a glance skywards. 'It's just not done. I don't show the rushes of my films to people I don't know. Who are you, anyway?'

'Jane Bee. I'm one of the houseslu— housemaids.'

'Ah, yes, the Picture Gallery. I remember now.'

The director looked me up and down as if I was

a carcass for inspection and tapped his walking stick impatiently on the pavement.

'Why do you want to look at it, anyway?' he asked in a slightly more reasonable tone, though laced with suspicion.

This was the hard part. If I were an RCMP officer like my father, I could ask direct questions and get direct answers. I could at least put my prey in such a dither that he might give me useful clues. But with Wentworth-Desborough, and, as I was learning, with others, I would have to be careful to appear guileless. I couldn't very well go around asking a lot of people what went on in Servants' Hall Tuesday morning. It would arouse suspicion.

'Well, Robin was a good friend of mine . . . and you know he died yesterday . . .?'

Wentworth-Desborough gave a curt nod.

'. . . and so I have nothing for a keepsake, if you know what I mean. No photograph or anything. And then I remembered you had filmed him, so . . .'

His eyebrows knitted together. He glared at me. 'There's no keepsake in watching a film sequence,' he said brusquely.

'I thought you could give me a copy of some kind.' I tried a smile which I thought might make me look girlish and sweet and convincing.

'No. Absolutely not.' So much for girlish and convincing.

'But you'll be making copies, anyway,' I said. 'I was hoping to get the – what are they called – "out-takes"?'

'No. Look, I'm not going to be using that sequence anyway. It wasn't satisfactory.'

'But . . .'

'I'm throwing it out. In fact, I did throw it out. Yesterday, after I was told about the death. I had planned to feature Robin in another sequence, but now there won't be any continuity. So I decided there was no point. I'm sorry, you're out of luck. Now, Miss Bee, if you'll excuse me . . .'

He said all this at great speed, clutched his walking stick and left so fast that I couldn't get another word in. I was left wondering why he had been so short with me. I didn't think mine was that unreasonable a request, although perhaps the footage might appear to be an odd sort of 'keepsake'. What I wanted to view, of course, was the movements in Servants' Hall that morning. After all, it was only a short time later that Robin had died. If he had ingested something, there was a good chance it would have been there and then, and perhaps the film would reveal it.

How could I ask the others who were there? I thought about Neil, wondering if I could get him to tell me what he saw while they were filming. He had moved nearer but was bent over, sorting through bits of film equipment. He has quite a nice bum, so I lost my train of thought for a moment.

'Neil,' I began, trying to reformulate the question, 'Neil . . . um—'

'You know, I was just thinking . . .' he interrupted, straightening himself and glancing round to see if anyone was looking at us. Cyril was standing not far away, conferring with the Storeman who had suddenly reappeared. Neil lowered his voice. 'I was just thinking that I could get you a videocopy of the bits with your friend in it. It wouldn't be great, mind. But once the film is processed, all I have to do is run it in front of my video camera.'

'Brilliant! Would you do that for me?' I whispered back. 'That's great!'

'Sure, no problem. It won't be the sharpest copy—'

'That's all right. But won't Cyril mind?'

'He'll never know. Look, I'm responsible for the actual film and every other bloody piece of equipment. I take the stuff to the labs. I do the—'

'He said he'd already thrown away the film of that sequence.'

Neil was disbelieving. 'Couldn't have, the silly berk. He hasn't even had it processed yet.'

'Oh.' Odd, I thought. So why had he been so adamant? He could have just said no, without presenting all these other excuses.

Neil crooked his arm and began to wrap electric cord around it. 'There's something else.' He looked round again to make sure no one could overhear us. 'And I don't know if this means anything, but since you seem to be poking about in something . . .'

I frowned as if to deny it. He smiled conspiratorially.

'Anyway, last Thursday – I think it was – in the afternoon, we were packing up from a shoot in the post office. Everyone was out in the courtyard around the Ambassadors' Entrance, but I'd gone back because I'd left one of the lights. Cyril was still there, but he was having a bit of a barney with someone. I could see his jacket but I couldn't see who he was arguing with. You know how there's all these nooks and crannies in the post office. I didn't really pay much attention. Cyril's often got his knickers in a twist about something, so I just picked up my light and got out of there. But on Monday when we were filming in Servants' Hall I realized who Cyril had been arguing with as soon as he opened his mouth. It was the American accent that did it. Oh, all right, *Canadian,*' he corrected himself when I glared at him. 'You sound pretty much alike to us. Anyway, it was your friend the footman.'

'Are you sure?'

'Well, pretty sure. Unless you know of another Yank . . . er – Canadian working in the Palace.'

'Well, there's Chuck McCandless – Charles, I mean – one of the Assistant Press Secretaries. He's Canadian. But I can't imagine them arguing. McCandless is a fairly big deal in the Household. Cyril would really have to have some nerve to pick a fight with him . . . I guess you didn't hear what they were arguing about?' I added hopefully.

'Haven't a clue. Sorry, love. I could hear the tone of their voices but the words were a bit muffled behind all those wooden pigeon-holes for the letters. Maybe something will come to me later. We could, for instance, meet this evening, after Cyril's finished with me. By then I'll be sure to have remembered something.' He smiled slyly.

'The video and now this piece of information,' I said. 'Neil, you're making me feel like an ingrate.'

'Aren't I now!'

Chapter Five

The reason I couldn't go out with Neil that evening was simple. I was hoping to go out with Angela Cheatle instead. True, it wasn't exactly my idea of a fun date, but I wanted to talk to her about Robin. She had been his fiancée, strange as it seemed, and she had been one of the last people to see him alive. Or had she been the *very* last?

I found her just before noon, standing at the fire-place in the 1855 Room on the ground floor (so named after the visit of Napoleon III and Empress Eugénie of France that year), dabbing at her eyes with a lace handkerchief. She didn't see me at first. She was in front of the mirror, blotting away; then she raised herself on tiptoe and leaned over the mantel to get a closer look at herself, turning down the corners of her mouth so she looked sadder still. If it weren't for the fact that her eyes were red-rimmed and puffy, I would have said she was practising varying degrees of grief. She started slightly when she saw me, stuffed the handkerchief up the sleeve of her uniform and altered her expression again. 'Shining Through', you could have called it. Or 'Courage in the Face of Adversity'. Something like that.

Anyway, she *seemed* sort of grateful for my invitation. It made me wonder if I was the only one who had offered Angie any condolences. I had been about to suggest that we avoid both the Palace Staff bar and the favoured nearby watering-hole, the Bag O'Nails, but she beat me to it, suggesting a pub a little further into Belgravia, the Plumber's Arms, which I had never visited before. She said she had some other business in the area, although what business she might have in such a well-heeled neighbourhood I couldn't figure. Anyway, it was all right by me.

I was there at eight o'clock, as we had arranged. The Plumber's Arms turned out to be a snug little place, down a few steps from the street, not particularly crowded, with the bar propped up by what looked like a bunch of regulars – middle-aged guys, government types probably, business-suited, talking quietly among themselves, ignoring – somehow! – the infectious technothrob of the Pet Shop Boys' 'Go West' that, improbably for such a place, flowed from speakers over the fruit-machine.

The song was everywhere you went, from Capital FM 95.8 first thing in the morning to, well, cosy Belgravia pubs in the evening. Funny, I thought, humming along as I paid for a pint of lager, isn't 'go west' a euphemism for 'dying'? The barman, much younger and infinitely more ear-ringed and moussed than the punters, smiled conspiratorially as he dropped the change into my hand.

'Do you think we could have something other than that rubbish, Dennis?' one of the suits said, regarding me balefully while the barman rolled his eyes for my benefit.

As the music changed to Elvis mooning on about

something or other and the volume fell a notch or two, I moved to a seat in the far corner next to the fireplace and waited.

And waited. The wallpaper, I noted, was gold with burgundy flocking. The picture on the wall next to me was a pen-and-ink sketch of Queen Victoria receiving the homage of some young woman. Everyone ignored the flashing fruit machine and the dartboard. And the dumb waiter came up once with a plate of something hot. Elvis burbled on and on.

By 8.30 I wondered if Angie was going to show at all. So, between sips of my remaining lager and glances at my watch, I did a little reading of something gleaned at the Grosvenor Gardens chemist's on my way to the Plumber's Arms.

I had asked to look at their pharmacopoeia and I was able to sweet-talk the courtly gentleman behind the counter into photocopying the entry on Zolinane, the name on the empty prescription bottle I had found in Robin's drawer. After reading it, I figured the doctor who had prescribed the stuff to him should be shot. Apparently the drug was for insomnia – it was news to me that Robin even *had* insomnia – but people with emotional disorders such as depression were strongly cautioned against its improper use. A read between the lines suggested to me a kind of substance that could sharpen suicidal tendencies. I wavered for a moment after pondering that. Maybe Robin *had* killed himself, after all.

Then I thought: no way.

*

Finally, at 8.40, Angie arrived. Her long blonde hair, streaming over a blue cashmere coat (Nikki was right – how could she afford such things on £6000 a year?) glistened in the pub lights. She tossed her head alluringly to shake off the effects of the evening's light rain. From across the room I could see the high colour in her cheeks – whether from exertion or make-up I couldn't tell. She looked fantastic. Heads swivelled. Inwardly, I groaned.

I was pretty fed up by then but decided it would be better not to show it. She was unapologetic – no surprise. But her mood had changed from that of the morning. The grieving fiancée had vanished. Instead, she seemed agitated about something, even angry, hence the high colour.

'What'll you have?' I asked her.

'White wine,' she replied as she pulled a pack of cigarettes and a lighter from her bag and tossed them on to the table before she had even taken off her coat. I didn't know she smoked. Davey once said the only person allowed to smoke in the Palace was Princess Margaret.

'Are you sure?'

I thought she'd go for a Perrier or something non-alcoholic, being pregnant, but she looked at me like I was stupid. Then it occurred to me that she'd already had a drink or two somewhere. I signalled to the barman, but he didn't need signalling. The wine was delivered in double-quick time.

Angie lit up and puffed away hungrily, watching the smoke billow toward the sconces and the picture of Queen Victoria. She took her glass, sipped tentatively, and then, as if making up her mind about something, took a deep swallow.

'You know,' I said after reprising some of my sympathetic murmurings in the 1855 Room, 'I still can't get over it.'

'Can't you?' Angela said evenly.

'Well, no. I mean, Robin never seemed the sort of person who would take his own life. Mind you, he did seem a bit depressed, but . . .'

'He wasn't depressed. I don't know why people keep saying that. He was being serious. Serious-minded. Mature. He was going to get married. He had a kiddie on the way. He had decided to stop acting like those other idiots.'

I chose not to ask which idiots she was referring to. 'Then why would he end his life?'

'Well, I don't know, do I? He was perfectly happy with me. This isn't my fault, you know,' she added in an aggrieved tone.

'I know. I didn't say it was.'

'I'm sure that's what other people are thinking.'

'If they are, they have no business doing so.' I hoped I sounded appropriately indignant. In fact, of the few comments I had heard about Robin's death, at least one had been a snigger from one of the less heterosexually inclined about getting out of marrying Angela.

'Robin was looking forward to being a dad,' she said defensively. 'When I told him I was pregnant, he was really happy.'

'When did you tell him?'

'When we were at Balmoral.'

'Is that when you decided to get married?'

Angie nodded as she took another swallow of wine.

'Then why did you keep it all a secret for so long?'

'We just thought it would be better.' She shrugged. 'There were some things each of us needed to work out first.'

'Such as?'

Angela looked at me crossly. 'Such as none of your business.'

'Sorry.' I cast about for something else to say that wouldn't put her off. 'So when are you due?'

'End of March, early April. Around then.'

I counted backwards on my fingers under the table. That meant she must have conceived around the end of June or early July. Was it possible that she and Robin had had something going then? If they had, they were sure good at keeping it secret.

Then something else occurred to me. 'By the way, they were telling me you're having a boy. I guess you had one of those tests.'

'Amniowhatsits, yeah.'

'How was it?'

'Oh, fine. No problem.'

'Don't they stick a big needle in your stomach? It sounds kind of gruesome to me.'

Angie traced her fingers distractedly round and round the rim of her now empty wineglass. 'It didn't hurt.'

'And the baby was okay? Don't people usually have this done if they think there might be some kind of a problem?'

'I just wanted to make sure everything was all right. And it was. So . . . fancy another? I'll get this one.' She stubbed out her cigarette and rose unsteadily from her chair, glass in hand.

'I'll be all right with this, ta very much.' I was still nursing the dregs of my original pint, which had got warm and soapy. British lager is a tad over-rated in my estimation. I yearned for a Moosehead.

I watched the men watch Angie trip to the bar in her dangerous-looking heels, and thought about this pregnancy business. A whole lot of it just didn't ring true. I thought you had to be old, like over thirty-five, or have a family history of birth defects or disorders, to require the amniocentesis test. One thing I did remember was something that my sister Jennifer, the future doctor, had once said: the procedure is done around the sixteenth week of pregnancy. Which meant that Angie, if she'd really had an amniocentesis, could only just have had it.

But the thing that really made me doubt that she had had the test was what she said when she came back from the bar and I asked her if she had visited Robin in hospital.

'Oh, no. I couldn't,' she replied, shaking her head to fluff up her hair. 'I simply can't stand hospitals. All those tubes and instruments and machines and things. I haven't been able to go into one since my Mum died. She was in a car crash, you know. I was six years old. All I can remember is her all hooked up to those terrible machines. It was awful.'

'I'm sorry,' I said.

'Seems ages ago now.' She ran her fingers through that amazing hair.

'Did your father bring you up?'

'Did a flit, he did, early on. My Gran brought me up.'

'In London?'

'Yeah . . . well, council estate in Camberwell, if you must know.' She spoke with disdain – whether of me, or of the area, I couldn't tell.

'Then you've got a ready-made baby-minder,' I said cheerfully.

Angela looked into her glass. 'She doesn't know I'm having a baby. If she knew, she'd kill me. I mean, not being married and all.'

'That's a bit old-fashioned, isn't it?'

'It's the way my Mum brought me into the world. Got pregnant when she was sixteen. My Gran kicked her out – wouldn't have anything to do with her. Didn't even soften after I was born, according to Uncle Bert. You've seen my Uncle Bert?'

I must have looked puzzled. Angie rolled her eyes and took another greedy gulp of wine. Uncle Bert – her great-uncle, it turned out – was the old geezer, a figure of fun really, who spent his life trotting around the Palace keeping the hundreds of clocks wound up and on time. You'd be dusting or hoovering away in some room and Bert would pad in when you least expected it and make a bee-line for the clock. He never talked, but he did smell of whisky – which didn't, however, seem to affect the accuracy of his work.

'Is that why you're working at the Palace, then? I never knew.'

'Well, that's how I heard about working at the Palace.' She gave an alcoholic snort of dismissal. 'Anyway, what was I saying? Oh, right, my Gran. She brought me up after my Mum died, of course. She's a hard old bitch, my Gran, really. If I could tell her I was getting married, it might be all right, but . . .' She fell silent.

I felt a pang of sympathy for her. 'What are you going to do?'

'I'm leaving the Palace, for one thing.'

'To do what?'

She took a rather determined swallow of her wine. 'I've got some plans.'

The expression on her face suggested this was a closed subject. Still . . . Plans, plans. What would Angie's plans have been had Robin still been alive? I just couldn't see her living in some seedy flat somewhere while Robin continued at the Palace. Or would he have left, too? And done what?

'You guys started getting close at Balmoral, I gather.'

'Mmmph,' she said. She was in the middle of lighting another cigarette, and doing it clumsily.

'How did it begin?' With bated breath I awaited a tale of summer palace romance.

'I don't know! We just saw something we liked in each other.'

Dead romantic.

'Moonlight swims, I hear. With your clothes on, though.'

'Who told you that?' She regarded me suspiciously.

'Davey. He said the two of you looked quite peculiar.'

'Oh. Well, it wasn't anything. We were just being a bit silly and then I fell in the river.'

'And you pulled Robin in with you.'

'Yeah, that's right.'

She stared dreamily at the pale liquid left in her glass before downing most of it. Having had a few before she came in, she was now getting quite drunk.

'Angie,' I said, warming to the question I had wanted to ask earlier, 'if you only started going around in August, how can the baby be due in March?'

'What d'you mean?'

'It's only seven months. Pregnancies go on for nine, normally.'

She stared at me blearily. Slowly her face reddened. 'What are you getting at? Are you trying to suggest this baby isn't Robin's? The bloody cheek!'

'No, Angie. I was really thinking about the amnio-thingy – the test.' I lied. 'I thought maybe there was something wrong . . .'

'Didn't I just tell you?'

'Sorry.'

But Angela wasn't mollified. 'We fell *in love* in August. But we were *sleeping* together long before June. You don't have to be in love to sleep with a bloke, you know,' she said, raising her voice.

'Shhh.'

The dartboard was the other side of the fireplace and some of the men seemed to have decided there could be nothing more fascinating than darts, especially since it allowed them a better opportunity to do a little eyeball exploration of Angie.

'And he was brilliant in bed, for your information,' Angie continued. She looked at me disdainfully. The men at the dartboard gaped.

'Oh, yeah? When did you two last sleep together?'

She gasped and then, after a moment in which she appeared to be making up her mind, said with scorn, 'Monday night, if you must know. Robin decided he couldn't stand the hospital any more, so he discharged himself. And when he got back to the Palace he came straight to *my* room.'

Well, that might explain the fact that his bed hadn't been slept in. But there was still the gay thing. I wasn't sure how to bring it up. It was sort of sensitive. But I was in luck and I didn't have to. Angie beat me to it.

'He wasn't gay, you know,' she told me in a slightly slurred voice.

'Oh?' I said. 'Well . . .'

'I know that's what people thought. But it simply wasn't true.'

'I sort of wondered . . .'

'Fancied him yourself, did you?'

'Well, when I first came to the Palace, I . . .'

'You're hardly his type.'

'What about Karim, then?' I said, annoyed.

'That black twit, hanging about looking so moony-eyed – I can't stand him. I told Robin, "I don't want him hanging about. And he's not coming to the wedding." ' She drained the last drops from her glass. 'It's a phase, don't you see, Jane? It's something they go through. Robin went to a public school, didn't he? Oh, what do you call them in America . . . Canada? *Private* school, right. What do you think happens to lads who have no girls about? But they get over it.'

'I guess,' I said reluctantly. 'I don't know. I don't think, though, that I would want to sleep with a man

who slept with men. These days, I mean. You know –
the diseases and all. Didn't you worry about that?'

'I told you he wasn't gay!'

'But you just said . . .'

'I said it was a *phase*.'

'But how do you know there wouldn't be another
phase?'

'Well, I wouldn't care.'

'Funny kind of marriage,' I said, half under my
breath.

'It's the way marriages among the aristocracy work,'
she replied in a boozy huff.

'What? You mean all aristocratic husbands and
wives have homosexual lovers?'

'Of course I don't mean that! I mean they have
lovers, period. They marry for . . . *dynastic* reasons. You
don't think the Waleses married for love, do you?'

'I don't know. I never asked them.'

'Don't be funny. It was to ensure the succession, of
course. They really love other people.'

'But, Angie,' I said – this was getting truly loopy –
'you're not a member of the upper classes. You're just a
housemaid in the Palace, not the bloody Queen!'

Angie looked like she was about to explode. 'Well, I
could tell you a—' she said, and then clamped her
mouth shut.

'And Robin was just a footman. What were you going
to do once you were married?'

'You asked me out for a drink so you could – what? –
grill me on my relationship with Robin?'

'It's just that it all seems so unrealistic . . .'

'Look, there was nothing *unrealistic* about it. Robin had prospects . . .'

'Oh, for heaven's sake!'

'*Real* prospects, Jane. And I would have been his wife. I would have finally got what I deserve. What I'm bloody *owed*. But the bugger went and topped himself.'

'What are you talking about?' My head was spinning.

'Never mind. And maybe I mean someone else. Oh, look, I've had enough.' She rose unsteadily, and snatched her coat from the empty seat. 'I'm getting out of here.'

'Wait. I'll go back with you.'

'No. Get away. Piss off.'

I watched her go. So did everybody else, sadly.

Chapter Six

Rather than take a left turn and head up Ebury Street back to the Palace, I continued down darkened Lower Belgrave Street and across Buckingham Palace Road to the brilliant noise and clutter of Victoria Station. When you get up as early as we housemaids do you rarely see a morning paper, and by late afternoon you're too tired to care about the evening editions. Besides, having some insight into the bizarre inner workings of news-papers (thanks to my mother) I was off the things, anyway. I prefer books.

Still, I wondered if the papers had got the wind up about Robin's death. And if not, why not, particularly since there were few taboos these days when it came to reporting anything vaguely to do with the Royal Family.

The W. H. Smith's bookstall in Victoria Station looks like a modern folly. It's a little glass-walled sanctuary surrounded by ornate nineteenth-century brickwork. The selection is geared mainly to the passing traveller – lots of BTRs (Big Trash Reads) and magazines galore – but there's also some decent stuff and, since it's the closest bookstall to Buck House, it's often on my itinerary.

The newspaper bins are all at the front, usually

surrounded by people reading and not buying. I joined them under the fluorescent glare. There was nothing about Robin in any of them, downmarket or upmarket, at least not that I could find. This was a mercy. Most of the tabloids were too busy having fun with some new political group, the *English* Republican Army, that kept claiming *it* was responsible for the bomb scares and other such annoyances that had been plaguing London life recently, and not that *other* Republican Army, and all this was apparently irritating the *other* Republican Army no end. The quality papers, meanwhile, were more bothered about the declining fortunes of the Prime Minister and the declining pound, and decline generally.

The Robin no-show was curious, though. The Palace was not without leaks, the human kind, despite the documents of non-disclosure we're all made to sign when we're hired. There was the odd person who would blab to the press for a few quid or for whatever satisfaction it gave them, and if they were found out they were sacked. Sad to say, most of these people came, like me, from the lower orders. Those higher up had more to lose than just a job. They could be banished from Society.

Still, Robin had been well-liked among the Staff. I reasoned that ranks would close if some news hack started sticking his – or her – nose in. And the Palace itself would have no reason to release anything to the press about a death on the premises. There was only one thing that bothered me, though: wouldn't a death, suicide or not, have to be reported to the police? And couldn't a reporter get it that way? Of course, as I knew from my mother, the police could be awfully niggardly with the information they doled out to reporters. Maybe they were keeping it off the books until after the State Visit. *Then* there'd be an inquest and all that.

It was late. An over-polite voice announcing the closing of W. H. Smith's ushered me out of the door through Victoria's mêlée, past the taxi stand and on to Buckingham Palace Road.

It was a cold, damp evening. There had been patchy rain all day and you could see your breath in the air. Just past the Midland Bank at the corner of Victoria Street I suddenly saw Nikki. Or, rather, I saw Nikki looking at me over the shoulder of a tall man in a long olive-drab greatcoat, like army gear, who had bent down to give her a hug. All I got to see of him was a very nice-shaped head of long, dark hair, because as quickly as Nikki saw me the man released her and moved up Buckingham Palace Road and into tiny Allington Street at a brisk pace.

'Who was that?' I said when I caught up with her.

'Just a mate.'

'Oh, right. "Just a mate." Going out with army blokes, now? C'mon, tell.'

'Just somebody I went to school with,' she replied as we fell into step. 'I ran into him the other day and we decided to meet for a drink. For old times' sake. Name's Kevin. And he's not in the bleedin' army.'

'Seemed anxious to get away.' I was interested in her reaction but her face was in profile, half of it hidden under the upturned collar of her coat.

'He had to get home. Anyway' – she had to shout as we dodged traffic while crossing the street at the Royal Mews – 'where have you been?'

'I went for a drink with Angie.'

'What did you do that for?'

'I thought maybe it would cheer her up.'

'She doesn't look that sad to me.'

'C'mon, Nikki, they were engaged.'

She made a noise like a horse braying.

'I'll admit it's still pretty weird,' I said, and I told her some of what Angie had said to me.

'Wait till we get to our rooms,' Nikki whispered as we passed security at the gate and entered the Palace. 'I'll tell you something *really* interesting about Angie.'

Later, after I had got into my Tank Girl nightshirt (a fun gift to myself), Nikki joined me, full of the power of privileged information. So intrigued was I that I even allowed her to cut her toenails on my bedspread after she had brandished her clippers.

'I really shouldn't be telling you this,' she began coolly, settling on my bed, 'but since you're a mate of mine . . .'

'What, already!'

Nikki's face went into a grin of exultation.

'Angie's the Queen's cousin.'

'And I'm the Pope's wife.'

'Get away! Really?'

I turned from the mirror and hit her with my hairbrush.

'Ouch. I nearly lost my toe there, Jane. All right, you know how I grew up at Sandringham . . .'

'Right . . .'

Nikki's father had been a tenant farmer on the Sandringham estate, the Queen's home in Norfolk. He had died in a hunting accident when Nikki was twelve or thirteen.

'Well, Angie has a sort of family connection to another royal estate. Balmoral. Or, at least, she thinks she does.' Nikki concentrated her nail clippers on her big toe. 'It's daft, really. Let me see if I have it straight. Her grandmother's father . . . that's right . . . her grandmother's father was the illegitimate son of Edward VII, so that, in her mind, makes her some kind of cousin to the Queen.'

'I don't believe it!' I exclaimed.

'Don't. Because it's a load of cobbler's. Families with long histories on royal estates have all sorts of old tales, and being the illegitimate child of royalty is the oldest one of all, believe me. The trouble with Angie is she's stupid enough to believe it. Her great-great-grandmother, or whoever it was, was probably some sort of skivvy at Balmoral during Queen Victoria's reign and she probably never even saw Edward – much less, well, you know . . .'

'I suppose that accounts for her going on about aristocratic marriages and such,' I said, doubtfully. 'Still, she was talking as though her marriage to Robin was actually going to *fulfil* this fantasy in some way. I don't know. You're right, it is daft.' I tried brushing my hair up into a kind of sweep, the way Angie did sometimes. It didn't work. 'By the way, why did she tell you all this?'

'Because of Sandringham when I was a child. I think she thinks I was having a natter with the Queen all the time or something, so naturally I would understand her position as cousin-a-million-times-removed from Her Nibs. Bloody hell, we were miles away. And *they* were only ever there for a few weeks after Christmas. Besides, I don't know why Angie thought I'd give a damn about royal bloody connections. One of those royal buggers shot my father.'

Every once in a while Nikki would bring this into the conversation. It was really one of the first things she ever told me about herself, and you could tell that the hurt and anger had never left her. Her version – and it was the only version I knew – was that her father had been employed one winter as a beater to flush birds and game from the Sandringham estate for members of the Royal Family and their friends to shoot. Instead of pheasant, alas, it was Mr Claypole who got shot. Fatally, as it happened. An inquest declared the death an accident, with no blame attached to any member of the Royal Family or their guests. But that didn't satisfy Nikki. And it couldn't have satisfied Nikki's mother or her brother. Mrs Claypole sold the tenancy at Sandringham not long after her husband's death and moved to nearby King's Lynn. But the family unravelled. First her brother, Jon, then Nikki, left school and drifted to a kind of dodgy life in Camden Town. The fact that she had ended up working for the Royal Family was, well, ironic. I couldn't fathom it myself. But, as Nikki told me, there weren't many jobs in London, in a recession, for someone with no A levels.

'Have you ever wondered why Angie went up to Balmoral and the rest of us didn't?' Nikki asked, admiring her newly trimmed toenails.

'Heather went up, too,' I said, mentioning the other Buck House housemaid lucky enough to go north.

'A decoy, I say. Look, they don't usually take any of

us housesluts up to Scotland. They don't need to. There's people up there they can hire as temps.'

'So what are you getting at?'

'I think maybe someone high and mighty is interested in Angie Cheatle and that's why she went up.'

'Such as who? Chuck?'

'He's in love with the Rottweiler.'

'Andy?'

'It's possible, I suppose.'

'Eddie? Phil?'

She thought about it for a second. 'Naaah.'

'You said, "high and mighty".'

'But that doesn't mean "royal".'

'Well . . . there's the Prime Minister. He goes up now and again, doesn't he?'

'I don't think she's the PM's type.'

I cast my mind over various other members of the Household. Most of them, as far as I knew, stayed in London while the Royal Family was on holiday. But then there were always all kinds of guests popping in and out. Aristocratic types. Still, it's not like I had paid any attention to the summer's guest list.

'W-Dez went up, didn't he?' I said, lighting on one possibility. 'There's supposed to be a bit of Balmoral in his film. And he and his wife have split up. Maybe it's over Angie.'

Nikki looked up from her toes. 'Perhaps. But I don't know how W-Dezzie could bugger around with Palace staffing.'

'Maybe he insisted. Wanted Angie for his film. Wanted Angie for himself. She is attractive, and probably fancies the idea of herself in a film.'

'Well, possibly. But . . .'

'Who, then?'

'I don't know!'

'Then why are you winding me up?'

Nikki contemplated her toes again.

'How about Sir Julian?' I asked.

'Bit ancient.'

'Sexy, though. Powerful, rich, titled. Angie's type, on the whole. Or at least her fantasy type.'

'Married . . . but I think someone did tell me Sir Julian and his wife don't get along, or lead separate lives or something.'

'Where do you hear these things?'

'You've got to keep your ears open.'

'But the risk! If it's someone "high and mighty" and married, then what if he got caught? Can you imagine what the tabloids would do with it?'

'Serve 'em right, in my opinion,' Nikki said, folding her nail clippers.

'Still . . .' I continued, intrigued, 'if it were someone like Sir Julian, he would want to keep it absolutely quiet. The Queen wouldn't be amused.'

'Ha! Look what some members of her family get up to. Anyway, if the father of Angie's baby were W-Dezzie or Sir J. or anybody other than Robin, then we're back to my original question: why would Robin get engaged to her?'

'That's the mystery, isn't it? Maybe he was just being kind.'

'Kind people can cause a lot of bother, in my experience.'

'I suppose . . . oh well.' I give up on my hair – straight

and hopeless – and put the brush back on the bureau. 'When you guys were being filmed in Servants' Hall at breakfast yesterday, what were you drinking?'

Nikki lay back on the bed. 'Me? What an odd question. Coffee, I think.'

'No, all of you. Were you all drinking something?'

'Oh, I see. You're wondering if Robin put something into his coffee? Well, I suppose he could have. But I didn't see him do it.'

'How many cups did he have?'

'One? Two? I really wasn't paying attention, Jane.'

'What was Angie having?'

'Coffee. I think. And I'm fairly sure Karim was having tea. Why do you ask?'

'Just interested,' I said vaguely.

'Sounds like you're investigating a murder: Who Poisoned Robin Tukes?' She laughed lightheartedly and I joined her, though I didn't feel lighthearted.

'Anyway,' she continued, 'there's coffee and tea in the Page's Vestibule. He probably did it there.'

'Do you know,' I said without thinking, 'that Angie believes Robin went back to his room from Servants' Hall and died in his bed?'

'Oh. Well, I guess that's the official version.'

'Who told you otherwise?'

'I don't know. Let's see . . .' Nikki shifted on to her side and faced me, head crooked in her arm. 'Say, you *are* investigating something, aren't you?'

'Don't be silly. It's just that I find the whole thing so curious.'

'Then who told *you* he did it in the Page's Vestibule?'

Too late, I realized my mistake. I didn't want to tell

Nikki about the Queen's second tumble over Robin, or my involvement at the scene. That was between HM and me. Only Humphrey Cranston, the Page of the Backstairs, had seen me there, and his position made him a model of discretion.

'I don't know.' I fiddled with some books and tapes on my bureau. 'I guess I just picked it up somewhere. The grapevine.' I really had an urge to confide in Nikki, but I knew I daren't. Open eyes and ears, I had promised the Queen. My mouth had different instructions. 'What was he like at breakfast – you know, when they were filming?'

'Quiet. They were all quiet. I did all the talking. I doubt if we'll ever see that bit on the telly,' she added.

'He didn't say what his first duty was after breakfast?'

Nikki shook her head.

I sighed. 'What about his first suicide attempt? After last Thursday's party, when the Queen tripped over him the first— when the Queen tripped over him.'

Nikki smiled at the memory.

'I mean, when did he take the pills or whatever he used that time?'

'I don't know.'

'I suppose he could have swallowed them while he was in the Page's Vestibule,' I mused.

'Funny,' Nikki said. 'I was just reminded of something I had completely forgotten. It makes me wonder now if Karim knew what Robin was intending to do.'

I looked at her sharply, but she had resumed her position staring up at the peeling ceiling.

'After Robin dropped his bombshell about the marriage that night, we had a champagne toast – don't ask me where the champagne came from – but I was standing near Robin and Karim was standing near Angie. When they lifted their cups – Robin and Angie, that is – this absolutely peculiar expression came over Karim's face. He was facing Robin, you see. And I was facing him. It was sort of a look of horror and sadness, all mixed up.'

'As if he knew what was in Robin's glass?'

'Perhaps.'

'Then why in God's name wouldn't he have stopped him?'

'Well, I don't know, do I?' She sat up and groped for her nail clippers, lost in the bedspread's fussy pattern. 'Anyway, this is getting to be all too much for me, Jane. I'm knackered.'

'But . . .'

'Oh, give it a rest.'

She turned and planted her feet on the cold floor. 'Ooh,' she said as she put one foot against the other calf to warm it, 'goodness, these floors.'

I couldn't resist, and held up a cautionary finger. ' "If you have cold feet, put on slippers," ' I said in a squeaky voice. The Queen, the world's thriftiest billion-aire, was famous for telling people to put on a sweater if they found Buck House chilly.

Nikki curtsied and made a face before backing into the corridor. 'Yes, ma'am. Thank you very much, ma'am. Three bags full, ma'am.'

I couldn't get to sleep with everything rolling around in

my mind, so after ten minutes I switched the lamp back
on and grabbed the nearest thing from the pile of books
next to the bed – my copy of the *London A-Z* guide that I
had taken from Robin's room. That's when I realized it
wasn't my copy after all. (Where was mine, then?!)
Mine opened automatically where I had cracked the
spine, in the middle at the enlarged central London area
– central London being where I live, after all. My copy
had lots of marking in that area. This one was clean
inside, except for the page where it fell open, page 75,
the West Kensington area. In pen, someone (Robin?)
had circled Abbotsbury Close, a series of horseshoe-
shaped streets to the west of Holland Park. Who did
he know who was rich enough to live in that posh
neighbourhood?

I reached over to replace the book – the *London A-Z*
guide is not what you'd call a gripping read – when I
noticed the edge of a piece of paper slipping from
between two pages in the index at the back. Mildly
curious, I gave the book a hard shake and found that
what fell on my chest wasn't the expected bookmark,
but a fragile envelope about the size of a wedding invitation. It was blue and the handwriting on the front was
rounded and tidy, almost like a child's. It was addressed
simply to 'Karim Agarwal, c/o Buckingham Palace,
London, England'. No post code. And no return address,
although the stamps indicated that the letter had been
sent from India.

Well, of course I looked inside!

It began 'My dear brother Karim' and was signed
'Your loving sister, Meena,' and a disturbing letter it was,
too, written only a few weeks earlier. From what I could

gather, Meena was in the care of relatives in Burhanpur. Or perhaps the better word would be 'custody'. It seemed she was going to be married, and the husband-to-be was much older. An arranged marriage, apparently. You could tell Meena was frightened, having been taken from her home in England and finding herself in a country she had not been born into, with a culture that was nearly as foreign to her as it would have been to me. But you could also tell she had a sort of fierce determination to free herself from the situation. I shuddered as I read her description of the groom-to-be. He sounded like a subcontinental version of the moustachioed villain in *Perils of Pauline*, a sort of ageing Indo-lizard. And she kept bringing up another name, Geoff, evidently a boyfriend in Blackburn.

There was, she wrote, one way out, however. She could, she had learned from one of her would-be in-laws, buy her way out of the commitment. But it would take a sum well in excess of the dowry Karim's parents had agreed to pay the bridegroom – about £25,000, money which her family did not have, nor, I presumed, reading between the lines, would give if they did. Meena did not ask Karim for the money, for she must have known full well that such a sum would be impossible for a footman on Buck House pay. It was like she was trying to set a miracle in motion. She didn't say when the wedding was to take place, but it had to be fairly soon.

Poor Karim, I thought. What a worry. And what could he do about it, anyway? I replaced the letter in its envelope and determined to return it to Karim as soon as possible. I wouldn't tell him I had read it.

But then, after I had turned off the lamp and begun, finally, to sink into sleep, I wondered why Robin was in possession of the letter. Was it the one he was holding in the hospital that day? It certainly looked the same. And then I wondered if the letter, not his jumper, had been what Karim was really seeking when he had come into Robin's room the day before.

Chapter Seven

What can you say about these cavernous State Rooms in Buckingham Palace?

Well, they're cavernous. That's the word. It was Thursday morning and I was again in the White Drawing Room, although this time I was hoover-less and duster-less. A little note I had found in my mailbox had told me to be in the White Drawing Room at 9.30, which happened to be very convenient – oddly convenient – because my schedule had me cleaning the Music Room next door until ten. (If you ever see a picture of the back of Buckingham Palace, the Music Room is the curved one on the second floor. It sits over the Bow Room, which is where members of the Royal Family gather before joining the throngs at the annual garden parties.)

Even though the note was unsigned, I had an idea who had written it and I was suffering from a little trepidation. Being in the White Drawing Room didn't help. Everything there is so ornate and rich and complex and beautiful and graceful that it makes you feel small and plain and insignificant – particularly when, hoover-less, you have time to think about it. The enormous tiered chandelier in the centre of the room had not been switched on and so the room was rather dark, while outside the french windows the thick gloom of the November morning offered little solace.

I looked over the gardens for a moment. The grass was still green but the enormous urns, which in summer held clusters of dazzling flowers, were now empty, as if waiting to fill up with rain or snow. The statues, liberated from the lush seasonal foliage, looked suddenly stark and cold against the grey. I could see a couple of gardeners rooting away at something in the soil, and a bright yellow kayak seemed to be parked by the artificial lake in the distance, although I knew it had to be something other than a kayak.

Early for the appointment, I wandered around the room, running a hand now and again over the cabinets almost as if I were checking for dust, but in fact going over in my mind what I was going to say. I stopped for a moment in the centre of the room, where the chandelier dangled like an immense stalactite over the floral centre of the Axminster carpet, and then, just as I was about to move on to the fireplace, I found that my foot wouldn't move.

Well, not so much my foot as my shoe. It was stuck. And I could tell from the resistance that the culprit was once again, of all things to adhere to a carpet in Buckingham Palace, chewing gum. Only this time it was fresh. A great bloody wad of fresh chewing gum.

I was so absorbed in this little dilemma that I was completely oblivious to the presence in the room. When the sound of my own name pricked my ears, I nearly jumped out of the offending shoe and careened into the chandelier.

'Your Majesty!' I gasped, hand to heart, turning

around awkwardly on the sticky carpet. It was as though she had materialized from thin air.

'Whatever is the matter with your foot, Jane?' the Queen said.

'Chewing gum,' I replied as apologetically as I could. 'I don't know how it got here.'

The Queen looked at the Axminster, then at me. And then she looked exasperated.

'There was some on the carpet in the Green Drawing Room the other day, too,' I continued nervously.

She looked even more exasperated. 'Are you able to free your shoe?'

I lifted my foot in its shoe, but great strings of pinkish goo clung to the sole. If I put my foot down, I would merely contribute a wad of gum to another part of the carpet.

'I think I'd better take my shoe off, Ma'am.'

'Then do, and follow me.'

The Queen turned and made her way towards the pier-glass to the left of the room's dominant painting, a portrait of Queen Alexandra, Edward VII's wife. Much to my amazement, the glass and the table beneath it were now set at a ninety-degree angle to the wall. Hobbling slightly, one shoe in hand, and feeling a little like Alice, I followed HM through the opening in the wall and found myself in another room, a smaller one, with furniture that was much less grand than that in the State Rooms and more quietly elegant. The walls were covered in a crimson damask.

'Are you surprised?' the Queen asked, noting my reaction.

'Well, yes.'

'Good,' she said firmly. 'We often greet our guests like this. One is always interested to see their reactions when we pop through the wall. Rather fun, don't you think?'

I supposed it was. But I felt rather more silly clutching my shoe in front of the Queen of England.

'Ah, yes, your shoe,' she said, glancing around the room. 'Don't put it down on the rug or the dogs will have it.' She looked sternly at two of them who had padded into the room, tongues hanging at a lascivious angle. 'Perhaps you should put it there.'

She indicated a large table near the window. There was a picture of sorts lying in the middle of it, but when I got closer I saw it was a jigsaw puzzle, virtually completed except for parts of the top border. I placed my shoe, top side up, off to the side.

'Oh! It's one of the Stuart kings, isn't it?' I recognized a man on horseback with a cascade of long sausage hair who seemed to be trampling a host of huge snakes.

The Queen joined me at the table and ran her fingers over the puzzle's textured surface.

'It's called *The Triumph of Charles II*. The original is in the Royal Hospital in Chelsea. I've been working on it for some while,' she added pensively, tilting her head to see better through her bifocal lenses. 'Three thousand pieces, one of the most difficult I've ever done. I do love a good puzzle.'

'And you leave the borders to the end. Wow. You must be good.'

'Worse, there are pieces missing. Look there.'

The Queen pointed to a blank spot I had missed before. Where there should have been a continuation of deep purple among a series of allegorical figures around the King there was only the walnut of the table. The remaining puzzle pieces were all blue and pink, clearly set aside for the sky.

'I've written to the firm. I expect the final pieces next week.'

I tried to imagine the effect of a letter of complaint from the Queen.

'Sit down, Jane,' she said, moving to a nearby arm-chair next to a large and ornate (and dead cold) fireplace.

I sat down opposite her. She was wearing a shirt-waister dress covered with purple and green poppies, the trademark three strands of pearls and a small brooch, a circlet of diamonds. Working attire, I guess you could call it.

She composed her hands very neatly on her lap. It seemed to invite me to do the same.

'What have you learned?' she enquired.

Well, what *had* I learned? That Angie had preten-sions to the aristocracy? That Karim needed a huge sum of money quickly? That Robin had had some sort of argument with Cyril Wentworth-Desborough? Sud-denly, faced with having to explain everything to the Queen, I felt hopelessly inadequate. Was any of this information pertinent?

Nevertheless, I plunged into the details. HM lis-tened attentively, interrupting only for a quick clarifi-cation now and again. Occasionally she would lift an eyebrow at something I said, but otherwise her expression betrayed no emotion. I was hard pressed to know whether she found anything I had to say meaningful or relevant at all, yet I wasn't discouraged from speaking my mind. HM has this odd talent for making you feel, for the time you are with her, that you are the most interesting thing in the world. She is surprisingly easy to talk to if you can get past the whole 'majesty' bit.

'Are you still convinced Robin Tukes' death was anything other than . . . self-inflicted?' the Queen asked.

I searched my mind for a moment. I had to admit that what I had learned amounted to very little, and yet in my heart of hearts I was certain Robin had met with foul play. Although he had been solemn and earnest that day in the Devonshire Hospital, he had betrayed none of the deep despondency or utter embarrassment I imagined a failed suicide would exhibit. Robin might have been prone to depression, he might have retreated to the Palace from a disagreeable period earlier in his life, but he didn't seem to me to be someone who wanted retreat from the *world*. His mind had been set on one objective – reaching the Queen. And he had been thwarted.

'Yes, Ma'am,' I replied firmly. 'I'm sure Robin did not die by his own hand.'

'I see.'

Her Majesty ran her fingers thoughtfully along one strand of her pearls. 'One has had, informally, word on the results of the post mortem. A fatal amount of the drug Zolinane was present in his bloodstream—'

'The drug I found in his room!'

'Yes, but some other information has also come to light.' Here the Queen paused as if she couldn't find the words. 'He was also . . . ill, or potentially ill,' she said finally. 'Jane, Robin Tukes was HIV-positive.'

'Oh, no!'

'You had no idea?'

'Ma'am, I had no idea at all.'

In truth, I was shocked. Not *morally* shocked. Just shocked. Stunned. Surprised. And confused in a miserable sort of way. Poor Robin. It must have been this knowledge that had caused him to withdraw in recent weeks. Yet in the face of that, why do something as nutty as get engaged to be married?

'It does suggest that this boy might have had a reason to do what he did,' the Queen was saying.

'Yes,' I said reluctantly, 'I suppose it does.'

I regarded the sovereign. Was she leading me to the irrevocable conclusion that Robin's death was indeed a suicide? That I should drop my inquiries? Yet nothing in her startling blue eyes persuaded me that this was her thinking.

'But, Ma'am, he was still found right outside your door.'

She gave a barely audible sigh. 'Apparently he was placed there. Two footmen found him in the Page's Vestibule. They thought he had passed out after having had too much to drink and, as a prank, they carried him into the corridor when they noticed the missing police guard.'

'Oh,' I said, slightly startled. Then I wondered how she had found out.

'They confessed to Mr Dowse,' she said, as though reading my mind. 'I'm told the two young men were quite distraught. They thought they might have been able to do something for him if they had realized that he was not merely drunk.'

I had a good idea who one of the footmen might be. It was just the sort of thing Davey Pye would get up to. And it would explain his relatively subdued behaviour over the past two days. My guess was that both footmen had been severely reprimanded – severe in Palace terms, at least.

'Still,' I persisted, 'I think he was determined to speak with you, Ma'am. That doesn't argue for suicide.'

'I'm inclined to agree with you, Jane. But . . .' and here the Queen seemed to choose her words with care, 'there is the opinion that no motive exists for anything other than suicide. Neither has anything been found to suggest that the poison was administered by another person . . .'

'But, Ma'am, what about the cups in Servants' Hall?'

She gave her head a little shake to indicate that this avenue had been explored and found wanting.

'There is also concern pertaining to the arrival of the King and the State Banquet next week. It is a question of security and' – she gave the slightest of grimaces – 'of an untroubled relationship with the press during delicate trade negotiations between our two nations. The coroner will not be making an official ruling until next week, the inquest will be delayed and the press have not been informed.'

I was to realize later just how captive a creature the Queen really is – how she must accede to the advice of others, or at least appear to accede, often against her better judgement. But at the moment I was angry. It sounded as if this whole thing was being swept under the Axminster just because in the scheme of things Robin was a nobody, whose death was nothing more than an inconvenience to the running of the Palace. I must have looked like I was boiling over, because the Queen held up a cautioning finger.

'I, however,' she continued, stressing the 'I', 'am of a different opinion, and that is why I wish you to carry on as you have been doing, Jane.'

'Brilliant!' I exclaimed.

The Queen smiled one of her more dazzling smiles. 'Now, there are two things,' she continued. 'This afternoon, a Miss Katherine Tukes is arriving to gather her brother's belongings and to attend to other arrangements. Normally, these would be conveyed to Miss Tukes at the Household Offices and every assistance would be given to her there. However, if you go to the footmen's quarters at about three o'clock, I believe you will find her in Robin's room. Secondly, you told me you found a card in a book bearing the name of a firm of solicitors, Cholmondeley & Featherstonehaugh. Coincidentally, that is the name of *my* solicitors.'

'*Your* solicitors, Ma'am?'

'One occasionally has need of them,' she said drily. 'Now, I would suggest you pay a visit tomorrow morning to Sir Terence Featherstonehaugh at his offices. If you look in your pigeon-hole you will find something in your post to take with you.'

'But, Ma'am, I'm supposed to be working that morning. Mrs Harbottle has me on the rota for more of the State rooms.'

'Yes, I can see that might be a problem.' The Queen appeared to be considering something as she reached for her handbag, rose purposefully and began to usher me across the room. The corgis followed faithfully.

'Hmmm,' she said. 'Well, you'll have to use your own ingenuity, I'm afraid. One is somewhat powerless as far as Mrs Harbottle is concerned. But mornings are the only time you will catch Sir Terence in.'

I curtsied and walked back through the wall.

'Good luck,' she said. The pier-glass closed behind me and I was back in the White Drawing Room, alone. Minus one shoe.

The wall opened one more time and a regal hand reached out.

'You forgot your shoe.'

'Thank you, Ma'am.'

'And will you tell Mrs Harbottle about the chewing gum?'

'Absolutely, Ma'am.'

Chapter Eight

I have to admit I was still wondering why the Queen was involving herself in all this. If she thought, as I did, that there was foul play involved in Robin's death, why didn't she bring it to the attention of the Palace detectives and security staff? I was to learn the exact reason later, but at the time it struck me that perhaps the Queen was a person who actually *liked* things to be a bit wrong so she could have the challenge of putting them right. After all, she had been doing the same job for forty-odd years – visiting old folk's homes, signing legislation, opening Parliament and the like – so that much of her life ran like clockwork. Solving a murder was a diversion, the way her jigsaw puzzles were. Perhaps it was just the tonic she needed after her *annus horribilis*.

At three o'clock I was standing outside the door of Robin's old room. I had a story prepared: I had come to retrieve my copy of the Jack the Ripper book.

I pushed the door open quietly and saw silhouetted in the light from the window a tall, angular figure in what appeared to be a dark blue suit. The woman's back was to me, but when I said, 'Oh, excuse me,' in what I hoped was a convincingly surprised tone, she turned sharply. She revealed no alarm at my sudden intrusion, however. She merely examined me without interest for a moment and then turned back to what she was doing – trying to fold clothes. Of course: I was wearing my boring housemaid's uniform, a dead give-away that I was someone of no importance.

'Yes?' she said.

'I just came to get a book that belongs to me.'

Katherine Tukes turned and looked at me once more, this time coldly. Her resemblance to Robin was strong – the same dark eyes, the same honed cheek-bones. Only the hair was different, steel grey instead of black, and cut in a short and severe bob. She was obviously much older than Robin. Somewhere in her mid-thirties, I guessed.

'You're not English,' she bristled, turning back to her task.

'No,' I replied.

'I was told the servant girl he was marrying was English.'

The disdainful tone got my back up a bit. 'Yes, but she's not me, if that's what you mean. There are twenty-six of us "servant girls" who work here. I just came to get my book. My name's Jane Bee. I was a friend of Robin's, not his fiancée.'

'Then would you get your book and please leave.' It wasn't a question.

'I'm really sorry about Robin,' I persisted, more reasonably, needing to mollify her if I was going to get her co-operation. 'You must be related. You look a lot like him.'

She didn't reply but just continued fussing over the folding. It was Robin's Burberry.

'Have you found your book?'

'Could I talk to you about Robin?' I moved past her in the narrow room and picked the Jack the Ripper volume from the table.

She more or less threw the coat on the bed. 'Can't you see I'm busy?'

'I'll help you, then.'

'I don't need any help, thank you.'

'Please. I don't want to, you know, intrude on your grief, but I really want to understand about Robin. You're his sister, aren't you? He told me about you.'

'Oh, yes,' she sighed noisily, 'and what did he tell you?'

'Well, that you were a lawyer and – ' in truth Robin had hardly told me anything about his sister – 'and that you live in London . . . Ontario, that is.'

'And that's it, is it? I doubt that my brother told you very much about his family at all.'

'Well . . .'

'Did he tell you, for instance, that our father also killed himself? I'll bet he didn't tell you that, now, did he?'

'No,' I replied, somewhat subdued by this grim information and the very bitter way she had revealed it. 'No, I didn't know that. Are you saying it's sort of hereditary or something?'

'Robin was thirteen when his father died. It's a cruel age for that kind of shock . . . or any shock, for that matter.'

I had begun to gather up the Walkman, tapes,

jewellery and other things from the top of the chest, and the noise drew her attention.

'Put those down,' Katherine commanded. 'I'll do it.'

'I don't mind.'

'Well, I *do* mind! Now, aren't you leaving?'

'No.' I held my ground. 'I really want to know more about Robin.'

'Why?' Under closer examination her face looked gaunt, almost haggard. Her eyes, as blue as Robin's, were glassy and hard, the likely result of jetlag as much as grief, though a kind of anger flickered briefly in them as she stared at me.

'Why?' she repeated, this time more insistently, crowding me away from the chest of drawers.

'Because he was a mate, a friend,' I replied stubbornly, sitting on the bed next to the half-packed suitcase. 'We're all kind of shocked around here. I just thought if I knew more about his background, then—'

'God, what does it matter?' she exclaimed, half to herself, and then added wearily to me: 'Fine. Okay. We'll be like strangers on a train. I don't know who you are. Evidently you really don't know who I am. And I'm sure I don't care. Robin certainly didn't care about us. He hasn't bothered to communicate with me or with our mother in over a year. We knew only that he had left university on some fruitless acting quest. My mother, who is a frail woman, has been sick with worry. And then, on Tuesday, she gets a call from Buckingham Palace of all places to tell her that her son is dead.'

She slammed shut the drawer she had been rooting around in and opened another. She slammed that shut, too.

'Why did your father take his own life, if you don't mind my asking?' I asked, watching her methodically troll through the next drawer.

'He was depressed. Clinically depressed. They have words for these things, but as far as I'm concerned he was incapable of coping with life. That's all. He was weak. He did it just when I was about to be called to the Bar.'

'What did he do for a living?'

'He was a lawyer.'

'Was it a drug overdose?'

'Yes. So, if you want to believe that sort of thing is hereditary, then it was hereditary. Hereditary on the male side.'

'But Robin could cope. He was coping here in London, on his own, just fine. He was quite popular.'

'I'm sure he charmed you all. My father was like that. Charming some of the time, withdrawn some of the time, but no real backbone at any time.'

This just wasn't true. Robin had plenty of backbone. Not only had he made his way in a foreign country, he had borne his disappointments in the acting sphere with good grace. It also took courage to deal with depression, I thought, not to mention with being HIV-positive. Hell, it even took some kind of courage to kill yourself, if that's what he had really done. I said as much to Katherine, with some prudent editing.

'Well, he's dead. What other explanation is there?' she retorted sharply, moving over to the wardrobe. 'And what am I supposed to do with this?' She lifted the scarlet livery by its hanger.

'Leave it. It belongs to the Palace.'

C. C. BENISON

Katherine quickly scanned the mix of colourful uniforms and sombre street clothes.

'Well then, what doesn't belong to the Palace can go
to Oxfam or whatever charity they have here. There's
no sense in taking much of this back to Canada.'

She pulled a second suitcase from the top shelf of
the wardrobe.

'The money spent on Robin!' she continued in a
kind of fury. 'The hopes and dreams invested in him!
For what? So he could end his life as a . . . a footman, of
all things? In Buckingham Palace as a *footman*, when
one day he could have been here as a . . . well . . .'

'As a what?'

'Give me those things,' she snapped, indicating a
watch and jewel case on the chest. 'You might as well
keep the books – there's no sense in my taking them.
And these posters . . .' She looked at the walls with distaste. 'Who was this woman he was going to marry?' she
demanded.

'Angela Cheatle,' I replied, handing her the bits and
pieces from the top of the bureau and trying to follow
her abrupt changes of subject. 'She's all right, I guess.
Blonde, attractive. Not quite as dim as that sounds . . .'

'Damned with faint praise.'

'Well, Angie's not my type, really.'

'And was she Robin's type?'

'Well . . .'

Katherine's face was a mask. I had no idea what she
knew about Robin in this regard, and I didn't intend to
be the one to break it to her, not when she had his death
to contend with. 'Sure, I guess so. And, well, Angie is
pregnant, so . . .'

'So Robin was being a gentleman,' she said witheringly. 'The footman who brought me up here told me this woman was pregnant. I guess he thought I knew. Tell me about her. I have a sudden crazy urge to know.'

So I did, with some judicious trimming, notably Angie's fantasy of royal blood. As I talked, Katherine's face seemed to grow more pinched.

When I had finished, she said: 'Basically, then, this woman is some creature of the lower classes. Her mother was a slut of Swinging London vintage. Her father abandoned her. And her grandmother probably abused her one way or another. Wonderful. And this is the sort of female Robin was intending to bring into our family.'

'She's not that bad . . .'

'Bad enough. Marrying someone like her would have been nothing more than another act of defiance on Robin's part. He has resisted or subverted or screwed up everything we've ever done for him.'

'I can't imagine Robin marrying someone just to get at you. Really I can't. And what difference does it make, anyway? He's – he was – an adult. If he wanted to make a bad marriage, it was his business, not yours.'

Katherine looked at me as if I was a complete dolt. 'Oh, but there's so much more at stake in this case. Of course, you don't know, do you? Robin wouldn't have told you.'

'Told me what?'

'That he would become – and probably very soon – a peer of this realm.'

She searched my face. I guess I was expected to respond with some kind of astonishment. But after

Nikki's story about Angie, I was beginning to believe everybody was having fantasies of noble birth.

I said, 'Oh, yeah. So, like, he was really Princess Anne's illegitimate son or something?'

Her face hardened. 'Don't be fatuous. Robin was the heir presumptive to the Earl of Ulverstone.'

'Meaning what exactly?'

'Meaning that he would have been the next Earl of Ulverstone. The current Earl, our father's cousin, is old and childless and, as it happens, quite ill.'

'But Robin's Canadian.'

'It doesn't matter. He was the heir.'

'So he would have got a nice title—'

'And the house in London, the house in Dorset, the seat in the Lords and a considerable fortune.'

'Really,' I said.

'Yes, really. You can look it up in *Burke's Peerage* or *Debrett's*, if you don't believe me.'

Well, if this was true – and it was hard to believe it wasn't, given Katherine's intensity – it was stunning news. Old Robin, lined up for a fancy title and a load of loot. And yet he'd never said a word to anyone. Or had he? Did Karim know? Or, better yet, Angie? She was the one with the visions of noble birth. Then I wondered what this knowledge could possibly mean in terms of Robin's death. If money was a motive, why murder Robin *before* he had any of it?

'He never mentioned any of this to us,' I told Katherine. 'Does the Palace know?'

'How would I know? I doubt that Robin would have told them. But I'm sure the Palace would have looked askance at the idea of a future earl hired as a footman.'

'Sort of ironic, isn't it?'

'Robin, unfortunately, did not take his legacy seriously. Or anything very seriously, for that matter.'

'He took acting seriously.'

'Oh, yes? That must be why he was a footman,' she said tartly. 'Robin has resisted us all along the line, whether it was going to Upper Canada College, going to Cambridge, or now, it seems, marrying a completely unsuitable woman.'

'What an earl's wife called?'

'A countess.'

Angie, Countess of Ulverstone. It made me want to giggle. I suppressed the urge and asked: 'Would you have tried to stop the marriage?'

'Yes, if I'd known. But then, I wouldn't have known, would I? I haven't known his whereabouts for the last year. Had they set a date?'

'Not that I know of. But I assume they were going to marry soon – I mean, what with the baby coming.'

'Well,' she said spitefully, 'if he was determined to marry, and if he was determined to kill himself, I wish he had done it in reverse order.'

'What an awful thing to say!'

'Don't you see? This child is illegitimate.'

'So? It's still a child. Your nephew, as it happens.'

'You don't see. If Robin had married this girl, then the child would be the heir. Everything would have stayed in our family. Now it doesn't matter. It's too late.'

'God! Is that all you care about – this silly title and the money? Your brother's dead!'

She didn't say anything, but just continued throwing things from the wardrobe on to the bed. The room

113

fell into an acrimonious silence except for the soft plump of cloth falling on cloth.

'Was the child even his?' she said at last, quietly, as though she had voided some of her ire.

'Well, I assume so,' I lied. 'Why wouldn't it be?'

She regarded me, for the first time, with some uncertainty. 'I've always believed that my brother was more attracted to men than to women.'

She looked hard at me, as though she were trying to read my expression. I didn't know what to say, so I decided to avoid a direct answer. 'If you think the child wasn't Robin's, then why are you so concerned, anyway?'

'Marriage would have *made* the child Robin's. That's the law. In this situation, that would have been good enough.'

There was a discreet knock and then the opening of the door interrupted us. Davey raised his eyebrows as if to ask 'What are you doing here?' and then, for Katherine, resumed the official look of imperial boredom that footmen sought to achieve in public and which he did so well.

'I *do* beg your pardon, madam,' he said in his most friggypoo voice. 'When you are ready, I would be most happy to assist you downstairs with your things.'

'Thank you,' she replied sourly.

'As you wish, madam.' As he closed the door he stuck out his tongue at me.

'I want to talk to you,' I quickly mouthed while Katherine's back was turned.

'Any time,' he mouthed back before the door clicked shut.

We were both silent. I waited for Davey's footsteps to fade down the corridor. Katherine was concentrating on closing the suitcase.

'Don't you think it's weird that Robin decided to get married and then, a few days later, to take his own life?' I asked.

'No.' Her tone suggested that the question was utterly imbecilic. 'People like my brother and my father are capable of a great deal of self-absorption. The consequences of their actions – the people whom they hurt – aren't that important to them.'

I couldn't believe how completely she was misreading her brother, but it seemed pointless to argue. I also didn't want to get her wound up over the possibility of murder. Not at this point.

'There,' she said, closing the locks with finality, 'I guess that's it.'

She looked around the room with distaste, as though trying to rid her memory of its unpleasantness forever. Her eyes finally rested on me, sitting on the bed.

'Would you mind helping me down with these things?' she said, putting her prim navy blue coat over her shoulders and picking up the smaller of the two bags. 'I'm not in the mood for footmen.'

I put the Jack the Ripper book in the pocket of my uniform, tugged at the larger bag and led her down the stairs to the Side Entrance.

'I'll tell someone about sending the clothes to Oxfam. And thanks for the books,' I told her awkwardly as she buttoned her coat at the foot of the stairs. 'I'm truly sorry about Robin,' I added, ushering her through the door. 'We were really very fond of him.'

For once, she ventured a smile. It wasn't a very good one. 'I don't expect I'll see you again,' she said. 'I hope whatever I've told you helps you to understand . . . or whatever. Anyway, goodbye.'

'Wait. Where are you staying?'

'Brown's. Why?'

I shrugged. 'Maybe, I could . . .?'

'Well, I'll be in London a few days yet – some delay in releasing the body – but I'm going to be busy. Thank you.'

And with that Katherine Tukes passed through the Palace gates and into the grey London afternoon.

I was still at the entrance a couple of minutes later, lost in thought, when Davey came up beside me.

'Did she leave?'

I nodded. 'Said she couldn't bear footmen. Is it any wonder?'

'But I was utterly charming to her.'

'I don't mean you – I mean with her brother having been a footman. She didn't think much of it.'

'The snob!'

'Look who's talking.'

Davey grinned.

'Did *you* take her up, by the way?' I asked.

'To his room? No, I think the Sergeant Footman did. After a cup of tea and the Palace's official condolences, I assume.'

'Let's go outside for a moment.'

'Why? It's freezing.'

'Come on, it's not that bad. You're English, for

heaven's sake. You're supposed to thrive on this pissy weather. You've got your tailcoat on. I've got something to ask you and I don't want others to hear.'

Without giving him an opportunity to respond, I led Davey out under the plane trees well away from the security sentry box at the gate. There was a shush of traffic along a damp Buckingham Palace Road, and a few late-season tourists peered through the iron bars of the fence.

'What?' Davey said, kicking at a little pile of leaves that had gathered around the trunk. Plane tree leaves always remind me of Canadian maple leaves.

'Were you the one who carried Robin out of the Page's Vestibule on Tuesday?'

'Wherever did you hear about that?'

'Never mind. I just heard.'

'We didn't know he was . . . unwell. He wasn't dead when we moved him, you know.'

'Who's "we"?' I asked, snatching at a leaf that drifted down towards my face.

'Nigel and me.'

'Oh, God.'

Nigel was the twittiest footman of them all.

'I was delivering something to Father,' Davey continued, referring to HM's husband. 'And Nigel popped out of the Page's Vestibule just as I was passing. You know he's mad for Paul, one of the pages. Well, anyway, Nigel said Robin had passed out, and wouldn't it be a laugh to move him to the corridor, where Mother might see him. Her minder had buggered off somewhere, so we had our opportunity. No one was around, so . . .' His face crumpled. 'Well,' he wailed, 'we didn't know he was going to die!'

'Shhhh! If no one was around, how come it's got about that you guys did this?'

'Oh, we confessed, actually. You see, I began to wonder if he had been murdered.'

I started. This was the first time the possibility had been voiced by anyone other than HM and me.

'Yes, I know, rather unlikely,' Davey continued. 'But we thought, or rather, Nigel thought – he's a bit of a nervous Nelly when you get right down to it – that we should own up just in case. Just so no one would suspect us, was his argument. Fingerprints on his uniform or something. But Nigel was a bit over the top about it. As it happens, we would have been better off, I think, keeping our gobs shut. The Sarge threw a fit. Threatened to sack us if we said a word about it to anyone. I think he meant it this time. I've got enough blackballs against my name. How *do* you know all this?'

'I don't know,' I lied. 'I can't remember now.'

'Oh, God. What if it gets back to . . .? Well, it wasn't me. It must have been bloody Nigel.'

He sighed ostentatiously as I twiddled the leaf by its stem, then let it float to the ground.

'Oh, well . . .' he said after a moment. The cloud that had briefly shaded Davey's face departed. He wasn't one to worry overmuch about consequences.

'Let's go back in,' he said decisively. 'I'll catch my death out here and so will you. Besides, the tourists are starting to stare. Should charge them 50p for the privilege. Oh, and look, there's Andrew Macgreevy pretending to be one of them.'

'Who?'

'You know, from that new paper, whatever is it called? – the *Evening Gazette*. That's it. Wonder why he's hanging about? Yoo-hoo, Andrew!'

Davey fluttered his hand. The man, a head taller than most of the tourists, with a hangdog face and a halo of short, fine, oat-coloured hair, scowled and swiftly retreated into the knot of people.

'You don't actually know him, do you?' I asked as we turned back toward the Palace.

'He's chatted me up a few times in the Bag O'Nails. New boy on the Buck House beat, trying to make his mark. Poor bugger. As if I'd spill the works for a few pints.'

'How about a lot of pints?'

'Oh, no, you mistake me, Jane, dear. I would never betray Mother.'

Chapter Nine

At 9.30 the next morning I found myself in the private offices of Sir Terence Featherstonehaugh in Lincoln's Inn Fields.

I was amazed that I was even there at all. Getting away from Mrs Harbottle's dominion at short notice hadn't been easy. After talking to Davey Pye the previous afternoon, I had gone to The Harbottle's lair, near the Palace's forecourt, with a dozen excuses for being pardoned from work rattling around in my brain, none of them convincing. Doctor's appointment? Dentist's appointment? These were about as original as the 'My dog ate my homework' defence at school. Mrs Harbottle, who was attached to the Palace Staff like a limpet to a ship's bottom, had heard them all before. I could just see the 'haven't you got a better one that that?' look in her stony eyes – not that I was one of the ones, like Nikki, who continually tried her patience.

Then I had an idea. It was so outrageous that I thought it might work. And it did.

First of all I buttered her up by reporting the presence of fresh chewing gum mucking up the Axminster in the White Drawing Room.

'And I'm sure that was what was on the carpet last

week when I was doing the Green Drawing Room,' I elaborated earnestly.

The Harbottle scribbled on her clipboard. 'Chewing gum . . . GDR . . .' I could hear her muttering as she wrote.

'Why didn't you report this at the time?' she demanded, looking up. Mrs Harbottle has large, luminous eyes behind her serviceable wire frames and could probably be quite attractive, I thought, if she loosened up, let down her hair (literally) from its lacquered tower and smiled once in a decade. She couldn't have been much older than my mother, but she seemed ages older still. The 'Mrs', by the way, is a courtesy title. Mrs H. was not married, nor had she ever been.

'I wasn't sure what it was,' I said in answer to her question. 'It was only today that I made the connection. I stepped in it. It was quite fresh.'

'I see.' Her lips pursed. 'Have any of the other girls mentioned a similar experience?'

'No,' I said. (As if all we talked about was cleaning, for heaven's sake!)

'I see. Well, I've spotted it in the Bow Room and the State Dining Room over the last fortnight. And I very much want to know who could possibly be so careless . . .'

'Or could manage to put so much gum in their mouth at one time?'

'I beg your pardon?'

'Oh, nothing.'

'. . . so I expect you girls to be vigilant. These splendid carpets belong to the nation. The Queen is quite mindful of her custodial responsibilities, and I don't want Her Majesty troubled.'

Too late, I thought.

'So I will be posting instructions presently on the removal of chewing gum,' Mrs Harbottle continued, scribbling again on her clipboard and muttering, 'Gum. Removal. PI. Is there something else you wished to see me about?'

'Yes,' I said, 'I need to take a few hours off tomorrow morning.'

'This is extremely short notice, Jane. What, may I ask, is the reason?'

'I need to see a lawyer . . . a solicitor, that is.'

The Harbottle's eyebrows rose a fraction of an inch. 'A solicitor,' she echoed. 'I see. And what, if I may ask, do you need to see a solicitor for?'

'About a will,' I said.

'I see. A will. Are you unwell?'

'No.'

'Sudden inheritance?'

'No. Well, I have some money.' About £156 in a savings account at the Clydesdale Bank, actually, but she didn't need to know.

'I see. You seem to me to be rather young to be worrying about such things.'

'It has to do with Robin's death, Mrs Harbottle,' I explained pleadingly. 'It's made me think about life . . . and death.'

'I see.' She tapped her pen against the blotter on her desk. 'This couldn't wait, I suppose?'

'Well, they're very booked up, but they phoned and

said they had a cancellation tomorrow morning at 9.30 and could I come then.'

'Which firm is it?'

'Cholmondeley & Featherstonehaugh.'

Mrs Harbottle's eyebrows travelled higher. 'Those are Her Majesty's solicitors!'

'That's how I picked them. I remembered the name from a newspaper article way back when the Queen was, um, suing one of the papers for . . . for leaking her Christmas speech.'

'I'm tempted to call their offices,' she mused.

'Oh, then you should,' I replied earnestly.

Eyebrows at twelve o'clock. 'I think you are over-wrought over this young man's death,' she said, tapping her pen yet more furiously, 'but you've given me no reason to doubt you in the past, Jane. However, I expect you back here, in uniform, by eleven o'clock. And I won't tolerate any deviations from the schedule until the State Banquet is over. Do you understand?'

'Yes, Mrs Harbottle,' I said with appropriate meek-ness, rising and almost dipping into a curtsey. Davey's right when he says there's more than one queen in the Palace.

Well, I hadn't lied, had I? I said I had to see a solicitor about a will. It was Mrs H. who assumed it was *my* will.

Of course, I was assuming it was a will we were dealing with, and I assumed that was HM's assumption as well, particularly since the unhappy HIV revelation. Why else would someone as young as Robin seek a lawyer? As it turned out, I was correct.

Sir Terence Featherstonehaugh came into the room carrying the letter I had given to his secretary. I had found a plain brown envelope in my pigeon-hole at the Palace earlier that morning. Inside was another envelope, sealed, with a typewritten address and some tiny and rather cryptic-looking handwritten markings in the lower left corner. The stationery was rich and creamy, with such a lovely texture that I couldn't help fingering it inside my bag as I travelled by Underground to Holborn.

I had half expected the offices of Cholmondeley & Featherstonehaugh to be terribly forbidding – Gothic and impenetrable and scary – but it was all very cosy, more like an elaborate rabbit warren with many doors and many rooms beyond. The impeccably dressed secretary greeted me cheerily, even though I must have looked like some London scruff blown in off the street in my damp jacket. The distinctive envelope elicited a tiny 'oh' and then a dainty, almost conspiratorial smile. And it had a magical effect. She darted off with it and fifteen minutes later, after a nice cup of tea and some idle chit-chat in the reception area, I was in the inner sanctum, a richly panelled room with heavy green curtains drawn and a *real* fire lit – not one of those Buck House electric jobs.

Sir Terence was an absolutely huge man. He must have weighed twenty stone and looked, from my piddling five feet and nothing much, to be about six foot six tall. But the solicitor glided into the room ever so gracefully, like a great ship docking at port. His head was shaped like an egg, tonsured on top, with tufts of hair sprouting from his ears that happened to match the ones sprouting from his eyebrows. His face was florid and his eyes deep-set and, at first glance, he looked quite fierce.

'I'm Terence Featherstonehaugh,' he boomed enthusiastically, taking my hand in his.

'Jane Bee,' I replied, feeling my fingers scrunched.

' "A swarm of bees in May is worth a load of hay",' he sang, as he turned and distributed his girth into a commodious armchair. ' "A swarm of bees in June is worth a silver spoon . . ." '

' "A swarm of bees in July is not worth a fly!" ' I chorused, taking a seat opposite him.

'Oh, you know that one, do you?' He looked quite pleased.

'My grandfather used to recite it to us when we were kids. He was from here. England, that is. I haven't thought of it in a long time, though.'

'Let me see . . .' Sir Terence paused and considered the ceiling. ' "All nature seems at work. Slugs leave their lair/The bees are stirring – birds are on the wing/And Winter slumbering in the open air/Wears on his smiling face a dream of Spring!/And I the while, the sole unbusy thing/Nor honey make, nor pair, nor build, nor sing." ' He eyed me slyly. 'Coleridge. Do you know that one?'

I shook my head.

'Pity, Miss Bee.' He chuckled. 'Bee by name, but not by nature, I expect.'

'Depends on whether you mean insect bee or letter b.'

'Oh, insect bee, of course, Miss Bee. Then you must

be a bee by nature, after all. Buzzing about for Her Majesty?'

'Buzz, buzz.'

'You must be busy. Or perhaps should I pronounce it "buzzy"?'

He let out a roar of laughter. From poems to puns, Sir Terence Featherstonehaugh evidently enjoyed himself very much. It was hard not to be carried along with laughter loud enough to make a room shake.

When we had recovered our sensibilities a little, he continued: 'According to the note, you wish to gather some information about a Mr Robin Tukes, lately deceased. Let me see . . .' He pulled closer to him a folder that had been sitting on his desk and opened it.

'This is actually somewhat unorthodox,' he said as he positioned a pair of spectacles on the end of his nose, 'but as Her Majesty is the fount of law . . .'

I remained silent as he scanned the pages in front of him. Tiny frowns fell about his mouth and eyes.

'Nothing too unusual here,' he said. 'I presume it is the details of the will that are your concern?'

'Well, yes, in a way,' I replied. 'Actually, I wasn't sure that he had a will to begin with, but I knew he had been to this office, and I really couldn't think why else he would want to do that until, well . . . until I learned that he was ill, or might become ill, if that makes sense.'

'I see,' he said, not seeing. 'Not many men of Mr Tukes' youth or station entertain the idea of wills, but sometimes circumstances oblige. I gather the death was self-inflicted . . .?'

I hesitated, and that hesitation was enough to put a

little twinkle in Sir Terence's blue eyes – a twinkle about what, I wasn't sure.

He leaned back in his chair. 'Her Majesty is, you know, an excellent judge of character. As good a judge of character as she is a judge of horses, I would venture to say. What do you say?'

'I hardly know her, really,' I replied, wondering at the turn in conversation.

'Ah,' Sir Terence smiled and continued: 'Well, people think the Court insulates her from the world, but really, she has had an opportunity to meet the most amazing number of people, from all strata of society, all over the world, for forty-odd years. She assesses things quickly and confidently: situations and, of course, people. And she is rarely wrong in her judgement. When I was at Windsor a fortnight ago, she, well . . .'

The pause was a tiny bit theatrical. Of course, people who have any kind of intimate association with the Queen know better than to blab on about it, and Sir Terence was surely one of those people. But he seemed to be endeavouring to get another point across to me, and I guess I was a little slow on the uptake. His point, as I took it later, was that the Queen had judged me trustworthy, a trust not given to many. I was sort of flattered, when I thought about it afterwards, but at the time, in Sir Terence's office, it seemed more like he was inviting me on some philosophical voyage around Her Majesty.

'I've only been a housemaid less than a year,' I said, following his lead, 'but sometimes it seems as though the Queen is less a queen than a sort of captive. And I mean just as far as her own Household is concerned.

It's all so snobby and hierarchical at times, with people so concerned about their little perks and privileges. It's like a hive. The Queen is the most important member in theory, but actually she just exists to service everybody else – well, that's not quite the right expression. To justify their existence at least. Do you know what I mean?'

'Bees, again.' He laughed, and a tiny golden gong on his desk rattled. 'But, yes, I do know what you mean, Miss Bee. Two things, however: Her Majesty views us – all of her subjects – without differentiation. This is due in part, I think, to her personality, but it is also due to her position at the pinnacle of society—'

'When you're at the top of a mountain, everything sort of flattens out before you . . .'

'Quite. Very perceptive. Her Majesty sees no difference between a duke and a lorry driver. The duke and the lorry driver do, of course. The other point I should make is that Her Majesty may seem at times, as you say, "captive" of her Household, but in fact she knows quite well when and how to exert her wishes and get the things done that she deems important. She does it patiently and meticulously and so subtly that those around her are barely aware it is happening. There are exceptions, of course . . .'

He smiled, leaving the rest unsaid – not, at that point, that I had the fullest understanding of what he was talking about. Contrary to most English interiors, it was quite warm in Sir Terence's office. The flames were crackling away nicely, sending both heat and a lovely scent into my pores. It made me feel sleepy in a cosy sort of way and I was starting to drift from my purpose. He must have noticed the tiniest droop of my eyelids, because he moved to reacquaint himself with the file before him.

'I should tell you,' he said, clearing his throat loudly, 'that Mr Tukes' appointment was with a junior member of this firm. I did not have the opportunity to meet the young man myself.'

'Oh,' I said, newly alert. 'I was hoping that Robin might have said something or other in conversation that could be important. Could I meet this junior member?'

'That wouldn't be possible, I'm afraid, given that you are, in a sense, on Her Majesty's secret service.' He chuckled again, softly. 'I did speak briefly to Mr Woodings, however – that's the gentleman who drew up Mr Tukes' will and who also happens to be the executor – but I'm not sure what I can tell you that will be of any use.'

'Oh,' I said, disappointed. 'What does the will say, then?'

Sir Terence regarded the document once again. 'He had, I gather, decided to devise a will in contemplation of marriage. He was also to come into a certain sum of money from his father's estate on his twenty-first birthday, which was—'

'—last week.'

He turned to a different page. 'Indeed,' he said. He pulled a slip of paper from a pocket in the folder. 'The sum from his father's estate is not inconsiderable, about, let me see, in dollars that would be . . . oh, it would be Canadian dollars, wouldn't it? I'm not sure about Canadian dollars. In American dollars it would be approximately three hundred and seventy-five thousand. That's Mr Tukes' reported estimate.'

'Wow!'

Sir Terence raised his bushy eyebrows in my direction.

'Well, I knew his family was comfortable,' I told him, 'but I didn't realize Robin was in line for that kind of money.'

Gosh, I thought. Think what he might have done with it! Travel, join one of the great acting schools, buy some quality stuff. But then I thought of his potential illness and how his life might have gone, and felt a sting of sadness.

'Who does it all go to?' I asked.

'Half is bequeathed to his wife, whoever that may be – the name is not given. And the remaining half goes to a Mr Karim Agarwal. Is that name familiar to you?'

'Yes,' I said, startled. 'He's a footman at the Palace.'

'Indeed? A good friend of Mr Tukes', I assume.'

'Well, yes . . . I guess . . . When was this will made?'

'About three weeks ago.'

Just after they all got back from Balmoral, I thought. And how peculiar that Karim should be beneficiary just at a time when he needed a large sum of money. A feeling of dismay came over me. Was it possible that Karim felt so desperate over his sister's plight that he was willing to take a life? Surely not. Surely Robin would have given him the money if he had had it and his friend needed it so badly. And yet there was the estrangement between the two since Balmoral, at least up until that moment in the Devonshire Hospital.

'The wedding never happened, though,' I told Sir

Terence. 'Does that mean Robin's fiancée gets half the money anyway?'

'No. There's no mention of another beneficiary. By right, half of an estate this size passes to the wife. That is the minimum required by law. I assume that Mr Tukes' concerns in coming here were for the remainder of his estate – the half which did not automatically go to his spouse.'

'As I said, there never was a wedding. So who gets the other half now?'

'According to this, the entire estate now passes to Mr Agarwal.'

'The whole three hundred and seventy-five thousand dollars!' To my mind, it was a liberating sum of money. Not only would Karim be able to free his sister from a feudal marriage, but he could free himself to do what he wanted; $375,000 – over £200,000 – was a powerful motive.

'There is also mention,' Sir Terence continued, frowning slightly, 'of an enterprise of some unspecified nature. Mr Tukes expresses the hope that Mr Agarwal will now be able to succeed in establishing, and I quote, "the business of which we so often talked".' He looked at me inquiringly.

I shook my head. 'I don't know what it means,' I said.

The whole thing seemed so melodramatic anyway. Even if Robin had been HIV-positive he might never have got full-blown AIDS, or he might have lived for years, or they might have found a cure in the interim. Maybe the melodrama was a result of the shock of learning of his illness. And maybe he wanted to make amends to Karim. Guilt? Worry that he might have infected Karim?

'How long does it normally take for a beneficiary to get his money?' I asked Sir Terence.

'Mr Woodings must first apply for probate; that is, the will must be deemed by the court to be valid and Mr Woodings must be confirmed as the person named in the will as executor. After that, well, I'm sure it would take a month before the assets might be distributed. Of course, things can be hurried along if need be . . . Why? Is it important?'

'I don't know, really.'

I thought about Karim's sister's letter. Was a date for the wedding in India mentioned? I didn't think so. And yet I was certain the letter was full of urgency.

'What if Robin had never made a will at all?' I asked.

'Then his parents would inherit his estate. If his parents were deceased, his brothers and sisters would inherit equally.'

I had wondered earlier about Robin's other inheritance: the aristocratic title and the money attached to that, but I realized these were not his to give away, nor would they have been. There was no point in mentioning it. No one benefited. Or so I thought at the time.

That was really the end of my interview with Sir Terence Featherstonehaugh. We chatted for a few more moments about the Englishman's favourite topic, the weather, and about my recent life and times, which seemed to satisfy him in some way, and then he ushered me from his office with a cheery 'Be good, Miss Bee', followed by a rich chuckle.

I stepped down the high curving staircase outside the offices of Chomondeley & Featherstonehaugh – quite the grandest building in Lincoln's Inn Fields, actually – lost in my own thoughts, intent on retracing my steps to Kingsway and Holborn Tube Station. At Remnant Street, I stopped myself just in time to avoid being run over in a sudden burst of traffic that seemed unbecoming to this calm, dignified part of London. Even though I had been in England for nearly a year, I was still apt to turn my head to the left first before crossing streets. Many's the time I had been saved by a friendly hand from walking into an oncoming car.

This time it was some inner alertness that kept me from being squashed like a bug. Suddenly aware of my surroundings, I noted in a knot of people across the street a familiar face and realized, in that intuitive way you have about these things, that the familiar face had been looking at me. His knot of people and my knot passed each other, and while I affected not to notice him, I could tell he was studying me. Where had I seen that face before? The memory floated tantalizingly out of reach until I reached a news-stand in Kingsway and realized it was the man whom Davey Pye had yoo-hooed to the day before outside the fence in Buckingham Palace Road – Andrew Somebodyorother from the *Evening Gazette*. What a coincidence, I thought. Eight million people in Greater London and I run into the same guy twice in less than twenty-four hours.

Or was it a coincidence? I suddenly had the chilling thought that the reporter might have followed me to the offices of the Queen's solicitor. Had some kind of rumour about Robin leaked from the Palace? Was I being followed?

I dismissed it from my mind. After all, I was just a housemaid. Would a newspaper reporter reasonably expect me to be party to all the inside gossip at the Palace? No way, thought I. Maybe this was why I could be so useful to Her Majesty. Who in the world would expect a mere housemaid to be investigating a murder?

Thinking all this made me feel better. I looked around. No Andrew in sight. Then I looked at the newspapers ringing the borders of the stand like bunting at a journalist's wedding, and realized it had been two days since I had last looked at a newspaper. And then something popped into my head, something that hadn't struck me when I was leafing through the papers at Victoria Station on Wednesday evening. When I went to help the Queen up off the floor that morning, I had scooped up a newspaper first. I remembered holding it in one hand as I extended the other to HM. What had I done with that paper? I couldn't remember. And yet this detail, discarded from my mind, suddenly seemed significant.

I looked again at the newspapers. The quantity of them, the noisy colour and their blaring headlines, all seemed to blur together. I had no time to browse now. I reached into my bag and dug out a few quid to pay for a bunch of the worst for quick reading on the Tube. Maybe something going on at the Palace had found its way into the press after all.

But there wasn't much. As I rattled along on the Piccadilly Line towards Green Park, I flipped quickly through the *Sun*, the *Daily Mirror* and the *Daily Star*, all of which were either not taking the English Republican Army threat seriously ('Worra Cheek!' said one, as if it were the *other* Republican Army's prerogative to create urban mayhem), or they were doing yet another variation on the vicar and the Bayswater bordello, or they were each crowing over circulation gained in another round of price-slashing. The only item on the Royal Family I could find was a piece on the Princess of Wales pouring scorn on those who were saying she was having another bout of bulimia. Gee, her life is hell.

The stuff in the *Evening Gazette*, for which Andrew Somebodyorother – Macgreevy! – wrote was pretty much the same, but, as the train pulled out of Piccadilly Circus and I closed the papers and prepared myself to change trains for the Victoria Line at Green Park, I noted something which had escaped my attention earlier. Inside a coloured box on the first page, at the top right corner, was a highlight for an upcoming story. 'Royal Diary Shocker', it read, 'Sunday, only in the *Gazette*.'

Chapter Ten

'I've got some news for you.'

Nikki was practically overcome with a kind of malicious glee. She and I were in the Music Room. It was just after one o'clock, and I was trying to make up for the time lost through my visit to Cholmondeley & Featherstonehaugh. I hadn't quite made it back by eleven o'clock as I had promised The Harbottle. There had been a security alert in the Underground, which meant being stuck between Green Park and Victoria for forty minutes while the train grew hot and sticky and everybody pretended in their best English way that nothing unpleasant was happening. The damp and dirty – but cool – air along Buckingham Palace Road was an enormous relief after that.

So there I was, polishing the lid of the grand piano with as much speed as I could muster, hoping to get to Servants' Hall for a bite of hot lunch, when in popped Nikki. She drew me over into the shadow of one of the great windows with the heavy red muffling draperies which overlooked the garden. Sound in the Music Room carries so – it's probably something to do with the bow shape of the room and the gilded dome overhead. I always wondered why the Princess of Wales took her tap-dancing lessons in this room in the early days of her doomed marriage. The clatter would have given most people terrible headaches.

Anyway, Nikki hadn't dug me out to talk about acoustics. She had an interesting piece of gossip to relay. About mid-morning, it seems, she had slipped into the Queen's Cinema on the ground floor – not, I should hasten to say, to do any cleaning. Kipping was her objective. She was a bit tired, having been out late with her mates and so forth, and was feeling knackered after a mighty scouring of some of the second-floor guest bedrooms where the RamaLamaDingDong's entourage would be staying during the State Visit. She'd had to look particularly diligent, it seems, because Cyril Wentworth-Desborough and the film crew had decided to shoot her and a few of the other girls in full froth.

So she ducked into the cinema – which is about as far away from the second-floor bedrooms as you can find – put up a few of the armrests, turned off the lights and plopped herself down across several of the seats. As she tells it, she fell into a light snooze, some little time passed, and then she found herself aroused by voices. She froze, expecting the lights to be switched on at any moment, but the voices continued in the dark in a noisy whisper. It was evidently as important for the speakers not to be noticed as it was for Nikki.

One voice belonged to Angela Cheatle. Angie was aggrieved about something and it soon became evident that the best-laid schemes o' mice and men gang aft a-gley, as Robbie Burns put it (I think Sir Terence Featherstonehaugh's poetry bent was still affecting me.) Angie's plan to marry Robin and, as I now knew, eventually share an aristocratic title and a load of loot had, of course, gone for nought. She was now pregnant and unmarried, with a low-paid job in one of the most expensive cities in the world, who would shortly be losing her job because the Palace would not employ a pregnant woman – which is sort of outrageous, when you think about it.

According to Nikki, Angie was saying frantically that something *had* to be done about the pickle she was in. Or else.

'Or else what?' I asked Nikki.

'Or else she blabs to the tabs.'

'Really! Then who was the other person?'

'Guess.'

'You do know who it was, don't you, Nikki? You're not winding me up again?'

'Oh, all right, I won't make you guess,' she pouted, though her green eyes were sparkling. This is where she became practically overcome with glee: 'It was Sir Julian Dench.'

'Never! That *is* interesting. Wow.'

Nikki looked enormously pleased with herself.

'It's almost too hard to take in,' I said. 'I always thought these upper-class types liked to go off to knocking shops and have their bottoms slapped. But to get involved with someone at the Palace . . . I mean, the Queen's Private Secretary! Sir Julian must be off his nut.'

'Arrogant bastards like him usually think they're invincible,' Nikki said.

'I suppose . . . well, anyway, I guess there isn't much doubt who the father of Angie's baby is.'

'Sir J. didn't deny it.'

'Then what the hell was Robin up to?'

This, of course, was the question that had been vexing me for days. But Nikki merely shrugged.

'So what did Sir Julian say to her?' I asked.

'It was a bit hard to hear him, actually, since they were practically whispering and his voice was so low, but I gather Sir J.'s going to set her up in a flat somewhere. I think he wanted her to have an abortion, but it's too late for that.' Nikki cackled. 'You should have heard Angie. She was practically in hysterics.'

Odd, I thought. When I had spoken with Angie the other night at the Plumber's Arms she had seemed quite confident about her plans for the future, almost as if she had just resolved them before coming to the pub. Or had it just been bravura fuelled by drink?

'Did they mention Robin at all?' I was thinking about Robin's titular and monetary inheritance. Should I tell Nikki what I had learned?

'Not really.'

'They must have. I mean, it all hinges on Robin, somehow. I wonder if he knew it was Sir Julian who was the father and not someone else?'

'Maybe he didn't know. But then he found out and that was what really drove him to, you know, do himself in . . .'

'Well, he knew *he* wasn't the father, so why would it have mattered exactly who was?'

On the other hand, I wondered, was this the reason Robin had been trying to see the Queen? To warn her that her Private Secretary had got some housemaid pregnant and there might be a juicy scandal in the offing? Might this be the reason he had been murdered? But why would Robin do that? That sort of snitching wasn't in his nature. And besides, he was marrying Angie. He was the one preventing any scandal. Or had he changed his mind for some reason? Well, curiouser and curiouser, as old Alice might say.

'. . . maybe the idea of Sir J. was just too bloody awful . . . Jane?'

'Sorry,' I said, jolted from my reverie. 'I was just thinking about something.'

I had a real urge to confide in someone. I wanted to tell Nikki what Katherine Tukes had told me, about Robin's will, and about him being a potential AIDS victim, and see if she could make any sense of the mix, but I hesitated.

As it happened, I didn't have to keep battling the impulse. A tall figure came into the Music Room and cleared his throat rather noisily, causing both Nikki and me to start. It was Humphrey Cranston, the Page of the Backstairs.

'What the bleedin' hell does he want?' Nikki whispered.

'Beats me,' I replied, peeping around the curtain.

Nikki looked at me indecisively for a moment, gave a tiny shrug, and called out in her 'polite' voice: 'May I help you, Mr Cranston?'

'It is Jane with whom I wish to speak,' he drawled.

'Ooooh, lucky you,' Nikki murmured sarcastically under her breath as we crossed the room together. 'Humphrey-flamin'-Cranston. Maybe he'll take you to tea to meet his Mum.'

I elbowed her to make her shut up. I had an idea what Humphrey really wanted, and it wasn't me.

'What can I do for you, sir?' I said to him, but he held his eyes on Nikki, saying nothing. Humphrey has one of those pale, drawn English faces suggesting a childhood diet devoid of vegetables.

'All right, I'm leaving, I'm leaving,' Nikki said airily, taking the hint, but as she went out the door into the Picture Gallery she turned and flashed me a deeply puzzled expression.

'Her Majesty wishes to see you in the White Drawing Room at four o'clock,' Humphrey informed me when Nikki had gone.

'Oh!' I said, surprised, 'Won't she have gone to Windsor by then?'

'Her Majesty has been detained.'

'Oh . . . Mr Cranston . . .?' I longed to ask him what he knew. Didn't he find it completely bizarre that the Queen wished to see me – a mere housemaid – privately?

'. . . oh, nothing,' I replied to his left eyebrow, which had risen imperceptibly.

Humphrey looked down his nose at me. Not snottily. It's just that he's so tall and has such a big beak he can't help looking down it.

'I would suggest,' he drawled, 'that when you are talking with your . . . friend that you fashion a *plausible* reason for our conversation.' His lugubrious expression didn't alter but there was the tiniest twinkle in his eye. 'My mother is deceased.'

I stared at him for a moment, then I remembered

Nikki's comment. I smiled. Humphrey turned abruptly and vanished into the Picture Gallery.

I wasn't sure what to make of this. Not so much that HM wanted to see me, but that Humphrey Cranston was her messenger. I realized now that it was he who had put HM's letter to Sir Terence into my pigeon-hole. Of course, who else could it be? Humphrey was in direct attendance on Her Majesty and had been, I gathered, for years. He had to be someone she could truly trust.

It was good to know, in a way. But, the problem was, what *was* I going to say to Nikki? Pages of the Backstairs don't usually seek private conversations with house-maids. Nikki might easily get everyone else's curiosity up if she was of a mind to chatter about it. And, after that funny look of hers, I didn't know what frame of mind she might be in.

Half an hour later I was in Servants' Hall, seated alone, nibbling on a cheese salad. The hot food had ended, but I was just as glad. Stewed eels in parsley sauce with mash didn't much appeal to me.

The place was nearly empty. There was no one to talk to, so I found my mind wandering over the topic of trust. In a place like Buckingham Palace, who could you really trust? People mightn't be deliberately malicious, but they had privileges to protect, hierarchies to maintain, underlings to oppress, higher-ups to circumvent, and any serviceable bit of information was leaped upon like a long-lost relative with stock in Microsoft. Even the Queen wasn't immune to this, I imagined. It explained, in part, her private interest in a tragic incident that might just as easily have been left to the usual authorities. I inwardly moaned: if only Robin were alive. I could have talked to him about all this. But, of course, that was impossible.

I looked up as I shovelled another forkful of lettuce into my mouth and saw Davey Pye come in. Could I trust Davey? He didn't seem very discriminating. Much too talkative, too. But something he had said the day before echoed in my head. 'I wouldn't betray Mother,' he'd said. I think he meant it. Odd, the subterranean depths of loyalty some people had despite their surface behaviour.

'Davey! Over here.' I gestured to my table and watched as he poured himself a cup of tea. He walked over, put his cup on the table and sat down.

'Rumour has it Humphrey Cranston is about to break his vow of celibacy, and you, my dear, are the reason,' he said by way of greeting.

'Oh, damn that Nikki,' I muttered.

'What did you do? How did you seduce him? Do tell.'

'Cor, blimey, mate, it t'were me huuuge knockers!' I replied in my worst Eliza Dolittle voice. 'Oh, come off it, Davey. Humphrey Cranston is too high and mighty to be interested in the likes of me.'

'Yes, old Humpy does project a certain air of purity, doesn't he? Tiresome creature really.' Davey slurped his tea noisily. 'I happen to know, however, that he's about as pure as the driven slush. There's a very nice vicar somewhere in north London who he has a *very warm* friendship with, if you catch my meaning. Cosy little weekends. Humpy's rather a closet case, really. Which is odd. In this place.'

'Does Her Majesty know?'

'Does Her Majesty *care*? Of course she *knows*.

C. C. BENISON

Mother is, as you Americans might say, quite a sharp cookie.'

'Canadian, for the two-hundredth time. And what 1940s' movies have you been watching, anyway?'

'Eh? Beg pardon?'

'Oh, never mind. Funny, though,' I mused, chasing the last bit of cheese across the oily plate with my fork, 'someone else was telling me roughly the same thing this morning . . .'

'What?'

'That the Queen is . . . a sharp cookie.'

'Well, of course. How do you think she became queen?'

'Accident of birth, obviously,' I said, amazed that anyone could be so obtuse.

'Yes, quite,' Davey said impatiently, 'but what I meant was that she has filled the role so admirably. She has *become* queen, not just become Queen, if you catch my point.'

'Sort of. Davey—'

'You know, there's this wonderful story about Queen Victoria. Like Mother, she was surrounded by fairies. You can't have a fairy kingdom without fairies, I always say. Anyway, someone apparently told old Queen Vic that some women, too, engaged in homosexual activity. Lesbians, would you believe! She was absolutely appalled. Couldn't believe it. Refused to believe it. Amazing, isn't it? . . . Gosh, this tea's poisonous today. What *are* they putting in that urn?'

I glanced over at the tea table. What indeed, I thought, feeling utterly cheerless.

'Davey . . .' I said, 'speaking of becoming queen and

144

accidents of birth and so on, there's something I want to tell you . . .'

He looked up from examining his cup.

'. . . but you have to promise to keep it to yourself.'

'Oooh, another secret. I don't know. I've never been one to keep my mouth shut, Jane. On the other hand, I've managed to keep quiet about what Nigel and I got up to with Robin. Of course, threat of the sack does concentrate one's mind wonderfully. Still . . .'

'Davey, you're babbling.'

'Yes, I am, aren't I. What is it you want to discuss?'

'You have to keep it to yourself.'

'I'll try.'

'You have to more than "try". You said yesterday that you would never betray Mother.'

Davey's brows knitted. 'What's Mother got to do with this?'

'Well, I don't really know,' I dissembled. 'But it might have something to do with her.'

The brows knitted further. 'Is this why old Humpy was talking to you?'

'In a way. Sorry to be so vague, but I don't rightly know myself.'

'Jane-Jane, you are a dark horse.'

'You meant what you said, though.'

'About Mother?'

'It's not just because it's a job and all that?'

'Of course not,' Davey said indignantly. 'I love the old sweetie. In my way, of course.'

He looked back down at his cup. I swear he was blushing.

'Okay, then. You know how I was in Robin's old

room yesterday with his sister when she came to get his things? Well, she told me something that was really astounding. Get this: Robin was going to become an earl, a peer of the realm, with money and a country house and a seat in the Lords and all that stuff.'

'Oh, give over!'

'Really! The Earl of Ulverstone. I swear. That's what his sister said.'

'Pull the other one.'

'I'm not kidding.'

'She's daft.'

'She said I could look it up in one of those books that list nobility . . .'

'*Burke's Peerage* or *Debrett's*?'

'. . . one of those. So I'm sure she's telling the truth. It's too easy to check. So here's Robin, working at these wages, and he's heir apparent to an earldom . . .'

Davey frowned. 'But I have it in my mind that Robin's father had joined the choir celestial.'

'He has . . . had.'

'Presumptive, then. Robin is heir *presumptive* to this title.'

'Apparent, presumptive. Tomayto, tom*ah*to.'

'You Americans – beg pardon, *Canadians* – are abysmally ignorant.'

'What?'

'Never mind, dear, it's not important. Who is the present earl, then?'

'Some ancient cousin. Practically dead, I gather.'

'Really? This is amazing.' Davey put his finger to his lips and appeared to lose himself in thought. After a

146

moment, he asked with a sidelong glance, 'House in London?'

'Yes,' I nodded, 'that, too.'

'Just think: he would have been able to invite all his old mates around from the Palace. What a pity!'

'Can you imagine Angie putting up with you lot?' I laughed.

'No, that's true. Still, one can dream . . . hmm, Earl of Ulverstone, well, bless my dangly bits. And he never let slip . . . So, this is what you were talking about with Humpy, is it? Thought Mother should be notified?'

'Yeah, something like that. Davey – you'll keep this to yourself?'

'Of course. Didn't I say I would? I don't know *why* I should. It's really quite . . . interesting, don't you think? I mean, it sets the mind to wondering . . .'

'Wondering what?'

'Well, wondering, for instance, if this is why Robin had come over all serious of late. And why he had become engaged to Angela, and so forth . . . I mean, I still can't figure that part out . . .'

'But he must have known he would inherit the title one day. It's not like he woke up one day this summer when you guys were at Balmoral and said, "Wow, I'm going to be the Earl of Ulverstone. I'd better get mature real fast." '

'Well . . . perhaps you're not far wrong, Jane. Look, he was only heir presumptive, not heir apparent.'

'What's the difference?'

Davey rolled his eyes. 'Tch! If Robin had been the Earl's son, he would be heir apparent. That is, it would be *apparent* that he was the heir. But since he was only a cousin or whatever, he is only *presumed* to be the heir, because the present Earl, who I assume has been childless, might yet have a son. You see what I mean?'

I digested this information for a moment. 'Yeah, okay, so . . .'

'So perhaps Robin learned when he was at Balmoral that the Earl was actually on his deathbed, that this cousin of his would be pushing up the daisies before very long, and that the chance of the Earl's having a son in his condition was pretty much out of the question. So, in other words, he *did* wake up one day and say, "Wow, I'm going to be the Earl of Ulverstone." ' Davey looked at me brightly, obviously pleased with himself. 'It's rather Prince Hal-ish, in a way,' he continued. 'Don't you think?'

'Prince Who-ish?'

'Hal-ish. Hal. *Henry V.* Oh, don't you know your Shakespeare, you benighted colonial?'

'*Julius Caesar, A Midsummer Night's Dream, Merchant of Venice, Tempest, Macbeth, Hamlet,*' I said, rattling off the plays we had read in junior and senior high school. '*Antony and Cleopatra* in first year university . . . so I know a little something about Shakespeare, you pompous Englishperson.'

'But not Hank *Cinque*, obviously. If only you had had the advantage of a comprehensive education.' He sighed. 'Anyway, here's the nub: Henry V, as the Prince of Wales, is a sort of Jack-the-lad type. His mates are all – how shall I say it? – well, they're not exactly from the *crème de la crème* of society in the year fourteen-whatever. Prince Hal hangs about in pubs. Drinking.

Wenching. The usual. Falstaff is one of his mates. You have heard of Falstaff?'

'Yes,' I said, piqued. 'Of course I've heard of Falstaff.'

'Beg pardon . . . Anyway, Prince Hal is not exactly engaging in princely behaviour. But he knows his destiny. It's in the back of his mind. There's this one scene in a pub where Falstaff pretends to be Hal's father, Henry IV – the King, that is. It's sort of a send-up and Hal plays along. At the end Falstaff tries to kiss up a bit, as if he has an inkling that things might change when Hal becomes king. "Banish plump Jack, and banish all the world," he says. And then Hal says, "I do; I will." And you just know he's dead serious. And then Hal becomes king and – surprise! surprise! – he rejects all his old mates.'

I thought this was all a bit far-fetched. 'So you're saying that Robin was just fooling around . . . play-acting . . .'

'Don't forget, he was interested in acting . . .'

'. . . but all the while he knew he had this great destiny, that one day he would have to knuckle under and become very proper?'

'Why not?'

'It's just not Robin,' I argued. 'Maybe he would have looked forward to the money, but I don't believe he would care much about the title and all that. At least not enough to make him change his character.'

'Or reveal his *real* character,' Davey countered, sipping the last of his tea. 'You never know what people really think, Jane, or what they really want. Look at Robin. He wasn't just some fun-loving bloke. He was working here at the Palace only because he was frustrated in his real ambition – acting. And then there were those bouts of depression, or whatever they were. Probably triggered by frustration. Perhaps this inheritance was what he was counting on all along.'

'Prince Hal went on to become king. Robin ended his own life,' I pointed out.

'Well,' Davey said glumly, 'I'll grant you the analogy does seem to break down there.'

We both looked towards the window, where a little sunlight was trying to break into the room.

'Davey, if I take your argument – and I don't, really – that some inheritance had the power to change Robin, then the announcement of that inheritance would have to have come at Balmoral. That's when you guys all say he seemed to change. I mean, what happened? Did he get a telegram from his cousin saying, "Hi. I'm nearly dead. You're about to become earl. Enjoy! Cheers, etc. etc." '

'Perhaps he hired a skywriter, then,' Davey said. 'I'm sure I don't know. Robin might have kept in touch with the old gent somehow.'

I found this unconvincing. 'When,' I said, 'did Robin really seem . . . changed?'

Davey pursed up his face in thought. 'I didn't pay that much attention to the lad, you know. He wasn't quite my type.'

'I know. You've said.'

'Don't be cross, darling. Let me see. I remember he wasn't exactly chatty the day he and Angie tumbled into the river, or whatever it was they were doing. That was in the evening, during the Ghillies' Ball—'

'Wait,' I interjected. 'You said last week at lunch

with Nikki and me that Robin and Angie looked "quite peculiar" after their dunk in the Dee.'

'Did I? Oh, yes. Well, they did look peculiar. Or I thought they did. I think I'd look very cross if I'd just fallen into that freezing bloody river with my clothes on. But Robin and Angie seemed so preoccupied, almost conspiratorial, even happy – which at the time was unusual for Robin.'

'The difference in Robin's manner – was that noticeable?'

'When I tried to talk to him about something earlier that day he had been virtually monosyllabic. He looked a little ill, in fact. But then, maybe he was. I remember he had cut his foot – or was it his hand? – well, he had cut something a few days earlier and had gone to town, to Ballater, to see a doctor. Mother doesn't keep one around at Balmoral. Perhaps he'd had a shot for tetanus or something and was feeling a bit peaky . . .'

'He had gone to see a doctor there, in Scotland?'

'Yes,' Davey drawled. 'I believe Scottish doctors are reasonably capable.'

This was interesting, I thought. Was this when Robin got the bad news about his health? Was this, not the stuff about becoming an earl, the event that had straightened him out, that led him to form an alliance of sorts with Angie? I looked at Davey. He was looking at me.

'Why are you bothered about all this, anyway?' he asked.

It was a question I was coming to hate. If you showed initiative or too much intelligence in the Palace, you were viewed suspiciously.

'I liked Robin,' I replied somewhat defensively. 'I'm

sorry he's dead. And now that he is dead, I keep learning all kinds of strange things about him. It's just odd, that's all. I can't help being curious.'

Davey seemed to accept this. He shrugged and pushed his teacup aside.

'Yes, Robin was a likeable chap,' he said, rising from his seat. 'And I'm sorry about that house in London. Pity. One meets so many titled and wealthy people carrying things to and fro here, but none of them ever invites you back to their place for what one might euphemistically call "a drinkie". Well, one did, once. But you'd be scandalized if I told you who.'

'Who?' I demanded, responding predictably to his bait.

'Well, since we're trading confidences . . .'

He leaned across the table and whispered a name to me. I *was* scandalized.

'Say,' Davey said, brightening, 'I wonder who's next in line after Robin?'

'Next in line for what?'

'For the earldom, silly. Oh, well, likely not anyone I know.'

'Yes,' I said to him as he moved away. 'Probably doesn't matter now.'

Chapter Eleven

There was still more than an hour left before I was due to meet with you-know-who, and I wondered, as I added my tray to the stack in Servants' Hall, how I might profitably use the time.

Newspapers, I thought. The idea of them still niggled at my brain from the time when I had stood outside Holborn Tube Station and bought a bunch. Had Robin been carrying a newspaper when he tried to see the Queen? Or had the Queen been carrying the paper into the corridor just before she fell? Each scenario seemed odd in its own way. As a footman, Robin might be called upon to take a newspaper to one of the male guests or to one of the members of the Household, but that certainly wasn't his mission that morning. On the other hand, it was hard to imagine HM toddling about the Palace with a rolled-up newspaper under her arm as if she were some City banker on the way to work.

The Press Secretary's offices were on the ground floor near the Privy Purse Entrance, which is the entrance on the far right if you happen to be facing Buckingham Palace. I hesitated before going in. There were some places that lowly housemaids like me weren't supposed to be, and among them were the

Household Offices, where the real work of the royalty business was carried out. However, over my months at the Palace I had had the occasional word with Charles McCandless, one of the two Assistant Press Secretaries. Like me, Charles was Canadian. He was also fairly new in the job and fairly young, all of which meant he wasn't the stuck-up sticky beak most of the members of the Household were. You could practicaly call him Chuck and get away with it. He was also quite good-looking, a fact that hadn't escaped his attention one bit. I think there was a wife somewhere, but that didn't stop him from some flirtation, though it was mild. Funny, isn't it, how you welcome it from some men, even older ones, and from others: yuck. Anyway, this is how I managed to have a word with him from time to time.

From all appearances it looked like what my mother, at the Charlottetown *Guardian*, would call 'a slow news day'. So slow, in fact, that there was nobody in the outer office when I entered it. There were six desks, one for each of the two Assistants Press Secretaries and four for the Information Officers. I had always associated the news business with grunge. That was the impression left me by the newsroom at the *Guardian* whenever I visited my mother: great piles of old newspapers, desks littered with coffee cups, ashtrays, dogeared dictionaries, notebooks, press releases on their way to overflowing rubbish bins. The Palace Press Office, by comparison, was as tidy as my grandmother's porch. It looked as though there was work in progress – there were computer screens switched on, and so forth

– but the stuff on each desk – the papers, the pens, the books – was neatly stacked and aligned. The place was absolutely shipshape, but this was no surprise. The Press Secretary, Roderick Beagley, had been in the Royal Navy.

I wondered whether I should knock on a door to one of the inner offices to announce my presence, but then thought better of it. There was the low rumble of male voices behind one of them. Evidently a meeting was in progress. Why interrupt it – and worse, get sent packing?

The nice thing about all this tidiness was that it was easy to find things. Against one wall was a honeycomb of shelves designed specifically for the dimensions of newspapers: broadsheets in one area, tabloids in another, all in alphabetical order, national papers first, provincial papers following, and some international papers at the end – not including the Charlottetown *Guardian*, no surprise.

I looked at the selection and thought hard. Broadsheet or tabloid? It would make a difference. There had to be about a dozen national papers, but few of them were broadsheets. I forced myself to think back to those painful moments when I found the Queen sprawled in the corridor and Robin dead. I had scooped up a newspaper from the floor, but had paid no attention to it and couldn't even remember where I had left it. It had been folded, I remember, but folded tight. Tabloids didn't fold the way broadsheets do, neat and tight. And I had no impression of the lurid colour that characterized tabloids. So it had to be a broadsheet.

But which one? I pulled Tuesday's edition of *The*

Times, the *Guardian*, the *Daily Telegraph* and the *Independent* from their respective piles and took them to a large table below a window that looked on to the Palace forecourt. There, under London's feeble autumn light, I turned page after page. What was I looking for, anyway? Nothing suggested itself to me as a clue. There was little on the Royal Family other than mentions of the forthcoming State Banquet for the RamaLamaDing-Dong and some speculation about what would be in the Queen's Speech when she opened Parliament in two weeks' time. Since the *annus horribilis*, things had quietened down considerably in the royalty beat, at least as far as the broadsheets were concerned.

In *The Times*, I glanced at the Court Circular which announced the day's events for members of the Royal Family. Might Robin have been trying to warn the Queen about something outside the Palace? But it all looked innocuous to me. That day nothing more than an investiture had been scheduled for the Queen. At Buck House, of course. Just another day in the life of a modern monarch.

In the *Independent* the editorial page contained an interesting piece on republicanism of the right-wing variety, apparently the latest in a long run of arguments, for and against, that had been ongoing since the *annus horribilis*. I had always thought it was the leftoids who were against the monarchy, but it was the writer's view that the real threat came from radical Tories who believed everything should be subject to an unfettered free market – the monarchy, after all, was a bloated, state-subsidized, inefficient, unmeritocratic (lovely word), clapped-out thing that couldn't posssibly compete in the global economy. This, I thought as I read on, was a bit short-sighted. I'm sure that if someone put a contract for monarchy services out to tender, the Queen of England would wipe the floor with the queen of Denmark or the king of Norway.

What really caught my eye about the article, however, stemmed from the subhead. This hinted darkly that the right-wing forces of republicanism had infiltrated the upper echelons of the Palace itself. The text named no names, but it suggested that new men around the Queen were not so much inexperienced and lacking in confidence (as they appeared to some Palace watchers) as quietly but deliberately sabotaging the monarchy's prestige. And they were doing this in league with certain – unnamed, of course – *other* newspapers.

Well, this was fascinating, I thought, and I immediately regretted not paying attention to newspapers except for their TV listings. But when you grow up with a mother who is obsessed with newspapers, you tend to turn off.

I had become so absorbed in this article that I practically jumped out of my uniform when the telephone rang on the desk nearest me. And it kept ringing. I wondered if thy were all dead in the other room or if I should answer it. *Buck House. Sorry, no vacancies.* But the door opened suddenly and Chuck McCandless darted out. He grabbed the receiver impatiently, listened for a moment, said 'yes' then 'no,' and put the receiver back on its cradle. He regarded it unhappily and then turned to me with a somewhat stern look of inquiry.

'Is it all right if I look through these papers?' I asked,

157

withering a little under his gaze. He didn't seem at all affable that afternoon.

'You shouldn't be in here' was his gruff reply. 'What are you looking for?'

'Um.' I wasn't prepared for this. 'Um. Someone told me there was a long piece about Prince Edward Island in one of the papers. I was feeling a bit homesick, I guess . . .'

'I don't remember it, and you wouldn't be likely to find it on the editorial page of the *Independent*,' Chuck said, glancing at the open page on the table. 'This isn't a lending library.'

'Please . . .' I attempted to look as small and cute as possible, which isn't that difficult because I am certainly small and, I daresay, somewhat cute.

Chuck thawed a touch. 'Well, be quick and put everything back exactly the way you found it. *Exactly*.'

He looked at his watch. A cloud of worry seemed to descend upon his face as he made for the door back to the inner sanctum.

I quickly pressed my advantage. 'Something else. Have any newspaper reporters inquired about Robin?'

'Who?'

'Robin Tukes, the dead footman.'

'Ah, yes. Just one, I believe. Someone asking if there had been a death within the Palace precincts. I didn't take the call.'

'What answer was given?'

'This really isn't your business, Jane,' he said kindly. 'Safe to say we are doing everything to make sure the State Visit runs smoothly. Okay?'

'Okay.' I sighed. Behind the door there was an eruption of acrimonious voices. 'Is there something going on?'

'Of course there's something going on. When is there not something going on?'

'Not "Royal Diary Shocker", by any chance, is it?'

Chuck frowned. 'Maybe. But that's not your business, either. Now you'll have to excuse me.'

He opened the door. There was a burst of noise, then relative silence as he shut it behind him.

Poor Press Office, I thought as I replaced some of the Tuesday papers. The last couple of years had been just one thing after another: royal separations, divorce, blab-all books, illicit tape recordings, the fire at Windsor Castle, income tax demands, endless stories in the papers and on television. It had been relatively quiet lately – and now this. And on the eve of a State Visit. At least Robin's death was out of the headlines. So far.

Nothing in the Tuesday papers struck me as anything that might be remotely linked to Robin's death. I thought I might as well give up, but then it occurred to me that the paper didn't necessarily have to be Tuesday's. Robin's first attempt to see the Queen had been the Thursday before. Of course! But I faced the daunting task of going through all the Thursday papers. 'Be quick,' Chuck had said.

I replaced the remainder of Tuesday's papers as quickly as I could. I think I put them back exactly the way I found them. Then I removed the previous Thursday's papers, just the broadsheets, stacked them on the table and began the task again – only this time, feeling pressured, I didn't linger over anything provocative other than an editorial in the *Guardian* which took the tabloids to task for trivializing the threat of this new English Republican Army. As it happened, I got only halfway through the piece, because I suddenly became aware of a malignant presence behind me.

It was Sir Julian Dench, the Queen's Private Secretary. The large face under the fringe of silvery curls was very dark – blood-infused, I guess you could say. While his lupine eyes regarded me suspiciously, there was no uncertainty in them. Everything about Sir Julian – his strong features, his immaculate suit, his self-possessed air – suggested a man accustomed to getting his own way. He reminded me of a very handsome but very angry animal of some new breed not normally found in the Palace. He was carrying a newspaper, tightly rolled.

'I want to see you in my office now,' he barked at me, slapping the newspaper roll against one hand so that the air cracked.

He didn't wait for my response, and I hesitated only a moment. I followed him down the corridor, my heart slamming against my chest.

'Shut the door,' he commanded from the other side of his desk. 'Sit down,' he added crisply when I had completed that task.

He himself remained standing, however, hands behind his back Prince-of-Wales fashion, as I lowered myself with as much cool as I could muster on to a very hard chair.

'It is evident to me that you are not the new Court Correspondent for the Press Association,' Sir Julian began, coldly eyeing my housemaid's uniform. 'Nor, unless I am mistaken, have you been recently employed as a member of the team in the Press Office.'

'No, sir,' I muttered.

'Then you have no business being in the Press Office. You are a housemaid, and your place in the Palace is to be in certain rooms at certain times under the deputy Housekeeper's direct supervision, after which you are to be neither seen nor heard.'

Unless you're Angela Cheatle, I thought. And thinking this gave me a spurt of confidence. *Sir Julian*, my mind declared, *you are a pig.* I looked up into his face, hoping that mine conveyed nothing more than the indifference of a servant, something I had cultivated as a waitress at Marilla's Pizza back on the Island.

'Yes, sir,' I said in reply to his last comment.

He glowered at me. I supposed I wasn't being satisfactorily contrite.

I continued: 'Mr McCandless said I might look through the papers.'

'Mr McCandless has not quite accustomed himself to protocol.'

'I wasn't doing any harm.'

'I beg your pardon?'

'I wasn't doing any harm, sir. I was just looking through some old newspapers.'

'Don't be impertinent, girl!'

He had made his little point. But he seemed in no hurry to dismiss me. A silence hung in the room, broken only by the whisper of good cloth meeting good cloth as he moved his hands to grip the front of his desk chair.

'The smooth operation of Buckingham Palace depends on everyone knowing his or her place in the scheme of things,' he continued in those oh-so-patient tones that assume the listener is an idiot. 'There are hundreds of people in Her Majesty's service, and the only way to bring the greatest efficiency to each and every task is to organize people the way they are organized in the army. I know you young people – particularly you young women – do not care for hierarchy, but it is the most practical and productive way to move any enterprise forward . . .'

Is this the kind of stuff Angela had to listen to? I wondered as he droned on. Or the Queen? Poor Queen.

'. . . and why there is – yes, it's true – a class system in the Palace. But it is no different from the army, or a business enterprise. It is why relations among the ranks are formal, why there are proper forms of address, why there are separate dining rooms for Household and Staff, why socializing between ranks is discouraged—'

'Then why were you in Servants' Hall early Tuesday morning, sir, if there shouldn't be socializing between ranks?' I interrupted. I don't know why, but the question just popped into my head.

'I was conferring with Mr Wentworth-Desborough about the film,' Sir Julian replied impatiently. But there was just the tiniest flicker of doubt in his eyes, as though I had caught him out somehow and he didn't know why. 'Her Majesty is interested in its progress.'

And so she sends her Private Secretary to Servants' Hall to investigate at eight o'clock in the morning? Not blinkin' likely, I thought.

'My position grants me wide admittance,' he continued imperiously. 'Yours does not.'

'Yes, sir,' I said. 'May I leave now, sir?'

He set his lips into a grim line. 'No, you may not.'

He moved from behind his chair and sat down. Even cut at the waist by the desk, Sir Julian Dench remained imposing, muscled and big-shouldered, as though he had been a sportsman at some point in his past. I supposed, if I looked at him a little differently, I could see the attraction, even though he had to be older than my own father. This aura of power, which he was now using to intimidate me, some women might interpret as sexual. It made me wonder how the Queen dealt with such subliminal stuff. Her last Private Secretary, from what I had heard, had been a skinny thing, about as sexy as a wet teabag.

He glared at me. 'You're Jane Bee, aren't you?'

Ah, the penny had dropped.

'Well, Jane Bee, it has come to my attention that you have been spending too much time intruding into something which is none of your business.'

'What do you mean?' I protested, all innocence.

'You know very well what I mean. You have become overwrought by the death of this young footman. I understand you were upsetting his sister yesterday, for one thing.'

'I was not "upsetting" her,' I said, the protest genuine this time.

'You were in his room when she was collecting his effects.'

'Robin was a friend of mine. I was offering my

163

sympathies to his sister. That seems like a perfectly normal thing to do, in my opinion.'

'I don't think your opinion is welcome,' Sir Julian told me bluntly. 'Furthermore, I understand that you neglected your work this morning to go to a solicitor's.'

'I had Mrs Harbottle's permission.'

'Indeed. You are a child. You have no need of a solicitor, much less the Queen's solicitor . . .'

'. . . it was the only name I knew.'

'Such urgency is little short of hysteria.'

How did he know where I had been that morning? The only way could have been via Mrs Harbottle. But it was surely not something Mrs H. would go and tell him, no matter how straitlaced a person she was? The chain of command didn't work that way. Mrs Harbottle, the deputy Housekeeper, is responsible to the Chief House-keeper, who is responsible to the Deputy Master of the Household, who is responsible to the Master of the Household. The Queen's Private Secretary is a whole other department. The Private Secretary acts as the channel between the sovereign and the government. He organizes the Queen's schedule and deals with her correspondence. Nobody would bother him about the Palace's domestic arrangements. Did Sir Julian think I didn't know this?

It all meant that he had to have been doing some inquiring of his own.

'. . . and now I find you poking about in the Press Office,' he was saying.

'I was just looking for an article about my home province, about Prince Edward Island.'

'I'm sure,' he said drily. 'As you are well aware, we

have an important State Visit here next week. There must be no interruptions, no mistakes, no trouble. Do you understand? I can tell you quite candidly that Her Majesty has been upset by the death of this young man in her home . . .'

I figure you can always tell someone's not being candid when they say they are.

'. . . and I don't want any further emanations of this unpleasantness to intrude upon what must be the careful execution of a visit that is important not only to Her Majesty but to the entire realm. Do I make myself clear? If you are intent upon making a nuisance of yourself, Jane, then I will be forced to recommend your dismissal.'

He gave me a tight smile as if to say there could be no misunderstanding of the lack of regret with which he would do this. I echoed his gesture. There was nothing more to say. Sir Julian pointed to the door, as if there could be any doubt about what I was to do next: leave, and not darken said door again.

Chapter Twelve

At five minutes to four, after a brisk but not-too-con-spicuous trot down the Privy Purse Corridor and upstairs to the principal floor, I was in the White Draw-ing Room.

And you'll never guess what I found on the rug. Chewing gum. Again. It wasn't as fresh as what I had stepped in the day before, but it was there nevertheless, a great wad of the stuff, all pink and rubbery-looking. And, as it had been the last time I was in the room, it was directly beneath the chandelier, right in the middle of the floral pattern in the Axminster. This couldn't be carelessness, I decided. It had to be deliberate. Who was getting turned on by leaving wads of gum on priceless carpets?

At Buck House just about anyone, I concluded as, at four o'clock precisely, the pier-glass slid forward sil-ently on its hinges. The Queen is nothing if not punc-tual, I thought, reflecting on a life that was beholden to schedules. However, no Monarch popped out from behind the pier-glass to invite me in, so, ignoring the gum and decided not to vex Her Majesty by even men-tioning it, I moved to the wall on my own impulse and slipped into the Royal Closet. No one was there.

'Your Majesty?' I whispered, and then felt immedi-ately silly. What was I expecting? The Queen hiding behind a couch, waiting to spring out at me?

A door opposite, one to the Queen's Audience Chamber, opened and Humphrey Cranston poked his head through, jack-in-the-box fashion.

'Her Majesty will join you presently,' he said. The door closed.

Since I figured it probably wasn't a good idea for the Queen to find me seated – protocol and all – I went over to the card table near the window and looked to see if any progress had been made on the jigsaw-puzzle front since the day before. Apparently not. There remained the gap in the allegorical figures around King Charles, and parts were still missing around the top border. I picked up a pink piece from the table that I thought was part of the sky but I couldn't make it fit. I didn't try any further, because I suddenly felt a sharp pain in my ankle.

'Joan!' came the voice of the Queen.

'Jane, Your Majesty,' I squeaked, turning and dip-ping into a curtsey. The pain in my ankle was intense.

'Yes, I know. I mean the dog. Her name is Joan. Joan, come here.'

I looked down at my tormentor. The way Joan bared her teeth, I swear she was grinning at me. I like dogs but I don't like having my ankles bitten. I had an urge to give Joan a swift kick but refrained, of course. You couldn't very well kick the Queen's dog in front of the Queen.

'Joan, come here,' Her Majesty commanded, and this time the dog responded, padding over to her mistress on her little feet and plunking herself down on the carpet with a breathy sigh that sounded to me pretty much like one of satisfaction.

I thought the Queen looked a bit tired – a hard day doing her Boxes, probably. The fan of lines around her eyes was more pronounced, and there was a sort of sober set to her lips. Over a light pink dress with little grey twiggy-looking things on it she was wearing a pale blue cardigan which she tugged around her as if the cold (and Buck House was always cool, if not worse) were getting to her. She looked like she could have used a nice cup of hot, sweet tea. Quite frankly, so could I. It *was* teatime, after all. But none was proffered. The Queen sat herself down and indicated for me to do the same. Joan regarded me greedily.

'Were you able to talk with Sir Terence?' HM asked, giving the front of her dress a brush to straighten the fabric. 'Or perhaps I should ask first if you were able to arrange something with Mrs Harbottle.'

'Both, actually, Ma'am,' I replied, and I told her about telling Mrs Harbottle I needed to see about a will.

'How very clever,' she said when I had finished, and the beginning of a smile flickered in her face. It does make a difference. The Queen can look quite forbidding when her face is in repose, but when a smile is in the offing, well, suddenly you can see why she is this sort of ultimate mother figure who keeps appearing in people's dreams.

'Now,' she said. 'was Sir Terence able to enlighten you in any way?'

'Yes, he was,' I said excitedly, 'but first I have to tell

you about my talk with Katherine Tukes, Robin's sister. It's quite unbelievable.'

And I told her about Robin's titular inheritance.

The Queen's reaction was certainly odd. At first she was quite absorbed in what I was saying – disbelieving initially, of course, but then persuaded, as I had been persuaded by Katherine's insistence and the possibility of easy confirmation in *Burke's Peerage* or *Debretts*. It was when she asked me to repeat the title, Earl of Ulverstone, that her manner changed and her face took on that acid-drop expression she gets when she's in a disapproving mood.

'Ma'am?' I said after she had been silent for an unusual length of time.

'It's most peculiar. The Earl of Ulverstone has not been in one's thoughts for –' and here a look of mild surprise crossed her face – 'for nearly half a century. And now his name has come forward twice in a rather short period of time.'

'What was the other instance, Ma'am?'

'My husband mentioned him.'

'I see,' I said, not seeing.

The Queen seemed compelled to explain. 'My husband was in one of his teasing moods. We were having dinner together a few days before we went to Balmoral, and he tossed out the name Ulverstone quite unexpectedly. I'm afraid, however, that I cut him short. So I don't know now why the name ever came to his mind. It's all so long ago. It's very odd.' Seeing the look of puzzlement on my face, the Queen continued: 'You see, the Earl of Ulverstone, Francis Tukes – yes, of course, that is the family name . . .' She looked away for a moment, her face growing increasingly soft while the corners of her mouth turned up as though she were about to break into laughter. 'As I was saying, the Earl of Ulverstone, well, how shall I put it? Modern parlance, I think: the Earl of Ulverstone fancied one.'

'Ma'am! Really?'

The Queen's face dropped. 'Yes, really. It was near the end of the war. He was an Equerry to my father.'

'Sorry, Ma'am. I didn't mean to suggest—'

'Of course,' she interrupted. 'I knew exactly who I wanted for my husband. And it certainly wasn't Francis Tukes. He was quite unsuitable – a strange man, really. Fortunately, my father came to dislike him once he appeared to overstep himself. Banned him from Court, in fact. It all seems rather amusing in retrospect. I think Francis retired to the West Country – poor man, I haven't seen him since, nor barely heard news of him. And now this. I wonder what possessed Philip to bring up his name after all these years? I suppose I shall have to ask him now that he's returned from Africa.'

The Queen regarded the corgi Joan thoughtfully for a moment. 'And you say that this footman, Robin Tukes, was Francis' cousin?'

'Father's cousin, I believe.'

'Yes, that would account for the age difference, of course. I can't recall ever hearing if he married. And there must be no children.'

'So Robin was the heir presumptive. Is that correct, Ma'am?'

'Yes.'

'I'm not sure I understand this system.'

'It's somewhat akin to my position. I, too, was an

heir presumptive. Heiress presumptive, I suppose one must say today.'

'But you were the first-born child of the King.'

'Yes, but I was a daughter. If my parents had had a son, he would have preceded me in the line of succession. I was presumed heir in expectation of there one day being an apparent heir, a male heir.'

I said impulsively, 'It hardly seems fair, Ma'am.'

'What doesn't seem fair?'

'That boys automatically go to the head of the line.'

The Queen sighed. 'Yes,' she said, 'I remember having to explain this to my daughter once. Inheritance is based on the principle of male primogeniture, according to which male heirs take precedence and the right of succession belongs to the eldest son. I can only say that that's the way the succession in England has always been arranged and it has worked well. I see no reason for it to be changed.'

Well, I thought, you couldn't say the Queen was exactly a raving feminist. Still, the custom didn't seem fair to me. But I could tell from the look on her face that there was no point in contradicting her. My goodness, I then thought: I have come a long way in a few days. Even the *idea* of thinking of contradicting the Queen would never have occurred to me before.

'Ma'am,' I said. 'There's something else: Robin was going to be a father. One of the housemaids, Angela Cheatle, is having his baby. They're not married . . .'

Her Majesty looked dismayed. And I felt suddenly embarrassed, realizing how inappropriate it might be to talk with the Queen about such intimate things. But it wasn't the fact of their unmarried state that dismayed her. After all, if Angela had been married, she wouldn't even *be* working at the Palace. It was something else.

'I wonder, did this girl know about the state of Mr Tukes' health before he died?'

'I . . . I don't know,' I said lamely. At that point I felt I just couldn't tell her that the baby wasn't Robin's and therefore in no jeopardy.

'Then she should be told, for the baby's sake. Perhaps one should have a word with Dr Baring.'

'Yes,' I murmured, 'that would be a good idea.'

But something else was on my mind. I said, 'Even though they were engaged, the fact that they weren't married means the child cannot inherit the title. That's what Katherine Tukes said.'

'Yes, it's true,' the Queen said.

'And, according to Katherine, their father's cousin, the present Earl, is not well – he might die at any time.'

The Queen nodded.

'Therefore, maybe there *was* some urgency about the inheritance . . .'

'You need to find out who, after Robin Tukes, would inherit the title.'

'And, Ma'am, the money and the property.'

'Yes, I seem to recall there was some wealth attached to the title. Ulverstone is a fairly old one.'

'According to Sir Terence, Robin also came into money on his twenty-first birthday last week,' I continued. 'That money now goes to Karim Agarwal.'

The Queen looked blank.

I explained, 'He's another of the footmen.'

'Yes. Of course.'

'As it happens, Karim is in great need of money at

the moment.' And I quickly told the Queen of Karim's sister's dilemma. I also told her about this curious reference in Robin's will to an enterprise that he might have been planning with Karim. ' "The business of which we so often talked," I think were the words Sir Terence quoted.'

'And yet,' Her Majesty mused when I had concluded, 'there remains no explanation as to why Robin Tukes was so intent upon seeing one. That seems to me to be the key. This footman who apparently benefits by Robin's death would have benefited whether the death occurred in the corridor, in his own bed or out on the street. It's all quite puzzling.'

'Ma'am,' I said, 'on Tuesday morning when you . . . had the accident, were you by any chance carrying a newspaper?'

'No.'

'Oh. Well, when I came out of the White Drawing Room and found . . . you, I happened to pick up a folded newspaper that was lying on the carpet near Robin. It was just something I did automatically – housemaid's training, I guess. I'm not sure what I did with it. I was upset . . .'

'I believe you may have left it in my sitting room. I recall Humphrey lifting a newspaper from a chair. I did wonder briefly how it had got there.'

'Would you know, Ma'am, which newspaper it was?'

'I'm afraid not.'

'Oh.'

Some consternation must have shown on my face, for Her Majesty said: 'Jane, you look perplexed.'

'Well, maybe I'm grasping at straws, but I can't help

wondering if Robin had a newspaper with him when he was trying to see you because there was something in it that had something to do with *why* he wanted to see you. In fact, I was even down in the Press Office a little while ago going through the back papers to see if anything leaped out at me, but I couldn't find anything that made a connection.'

You know those dimmer switches that some people use for their electric lighting? Well, it was as if someone had connected one to Her Majesty. A look of illumination just seemed to gather about her face.

'I wonder . . .' she said.

'Ma'am?'

'I wonder if he had deciphered my advertisement?'

'Ma'am?' I repeated. The Queen, advertising? A used Rolls-Royce flitted through my mind. *For Sale. Immac. cond. Loaded. Used to chauffeur Monarch to Windsor Fridays.* Tel. 0171 999 4832.

'Something very important belonging to my family has gone missing,' she explained, after taking a moment to consider. 'An advertisement had been placed recently in some of the newspapers through a third party with the hope of recovering it without public notice. The wording was deliberately cryptic. But the right person, or persons, would of course immediately understand it, as was the intent.'

I could feel my heart beat quicker. This seemed promising.

'What is it that's gone missing?'

'A journal belonging to my great-grandfather, King Edward VII.'

'Royal Diary Shocker!' I whooped.

'You've seen the *Evening Gazette*,' Her Majesty said drily.

'It screamed out at me at a news-stand.'

The Queen looked very unhappy. 'The journal came to light rather belatedly from among the things rescued from the fire at Windsor,' she explained. 'I don't know how it escaped attention before, but it did. I had, of course, wanted to read it, but one's schedule provides little opportunity, and my great-grandfather's hand-writing is really quite difficult to decipher. Neverthe-less, I had intended to have a go at it at Balmoral and I believed it had been packed and sent up there. But it was missing when I arrived – most annoying. And then it simply couldn't be found. So when I returned to London, I began to see if there was some way to recover it.'

'Stolen, do you think?'

'Of course it was stolen,' she replied briskly. 'And now that impossible newspaper has got its hands on it. However, it is private property, *stolen* private property, and one is taking steps to ensure that its contents remain private.'

I felt a sense of dismay. Had Robin, I wondered, stolen the royal journal? Or been involved in its theft wittingly, or even unwittingly? Had he been going to confess the theft to the Queen, hoping maybe for some kind of mercy? I had it in my mind that monarchs could pardon people if they wanted. Maybe he thought she would be in a more pardoning mood if they could have a conversation face-to-face. I expressed these thoughts to Her Majesty.

'One can grant a pardon only on advice from the

Home Secretary,' she informed me. 'On the other hand, people do seem to retain some very antique ideas about one's powers, Jane. There are still those who believe that one's touch can cure them of scrofula. There are even people who believe my daughter-in-law is capable of curing AIDS. It's really most sad and disturbing.'

'What about Robin, though, Ma'am?'

'Yes, Robin.' Here the Queen looked pensive. 'Perhaps he was able to decipher the advertisement. Do you believe he would have been capable of theft?'

'No, Ma'am, not really – certainly not for sale or money.'

'Then perhaps he knew who did.'

It's possible, I thought. But if Robin did know who'd stolen the royal diary why wouldn't he go to the proper authorities?

'When was the last time you saw the journal?' I asked the Queen.

'I believe some few days before leaving London for Balmoral. My husband had had it briefly and glanced at it, but I wouldn't say he would have had the patience for the handwriting.'

'Did anyone else have it?'

The Queen ran her fingertips along the strands of pearls at her neck.

'My Private Secretary,' she replied. 'He's also Keeper of the Royal Archives. I had asked Sir Julian if he would read it and give me a report on its contents.'

'And was Sir Julian the last one to see it?'

'*I* believe so.'

Her stress on the personal pronoun suggested a difference of opinion with someone. Sir Julian himself?

And yet the look on her face was an example of the kind of studied neutrality you have to cultivate if you're going to remain a constitutional monarch. Somehow her expression didn't invite further probing, which was too bad: in wishing to see the Queen, Robin had seemed extremely intent on circumventing Sir Julian. Now, with the additional mystery of the missing diary, it seemed like there might be something drawing in all the strange, disconnected elements to Robin's death.

'Ma'am, is there anything in the journal that might be—' I groped for the right word.

'Embarrassing?' replied Her Majesty. 'I'm afraid I don't know. Apparently Sir Julian had little opportunity to review its contents, and since my husband has been in Africa, I haven't had an opportunity to ask him what he might have read.'

'The *Gazette* used the word "shocker".'

'The *Gazette* is inclined to hyperbole. On the other hand, my great-grandfather was, as you may know, a rather – ' Her Majesty paused and gave a tight little smile – 'robust man. Lucky for him, though, he did not live in a world with such an intrusive press.'

'Still,' I said to HM, 'it's all ages ago.'

'There's been quite enough unwelcome attention paid to my family of late,' the Queen said severely. 'Attention paid to my great-grandfather would be no more welcome, even if it does involve something that occurred a century ago. But the point is this, however: King Edward wished his diaries to be destroyed upon his death. And they were destroyed, as he wished, all except this one.'

'But, Ma'am, what about the historical significance?'

'Those were the King's wishes.'

Clearly Her Majesty could not be moved on the subject. 'My great-great grandmother, Queen Victoria,' she continued, 'was an unflagging diarist. There are over one hundred volumes of her journals in the Archives at Windsor, but none of them are in her own handwriting. Princess Beatrice, her youngest daughter, transcribed them all, but expurgating them as she did so, leaving out . . .'

All the hot parts about Albert, I thought.

'. . . all the parts that might cause pain to those mentioned or to their relatives,' Her Majesty said. 'Then Beatrice burned the originals. Those were Queen Victoria's wishes. What do you think of that?'

'Well, Ma'am, it makes me question the point of even *keeping* a journal if it's going to be destroyed or censored. If you don't mind my asking, do you keep a journal?'

'Yes.'

'In your own handwriting?'

The Queen looked at me quizzically. 'Well, in whose handwriting would it be?'

The Queen reached down to retrieve her handbag, a sure sign that the interview was over. The corgi raised herself, and as she did so released a stream of pee on to the rug.

'Oh, Joan,' the Queen exclaimed. 'How could you!'

Joan looked up at her mistress, hardly mortified.

The Queen opened her bag and pulled out a cloth and a small bottle with some fizzy liquid sloshing around in it.

So *that's* what she keeps in her handbag, I thought.

A great mystery resolved: soda water, in case one of her corgis has an accident.

'Oh, I'll do that, Ma'am,' I said, taking the bottle and cloth from her.

'Thank you, Jane. I'm really very late for Windsor. And it's been rather a *dies horribilis*. Goodbye. Come along, Joan.'

'Goodbye, Your Majesty. Have a nice weekend.'

And you, you little *canis horribilis*, I thought as Joan departed with a canine smirk at me, you have a rotten weekend!

Chapter Thirteen

For a couple of days I had been trying to get a quiet moment with Karim Agarwal, but whenever I came into view he managed to veer off the other way, and in a place as big as Buck House there are a lot of ways to veer off to.

Finally, early on Friday evening, I bumped into him. Literally, as it happens. I was starting on my way to Long Marsham to visit my Great-Aunt Grace. I was standing at the Side Entrance, having buttoned my jacket against the evidence of rain, and had stooped to retrieve my knapsack from the marble floor. As I rose, I swung the knapsack through the air and hit Karim square in the face.

'Ow!' he exclaimed, glowering at me as if I had planned to attack him and lain in wait deliberately to do so.

'Sorry, Karim, I didn't see you coming.'

He looked so put out, I almost felt like laughing. 'Where are you off to?' Karim dashed out of the door, past security, and turned left into Buckingham Palace Road. I hurried after him.

'I'm going to see *Sunset Boulevard*.' He tossed this

over his shoulder, unfolding an umbrella as the rain became impossible to ignore.

'Lucky you,' I said, unfolding mine. 'How did you get tickets?'

'I bought them months ago. Queued for them when it first opened at the Adelphi.'

We walked together in silence for a moment, rain pattering against our umbrellas. I had intended to turn right and head for the Underground at Victoria Station, but following him now seemed the better plan.

'Going alone?' I asked innocently.

We had turned the corner and were passing between the Palace and the Queen Victoria Memorial. Karim looked through the centre gate across the barren fore-court towards the façade of the Palace. Here the dark-ened Portland stone was relieved only by the lights around the guards' sentry boxes. The great lamps flank-ing the centre gate captured a fleeting expression of anguish on his dark, handsome face.

'Yes,' he said finally in a tone that suggested it was none of my business, and then, as if thinking better of it, added: 'I had originally bought these tickets for Robin's birthday. I was going to surprise him.'

We stopped at the traffic lights on Constitution Hill. A rising wind buffeted our umbrellas. Karim looked down at me from under his, noting that we seemed to be shoulder to shoulder (well, shoulder to rib cage).

'Are you following me or something?' he asked peevishly.

'No, I'm not following you, Karim. I'm heading for Green Park Tube Station. I'm catching a train to Maryle-bone. I presume you're heading for Green Park, too. So

181

do you mind if I walk with you? London's not that safe at night.'

'No,' he said in an ungracious tone as the light turned green. 'I don't mind.'

'And, anyway, I've been wanting to talk to you, but you've been so elusive the last few days,' I persisted.

'I've had a lot on my mind.'

'I've been waiting to tell you I've got your letter.'

'What letter?'

'The one from your sister.'

He stopped in his tracks. We were just the other side of the ornamental Canada Gates that open on to Broad Walk.

'How did you get it?' he demanded, turning to me. There was a look of consternation on his face.

'From Robin's *A–Z* guide. The letter was stuck in the index at the back. Here . . .' I dropped my umbrella on the path, opened the strap of my knapsack and rummaged inside. 'You can have it back.'

I had intended to show it to my aunt when I arrived in Long Marsham that evening, but I figured I could give anyone the gist of the contents and so it would do no harm to return it to Karim.

'It's private bloody property, you know,' he exploded.

'I know! I'm just giving it back, for heaven's sake. I'd have done it days ago if you hadn't been avoiding me.'

'You could have put in my pigeon-hole.' His anger was unmistakable.

'Well, I thought it was kind of personal.'

Karim reached for the envelope, tilting it to look at the handwriting in the pale lamplight along the path.

But raindrops splattered the blue stationery, menacing the ink. Abruptly Karim stuffed the envelope in his coat and resumed walking.

'In other words, you read it!' he shouted over his shoulder as I hastened to do up my knapsack and gather up my umbrella, which had threatened to bound across the grass in a gust of wind.

'It was hard not to!' I shouted back.

'It's my name on this envelope, not yours. You've got a bloody cheek.'

'Karim,' I said urgently, when I had caught up with him again. 'Karim, do you really believe Robin tried to kill himself?'

For a moment, he didn't answer. There was only the noise of our boots scrunching the leaves and the soft thud of rain glancing off nylon.

I thought he hadn't heard me, and I was about to repeat the question when he replied impatiently: 'Yes . . . of course.'

'Why were you so anxious to get that letter back?'

'What's that got to do with anything?'

'On Tuesday, when you found me in Robin's room after, well, after you know . . . you said you had come to get a jumper you had lent him. But you didn't come for the jumper. You came for that letter.'

'So what if I did? It was my letter.'

Karim seemed to have become harder since I had last spoken with him. In Robin's room that morning he had been blustering and, finally, weepy – not surprising, really, under the circumstances – but now he was very taut and defensive.

'Karim, in that letter your sister practically begs you

to somehow get your hands on twenty-five thousand pounds.'

'So?'

'You wanted to help her. She's how old?'

'Seventeen.'

'Good God! And forced to marry some old geezer because of some family bargain. It's positively medieval.'

He moved his umbrella to block my view of him.

'It's just the way things are done,' he told me. 'Meena will make a good marriage. It's what my parents want. There are too many problems for Asians living in England. Society here is very different. She could end up marrying outside her caste. Or someone white.'

' "Outside her caste"? Talk about double standard!' I said indignantly. 'What about you and Robin? He wasn't your caste, your colour, and not even the opposite sex—'

'That's different . . .'

'And never mind any of that – your sister's letter is heart-rending. You're actually defending this practice?'

'Yes,' he said curtly.

'Really? Then why did you give the letter to Robin?'

Karim was hurrying along the path more quickly now. 'Why shouldn't I show it to Robin?'

'Because you and Robin had broken up, that's why. You've barely spoken with him in weeks. And suddenly you show him a letter about an intimate family problem?'

'I gave him the letter long before.'

'The cancellation mark, Karim. The letter arrived in England last Thursday, the day of Robin's birthday party. You must have got it on Friday. And you showed it to him the first time at the hospital on Sunday.'

'Well, I *told* him about Meena long before. This didn't all just happen, you know.'

'But your sister's plea for money to bargain her way our just happened, apparently.'

'So?'

'So, you thought Robin could help you. You knew he had money, or was coming into money—'

'How did you know about the money?' Karim interjected sharply.

'Robin's sister told me.' I lied. 'She was at the Palace yesterday, getting some of Robin's stuff.'

He glared at me.

'Anyway,' I continued, 'that suggests to me you don't really believe in this arranged-marriage thing for your sister. You wanted to help Meena badly enough to break your self-imposed decision to stay away from Robin and to avoid talking to him. Even though he became withdrawn up in Scotland, it was really you who broke it off with Robin, wasn't it? It wasn't the other way around.'

'He certainly did break it off! By getting himself involved with Angie, he bloody well broke it off. That was enough.'

'The engagement to Angie last week was a complete surprise to everyone. It doesn't seem like it was much of a surprise to you.'

Here Karim hesitated. He regarded me suspiciously from under his umbrella. I had to keep tilting mine sideways to watch him and my hair was getting damp.

Karim said harshly, 'He told me beforehand.'

'How beforehand?'

'Earlier in the day, I suppose.'

'But you knew about the relationship earlier.'

'Didn't I more or less say so?' he responded sulkily.

'Did he never say why he was doing this?'

'No! No, he did not.'

'If you were so angry about this thing with Angie, why did you go to a birthday party that you knew was going to become an engagement party?'

His eyes narrowed. 'What are you on about, Jane?'

'Nothing. Just curious. And what's this stuff about business? Were you and Robin going to start up something?'

'Bloody hell. That was between Robin and me. Who told you about it?'

'I don't know,' I lied again with astonishing ease. 'I thought everyone knew.'

Uncertainty flickered in his face. 'We had it in mind to open a shop, that's all. Do you think I want to be a footman for the rest of my life? Working at the Palace may be just a lark for you, Jane. It's just part of your Grand Tour of Europe. But it's reality for me.' He said it with such fervour, I felt my skin prickle.

'Then why did you start working at the Palace in the first place?'

'My parents sent me here,' he replied miserably. 'They thought I'd just get into trouble if I stayed in Blackburn. They thought the Queen would personally look out for me, that's how stupid they are. So they wrote to the Palace to get me a job.'

'You didn't have to come.'

'You don't know Indian families. Besides, what other

work was there? And I was just as glad to get away from the North.' He sighed. 'Robin and I were going to open a shop. The shop was going to sell all kinds of things related to the London theatre – posters and books and costumes and antiques and the like. Robin was planning to use the money he was going to come into on his birthday to help get it running. And after that we were going to leave the Palace.'

'And then Angie screwed it up.'

'Silly bitch.'

'Are you sure Robin never explained anything about their relationship?'

'Haven't I told you?'

'Didn't he try?'

'He may have. I don't know. I didn't care. Why are you asking me all these damn questions anyway?'

'I wonder if Robin made a will,' I mused, fishing about.

'I wouldn't know,' Karim said coldly, quickening his pace. We were practically dashing through the rain.

I had a feeling that Karim did know. I had a feeling that he knew a lot and had known it early. But something was making him hedge. If he was extremely angry with Robin, yet knew that Robin had included him in a will for a considerable sum of money, mightn't that give him a perfect motive for murder?

'Did Robin say he would give you, or lend you, the twenty-five thousand to help your sister?'

'It's none of your bloody business.'

'I can't imagine Robin would say no in a case like this.'

Karim ignored me.

In the distance, above Piccadilly, a floodlit building soared like a beacon. Directly opposite, burrowing under the raised earth that formed the boundary of Green Park, was the tunnel to the Tube station. There was little time. I decided to take a chance.

'Look, Karim, I don't believe Robin took his own life. I think he was murdered.'

The effect of this announcement on Karim was electric. He looked at me wildly, his dark eyes blazing, nostrils flared, jaw muscles moving, the whole bit.

'What! What are you saying? You stupid bloody girl, leave it alone. He killed himself! *Killed himself!*'

'It doesn't make sense,' I insisted stubbornly.

'He was depressed!'

'Not *that* depressed.'

'He tested for AIDS! He was HIV-positive! Now do you see?'

'I know all about it! Stop shouting at me.'

'How do you know?' he demanded incredulously.

I had to think fast. 'His sister told me. He had written to her.'

Karim looked at me warily. He said nothing.

'How do *you* know?' I asked in return.

'He told me.'

'When?'

Karim hesitated. 'At the hospital. On Sunday. You were there. Just before you came in.'

'It must have been a real shock,' I said sympathetically, though I didn't for a second believe him. I was certain Robin had learned of his illness in Scotland; he had probably told Karim soon after. 'Are you okay yourself?'

He looked away, towards the trees with their few remaining leaves. 'I don't know.'

'What about getting tested?'

His eyes glittered. 'I'd rather not know, thank you very much,' he said bitterly.

'But it's not a death sentence necessarily. People live normally for years. Sometimes it never turns into full-blown AIDS.'

'But more often it does.'

We walked in silence for a few moments. I broke it by saying, 'So you think Robin had a good reason for killing himself, then?'

Karim nodded.

'Then why would he do it in the Page's Vestibule? That's not the normal pattern for a suicide.'

'What?' Karim looked bewildered. 'I thought it happened in his room!'

'No, the Page's Vestibule, like the first "suicide attempt".' I decided there was little to lose now with this information. And Karim's reaction was fascinating.

'Well, people jump off buildings,' he countered defensively.

'Meaning . . .'

'That people sometimes like to make a spectacle of it all.'

'That wouldn't have been Robin's way,' I said, and meant it.

'Not make a spectacle? It was Robin's idea to streak through the Palace, remember.'

This was too much. Why was Karim so adamant that it was suicide? If you were in love with someone, and that someone killed himself, wouldn't you be gratified, in a strange sort of way, to learn that the death wasn't self-inflicted after all? It would absolve you of the blame or guilt that surely you would be feeling.

'Okay, let's put it this way, Karim. I feel it in my bones that Robin was murdered.'

Fear, not anger, now seemed to radiate from Karim. 'Have you told anyone?' The words came out in a gasp, as if the oxygen in Green Park had suddenly vanished.

'No,' I replied. 'But I might.'

We reached the steps leading down to the station. Karim stopped and grasped the gate rail. 'You just bloody well leave it alone, Jane,' he said in a pleading sort of voice. He looked stricken. 'He's dead. Can't you see? Nothing's going to bring him back.'

And with this he bolted down the stairs ahead of me. His umbrella hit the overhang and he snatched at it with a groan. I was left standing in the rain, wondering what nerve I had struck.

A few moment later, having pushed my monthly Travel-card through the electric barrier, I was making my way down the escalator, heading for the Jubilee Line. I was a bit shaken from my conversation with Karim. At first I didn't notice the man who sidled up to me, violating the 'keep right' rule on escalators that cleared a passage for those in a hurry. Some lost tourist, I thought, when I finally brought my attention to bear on the face that seemed to be staring at my profile expectantly. In London, tourists get asked questions by tourists. At least, I thought gratefully, I wasn't a tourist any more. I was a Londoner.

This pleasing thought vanished when I realized who the man was. It was that damn Andrew Macgreevy from the *Evening Gazette* whom I had seen loitering around Holborn Station only that morning, the man to whom Davey Pye had waved. One of the tabloid terriers.

'Your friend seemed to be in a hurry,' Macgreevy commented as we stepped off the escalator and continued down a tunnel where the delicate sound of a busker's mandolin competed unsuccessfully with the echoes of heavy feet.

His broad features seemed to glow pink from exertion, or perhaps it was just high blood pressure. It made his face, even in profile, look a bit pudding-like. I wish I could say he also had ferret eyes, like raisins in a pudding, and beery breath and other characteristics that should go with descriptions of tabloid reporters, but he didn't. Andrew Macgreevy was quite an ordinary-appearing guy, younger than I had thought, a bit unhealthy-looking, but on the whole someone you wouldn't look at twice if he weren't looking at you twice.

'Andrew Macgreevy's the name.' He extended his hand as we joined the smattering of people on the platform.

'Stella Rigby,' I said promptly, naming for some unfathomable reason a very minor character on *Coronation Street*. I kept my hand on my knapsack strap.

If my choice of name contradicted what he already knew, he didn't reveal it.

'You work at the Palace, don't you?' he asked.

'Yeah.'

'I've seen you about.'

'Like at Holborn this morning? A bit far from Buck House.'

'A coincidence.' He shrugged and smiled placatingly.

'Oh, sure. So what are you, anyway. A stalker who likes to introduce himself first?'

'A reporter. For the *Evening Gazette*. Surely you've seen my name?' he added, trying to sound jolly. 'I'm famous.'

'Yeah? Then what's a famous fellow like you doing in Green Park Tube Station, chatting up someone young enough to be his . . . daughter.'

'Fergie cancelled our date. Her baby-minder didn't show. Too bad, too. She had an effigy of her mother-in-law she was keen to burn.'

I moved down the platform where greater numbers of people were starting to gather. Macgreevy followed.

'I need information,' he said.

'About what?'

'About some goings-on at the Palace.'

A wind was beginning to rise in advance of the train as it emerged from the tunnel, a dull roar sounding from deep in the blackness. I turned my head to face the moving air. Although I had lived in London for close to a year, the rich smells and sounds of the Underground still exhilarated me. I loved to watch the train burst into view like some ruthless mechanical animal. I ignored Mr Macgreevy.

'And I'm willing to pay for it,' he continued, pressing his face closer to my ear to be heard above the escalating noise. I instinctively moved away. The platform was now quite crowded.

'How would you like to earn fifty quid?'

He was practically shouting but no one could hear. I moved hastily down the platform. I knew I could easily elude him in the jostle. The train was upon us; the crowd surged towards the opening doors. I thought I had lost Macgreevy to a different coach.

No such luck. I grabbed one of the last available seats, sat down, and then, as the train surged forward and those left standing sorted themselves out, found myself looking at the middle of a now-familiar dun-coloured trench coat. I looked up to see Macgreevy looking down at me, smiling with what I presume he thought was an ingratiating smile.

Of course, he couldn't go on bribing me within earshot of a train full of people, so we rattled along without further conversation past Bond Street Station to Baker Street. There I left the train to transfer to the Bakerloo Line. Once we had stepped back on to the platform, however, he continued as if he had never left off.

'Fifty quid, I said, Stella. That's more than you get in wages in a day.'

'Look, Mr Macgreevy,' I retorted, making for the right exit as swiftly as I could, 'I'm just a housemaid. The only Palace dirt I could give you would come out of my hoover. I'm not party to any fabulous fund of information. Get real.'

'Some of my best sources at the Palace are at your level.'

'Then why don't you ask them?'

He didn't reply. That there were moles in the Palace was no secret. Most of them, it was said, came from among the lower orders, whose poor pay and humble station gave them some incentive to pass on tittle-tattle. I thought of the newspapers I'd had a chance to glance at over the last few days. Why had nothing about Robin reached the trumpet ears of the press? Could it be because Robin was, like me, one of the lower orders? Had everyone closed ranks for once to protect one of their own? Maybe. Or maybe not. A murderer, lower orders or upper echelon, would no more welcome press intrusion than the Queen herself.

'Not many housemaids take the morning off to visit the Queen's solicitor,' Macgreevy said.

'I was at the *office* of the Queen's solicitor. Even a housemaid might have some legal stuff to attend to.'

'With the *Queen*'s solicitor?'

'Look, I'm not English, as you can tell from my accent. I don't know one London law office from another. I went to Cholmondeley & Featherstonehaugh because I'd seen the name in the paper, that's all. It's a name you could hardly forget.'

'And what did you go and see them for?' He certainly was persistent.

'None of your business, Mr Macgreevy.'

The passage to the Bakerloo Line was only a few yards long but a busker had laid claim to it anyway. He was making an awesome racket playing the bagpipes. The screech filled the chamber like a migraine.

'. . . in a laundry truck,' Mr Macgreevy was saying as the bagpipes receded. 'I know that truck and I know what it means.'

'What are you talking about?' I demanded, against my better judgement.

'The laundry truck. There was a laundry truck at

the Side Entrance on Tuesday morning. That particular laundry truck wasn't picking up laundry. The drivers were coppers.'

At first, this didn't make any sense. And then I felt a little jolt of horror as the truth dawned on me. So that's how they had removed Robin's body without anyone noticing!

'So?' I said, trying for nonchalance.

'Someone died within the Palace walls.'

'And this is the big-deal story you're chasing? Do you know how many people work at the Palace?'

'Three hundred and twenty-six, minus one as of Tuesday morning. And you know who it is. It's a footman named Robin Tukes.'

'News to me. I'm a housemaid. I don't pay attention to footmen.'

I hoped I sounded convincing. We were now on the platform waiting for the westbound train on the Bakerloo Line, and I was anxious for it to arrive so I could shuck this nuisance of a reporter.

'Then why were you walking across Green Park tonight with one of the footmen?'

'If you're so concerned about what happens to footmen, Mr Macgreevy, why don't you ask a footman?'

My guess was he had, and had learned nothing.

'Or,' I continued with an exasperated sigh, 'if you have other concerns, why don't you ask the Press Office in the Palace? Or contact the Queen's Coroner? Or phone Scotland Yard? Why are you bothering me?'

'Because I think you're a clever girl, *Stella*.' He laid a heavy emphasis on my hasty *nom de guerre*. 'And I'm sure that was you accompanying Katherine Tukes out of the Palace yesterday afternoon.'

Mercifully the wind was rising in the tunnel, signalling the train's imminent arrival.

'Young men don't die in their sleep,' he persisted.

The chamber rumbled as the train drew nearer.

'Maybe you should think about Her Majesty's safety.' His voice was now competing with the thunder of the arriving train. It was also growing increasingly unctuous. I looked down the track, impatient for the train to stop. Andrew Macgreevy was giving me the creeps. 'There's that State Banquet on Tuesday, remember? Have you thought about that? There's a lot of funny buggers about. More republican armies these days than you can shake a stick at.'

'Look, you,' I hissed as the noise abated and the doors to the coach glided open, 'I don't know what you're talking about. And if you keep following me, I'm going to scream bloody murder.'

And with that hoary old cliché I let the crowd sweep me on to the train. This time he didn't follow me.

'Good night, Mrs Rigby,' he called loudly at my back as the doors began to close. 'And give my regards to Bet Gilroy, will you?'

Chapter Fourteen

I love staying at my great-aunt's place. There's something about it that's just so comfortable, cosy in a way, though it isn't at all cottage-like or thatched-roof-ish or any of that sort of tourist notion of houses in English villages. It's actually quite modern, probably built after the Second World War, and plain on the outside. It's situated on a rather steep incline covered with all kinds of the trees and flowers whose names English people seem to know by heart and about which I'm clueless.

On the first floor, at the front, there is a garage on one side and a guest bedroom, rarely used, on the other. But most of the living space is actually on the second floor which, because of the incline, opens directly on to a garden at the back. Here there are two bedrooms, the bathroom and toilet, the kitchen and pantry, and a very agreeable sitting room at the front with french doors that open on to a tiny stone balcony from which you can look over the treetops towards the gentle slopes of the Chilterns.

There is one particularly enveloping sort of chair that I like to sink myself into. I cover myself with a blanket – because, of course, my great-aunt usually persists in keeping those french doors open even if it is

November – and read or look out over the top of the balcony while listening to some classical music or jazz from her fabulous collection of records and CDs. Aunt Grace has a terrific stereo system, which should give you some idea that she is not an old dear sitting around knitting socks while she waits for the Grim Reaper to come to tea.

Grace is around the same age as the Queen, a fact which only struck me that Friday evening when we settled down in our respective chairs shortly after my arrival in Long Marsham. The Queen is short (like me), getting a teeny bit plump (not like me!), and always looks as though she has just been to the hairdresser's. Grace, on the other hand, is tall and lean, sort of astringent in a way, and her steely grey hair is cut in so practical a fashion that I'm sure the Long Marsham hairdressers despair when they see her. Of course, the Queen is incredibly wealthy and famous, and Grace is not. The Queen has four children and six grandchildren, and Grace never married. But there are similarities in character. At least I think so. Both women have a quiet determination about them, both are very positive, and both have a surprising sense of humour under their reserve.

And they are both easy to talk to. Of course, this seems improbable with the Queen, doesn't it? I mean, she's the *Queen*, for heaven's sake, but once you get over the initial astonishment that you are having a conversation with the woman whose face has been on every postage stamp you ever licked, you find she is quite straightforward. Grace is much the same, only more so. There are still some things I couldn't ever imagine chatting about with HM, and of course you have to keep addressing her as Ma'am and all that, but with Grace you can talk about absolutely anything. It's wonderful. She's just so interested in what's going on and she doesn't come over all judgemental the way my parents would if I told them what I told her.

And another thing: she's not like middle-aged parent types who feel they have to get to bed at a certain time every night or the moral order will crumble. That night we stayed up until three talking. Well, of course, I had so much to tell her!

'How's your friend who was in hospital last week-end?' she inquired when I had unpacked my knapsack in the smaller of the two bedrooms and come into the kitchen, where she was boiling the kettle and preparing tea.

'Dead,' I replied.

That, of course, was my opening to recounting the events of the past week: the puzzling circumstances of Robin's death, meeting the Queen and my subsequent rooting about for the truth of the matter. Grace listened with great attention, interrupting only now and again to clarify one point or another. Her eyebrows moved heavenward when I described my exchanges with HM – for Grace, that's the highest expression of astonishment – but otherwise she took the whole amazing story in her stride.

'Goodness,' she said when I had given her the main bits, 'what an adventure you've had. Or you're having, because it really isn't over yet, is it?'

'No,' I said, draining my teacup. We had transferred to the sitting room and were sitting comfortably. Grace had lit a small fire in my honour and the room was warm, the way Canadians like it.

Grace reached for a piece of Battenberg cake. 'What's so very interesting is that the Queen has involved you.'

'I know. Isn't it weird? But I think it has to do in a way with her Private Secretary . . .'

'Yes, Sir Julian Dench,' Grace said thoughtfully.

'Do you know much about him?'

'Not really. Only what I read in the papers, and that was all before he became the Queen's Private Secretary, of course. But he seems like an odd choice for the position. Quite a Thatcherite, I should think. Very "free market" and all that sort of nonsense. I can't imagine that the man would have much sympathy for the idea of monarchy. To someone with his point of view, it must seem very inefficient and such.' She took a bite of cake and added thoughtfully, 'Perhaps that explains it, though.'

'What do you mean?'

'Well, criticism of the monarchy in this country used to come strictly from the left. People such as Tony Benn view it as undemocratic and unjust. They're the ones who have traditionally called for Britain to become a republic. Now republicanism seems to come from the right wing, from people such as – I would have thought – Julian Dench.'

'So he's at the Palace as part of a conspiracy or something?'

Grace laughed. 'Oh, dear, no. I shouldn't think so. Perhaps, though, Sir Julian represents a faction among Tories intent on reforms that would curb the remaining prerogatives of the monarch or make it more business-like, or less costly, or some such thing. They used to call these people "efficiency experts" in my day. Sir Julian has a bit of a reputation for that, I think.'

'I wonder if he's busy doing time-and-motion studies on Her Majesty. Clocking her as she does her Boxes.'

We both laughed at the vision of someone with a stopwatch observing HM race through the paperwork that comes to her daily in red boxes from Downing Street and Whitehall.

'But, you know, you wonder sometimes about conspiracy,' Grace continued, warming to the topic. 'All that talk of MI5 tapping the telephones of the Royal Family, and some of these newspapers – astonishing, really! Of course, I don't read them, Jane, but you do see the headlines on the news-stands, when you go up to London, and of course it's on television and on the wireless. It's so intrusive. I feel quite sorry for the Queen.'

'Which reminds me,' I interrupted, 'something I forgot to tell you. It was the last thing that happened. There's this guy from the *Evening Gazette* named Andrew Somethingorother – Macgreevy, Andrew Macgreevy – familiar?'

Grace shook her head.

'He's been bugging me for information. First he saw me with Katherine Tukes, then I spotted him lurking near the offices of Cholmondeley & Featherstone-haugh, and then he started talking to me when I was coming up here to Long Marsham tonight. He followed me on the Underground from Green Park to Baker Street and offered me money. He's sort of on to Robin's death, which is worrisome. I didn't tell him anything, though.'

Grace shook her head again, this time in dismay. 'The *Evening Gazette*. One of Reuben Crush's papers, of course. They're the worst. You must be careful, Jane.'

'Isn't Crush Canadian?'

'I believe so. But he seems to have lived here for a very long time, gobbling up newspapers and getting enormously rich. Now, there's a man I'm sure must dislike the monarchy, given the intrusive sorts of stories in his newspapers. It almost seems like a personal vendetta. Perhaps Her Majesty once refused to confer a knighthood, or grant him some honour.'

We both fell silent. Some classical symphonic thing that Grace had put on the stereo was reaching a crescendo. It was lovely, listening to it while the fire crackled away. I could see the stars outside and the last flickers of a bonfire someone had built for Guy Fawkes Night. The weather had changed in only a few hours. It was a wonderful crisp, clear autumn night.

'I would almost say Julian Dench would have more in common with the Reuben Crushes of the world than with the old-school types who must make up most of the courtiers,' Grace continued, picking up the thread of our earlier conversation.

'They're a pretty stuffy bunch, for sure. But I'll take them over Sir Julian. He's creepy.' I thought back to my unpleasant encounter with him in the Press Secretary's office.

'I wonder how the Queen gets on with him? It was often said she never got on with Mrs Thatcher, and Sir Julian must be the same type. The Tory party is really so different now from when I was young.' Grace sighed. 'There was a sense of *noblesse oblige* then. Years ago, I would have assumed that if the Queen was allowed to vote, she would have voted Tory. But now – funny to think – I venture she would vote Labour.'

'How about Communist!'

'Now you're being silly. Another cup of tea?'

'Ta.'

I waited while she poured in the milk and set the strainer over the top. Her tea's wonderful, a blend of five parts Orange Pekoe, four parts Earl Grey and one part Lapsang Souchong that smells heavenly – nothing like the toxin in the Palace tea urns that was strong enough to trot a mouse on.

'There are rumours,' I said, 'that the Queen's not a happy camper when it comes to Sir J. That's really what set this whole thing off, you know. When I told the Queen that Robin had been trying to talk to her, and absolutely would not go through her Private Secretary, this look came over her face. Not quite an "aha!" look, but something like it.'

A thought struck me. 'I guess you could say Sir J.'s sort of a . . . now, what's that word my mother uses when she talks about what stories she lets in and what stories she doesn't let in the *Guardian*? . . . Oh, yeah, a gatekeeper. Sir Julian is a gatekeeper. Maybe he's keeping important information away from the Queen and she doesn't like it.'

'Now you're the one suggesting conspiracy,' Grace said.

'Well, Robin was certainly disturbed by the idea of

Sir Julian. I know that from when I talked to him in the hospital.'

'Then perhaps Robin had some very damaging information for the Queen, information that Sir Julian wouldn't want reaching the Queen's ears because he was the one who would be damaged.'

'Well, the thing is, Robin *did* have some information damaging to Sir Julian, or at least I'm pretty sure he did.'

And I went into greater detail about Angela Cheatle's pregnancy and the presumption of Sir Julian, not Robin, being the father.

'The man's a fool,' Grace said when I had finished. 'But then, I guess some men are so arrogant they can't help themselves. If it got out, it would certainly mean the end of Sir Julian's career at the Palace, a most humiliating end indeed. There would be a motive there if your friend had been trying to speak to the Queen about it.'

'The thing is: I really don't think Robin would blab about something like that. He wasn't that kind of a guy, and besides, it would be embarrassing for him if people knew his fiancée was carrying another man's child even if he was, you know, gay.

'But the main thing is this,' I continued. 'Robin alive and well was the *solution* to Sir Julian's problem. Robin took Angie off his hands, and with the promise of money and title Angie was happy to go through the whole pretence, if that's what it was. But with Robin dead, Sir Julian has one heck of a problem to deal with again. All that good stuff has been snatched away from Angie and now she's just another pregnant and poor single woman. She won't even be allowed to keep her job at the Palace, and her only living relative, her grand-mother, is apparently really mean about girls who get pregnant with no husband in the picture. Given the pickle she's in, Angie could make some real trouble for Sir Julian.'

'Who else knows about this?'

'Unbelievably, no one. At least as far as I know. Sir Julian and Angie have been amazingly careful. I only know because Nikki Claypole told me, and she just happened to overhear them in an unguarded moment.'

'Then I presume from what you've told me about Palace life that Sir Julian's downfall will be in the Sunday papers.'

Grace rose from her chair and went to the CD player.

'No, I don't think so this time.' I watched her place the CD in its box and reach down to take a new one from the rack. 'Nikki hadn't told anyone but me what she knows about Angie and Sir J. Believe me, if she was blabbing it around the Palace, it would have been back to my ears in about fifteen minutes.'

As Grace carefully removed the CD from its box, I told her about Nikki's background, about her growing up on the Sandringham estate, and about her father's accidental death. Maybe, I suggested, because of both Nikki's and Angie's connection to royal estates – one connection real, the other probably imaginary – Nikki felt some odd solidarity with Angie. After all, they were both working-class girls whose lives had been a bit of a struggle. Maybe Nikki didn't want to spoil things for Angie, however absurd the latter's relationship with Sir J.

'Well,' Grace said when she sat down and the strains of something slow and soothing came over the room, 'Nikki sounds like a girl with a reason to dislike the Royal Family, however mistaken she is about the circumstances.'

'I know. Her father's death was ruled an accident. Still, it is odd, isn't it? I've wondered, since she told me, whether she got the job at the Palace in the first place out of sympathy. Anyway, it all happened years ago, and I don't think Nikki's brooding about it now. I mean, I've known her for ten months and she only just told me the whole story.'

'Still waters run deep.'

'Too true.'

'Mockery will get you nowhere.' Grace smiled as she offered me a plate bearing an assortment of goodies. I chose a thick slice of gingerbread. 'What about the other footman, Karim . . .?'

'Well, Karim sure has one whopping big motive. Robin's death means he comes into about two hundred thousand pounds. And, what's worse, he desperately needs money – twenty-five thousand of it – to get his sister out of hock, or whatever state she's in. He also has ambitions to start a business. He says Robin and he were going to use Robin's money to start some kind of shop with a theatre theme, but I take it that dream ended when he and Robin fell out at Balmoral. But he's known for some time that Robin was coming into money on his twenty-first birthday. He may well have known Robin had put him in his will. The odd thing is, I can't imagine Robin not giving or loaning Karim the twenty-five thousand for his sister. But then, there's that much larger sum . . .'

'And there's a role for anger, rage or jealousy, don't you think? You young people can be so emotionally extravagant sometimes.'

I thought about this as I took another sip of tea. I supposed it was possible.

'What worries me about Karim,' I said finally, 'is his sudden appearance in Robin's room on Tuesday morning right after Robin had died. He claims otherwise, but I'm certain he was there to retrieve that letter from his sister. Why? What was the urgency? If Robin's death was a suicide, then some letter from the sister of a friend could hardly make any difference to anyone—'

'Unless Karim, too, believed it wasn't suicide.'

'But earlier this evening . . . well, yesterday now,' I said, looking at my watch, 'when I brought up the idea of murder he was dead set against it.'

'You probably shocked him, Jane. You have that way.'

'Do I? Oh! Well, I guess maybe I might have. Still . . . oh, I don't know. And then I wonder about this: probably no one at the Palace knew Robin better than Karim did. Although they had been – what's the word? – "estranged" from each other the past little while, Karim would know what drugs Robin was taking and where he kept them and that sort of thing. Robin was poisoned by an overdose of a prescription drug he was taking. Things just seem to point to Karim . . . except for this newspaper stuff,' I concluded.

'Mr Macgreevy and the *Gazette*?' Aunt Grace asked.

'No, I mean the newspaper I found beside Robin's

body. I thought the Queen had been carrying it when she fell over him, but it turns out it was Robin. Footmen carry newspapers around sometimes to guests in the Palace, but Robin was really intent on seeing the Queen. Why did he have a newspaper with him? Was there something in the paper he wanted to show HM? Robin doesn't . . . didn't read newspapers much. None of us do, really. Most people my age think newspapers are dead boring on the whole, full of stuff about baby boomers and their problems. Who cares? At least baby boomers have decent jobs.'

'Jane, are you losing your enthusiasm for working at Buckingham Palace?' Grace regarded me with amused disbelief.

'No, I didn't really mean that.' I shook my head. 'It's just that sometimes . . . oh, anyway, I've kind of gone off on a tangent, haven't I? What I meant was, that newspaper might be a clue of some sort. The Queen placed an ad in the paper . . .'

'How very unusual . . .'

'Isn't it? But it's not what you think. She's not selling off the family silver, even if she does need to raise a few bucks to redecorate Windsor Castle. The ad has to do with the stolen diary I mentioned to you earlier.'

And I told Grace about how Her Majesty had gone about trying to retrieve her property and about the Royal Diary Shocker stuff promised for the *Sunday Gazette*.

When I had finished, she looked at me doubtfully. 'Robin's connection to all this seems to me to be a trifle remote,' she said.

'It does,' I agreed, 'and I asked HM about the newspaper only on a kind of impulse. But then, when she said her Private Secretary had been the last one to see that missing diary, I began to wonder . . .'

'Sir Julian again.'

I nodded. Despite all the tea I was getting tired, and we seemed to have gone in a circle in our conversation. Then Grace put her hand to her mouth to stifle a yawn. I felt an immediate pang of guilt.

'I've kind of babbled on, haven't I?'

'On the contrary, Jane, I've enjoyed it. Your adventure quite exercises the mind. It's like a puzzle. You must write it all down, you know.' She looked pensive, then rose from her chair to shut off the stereo system. 'What do you want to do tomorrow?'

'Well, I don't know. Anything you like. But there is one thing I wouldn't mind doing. It won't take long. I need to look up something in the library.'

'I'm going to the high street in the morning to get something nice for our Sunday lunch. If you come with me, you can go to the library while I shop. What are you researching?'

'I want to look up the Earl of Ulverstone in something called *Burke's Peerage* or *Debrett's*. You wouldn't have a copy of either here, would you?'

'Oh, dear, no. I'm afraid we Bees can only claim to be nature's aristocrats, not society's.'

'Not a single knight? Or a royal mistress?'

'We're plain folk. Sorry to disappoint!'

The next morning – well, the same morning really, only much later – after we had had a quiet breakfast, Grace

put on her serviceable Barbour coat and I my serviceable
Mountain Equipment Co-op jacket and we made our
way to the high street. The morning remained clear.
Only a few scudding clouds spoiled the pale English sky.

My aunt had clearly been pondering our conversation. 'Your friend, you believe, was deliberately poisoned,' she said. '*His* friend – Karim, is it? – is the one
most likely to know he was taking a certain drug. Do
you think anybody else knew?'

It was something that had been floating through my
mind for the past few days.

'I don't know,' I replied. 'I know *I* didn't know, but
that doesn't mean others didn't. The Palace is very
gossipy.'

'What about procuring the drug?'

'It's prescription.'

'No, I mean entering Robin's room and taking his.'

'Easy. There's supposed to be locks on the doors, but
half of them haven't worked since – God knows –
George IV decided to do a major renovation on Buck
House in the 1820s. The one for Robin's room didn't
work. Anyone could have gone in.'

'Not very narrowing, is it?' Grace sighed as we
turned a corner into Sycamore Road, the high street,
with its ranks of tidy shops.

'Unless someone else had the same prescription,
but I don't know how I'd find that out. Anyway, the pill
bottle in Robin's room was empty, so . . .'

It all seemed so unsatisfactory.

'We really didn't get an opportunity to talk about
opportunity last night,' Grace said. 'That sounds funny,
doesn't it? Opportunity, opportunity.'

'Well, opportunity opportunity is a problem. I'm sure the stuff had to have been put in Robin's coffee or tea, or whatever he was drinking at breakfast on Tuesday morning. But the film director, Cyril Wentworth-Desborough, had set up this contrived sequence where Robin and Angie and Karim and Nikki were all eating together, which isn't something they would normally do. So, anyway, there they all were, with W-Dez. Even Sir Julian was there, conferring with W-Dez, he says. He let that slip to me yesterday when he was yelling at me. So it could have been any of them.'

'What about the first opportunity opportunity? I really must stop saying that.'

'You mean the first time Robin tripped up the Queen? Probably in his drink. It was a "surprise" birthday party that turned into a real surprise engagement party. There might have been, oh, forty or fifty people there, including everyone I've mentioned. Well, not Sir Julian, of course. He wouldn't be at a party among the lower orders. And W-Dez wasn't filming that night, so he wasn't there. At least I'm pretty sure he wasn't. So, again, opportunity galore.'

We continued down the high street. It was quite crowded with Saturday shoppers.

'You remember me telling you about Neil, the guy in the film crew?' I asked Grace as we stopped outside the butcher's.

She regarded me indulgently.

'Well,' I continued, blushing, 'Neil said he was going to try to get me a copy of the breakfast sequence on videotape. I think it will be all unedited stuff, so maybe something will jump out at me. Who knows? It's worth

C. C. BENISON

a try, although I had to lie to him and say I wanted it to remember Robin by. I think he thinks I'm peculiar.'

'No more than the rest of us Bees,' Aunt Grace said placidly. 'Do you know anything at all about the birthday party . . . or engagement party, or whatever it was?'

'I just have Nikki's description of it. They were all drinking and so on, and then Robin made his announcement and someone called for champagne and then they drank a toast. The thing that Nikki remembered, though, was this very funny look that came over Karim's face when they raised their glasses.'

'Funny in what sense?'

'Well, I think she thought it was a frightened look, or a look of shock or something like that. Horror, maybe.'

'Really?' Grace considered this for a moment. A woman who had been tugging at a stubborn-looking child stopped near us and began scolding him. The child let out a piercing scream.

'Perhaps I've read too many Agatha Christies in my life.' Grace watched with disapproval as the woman cuffed the child's backside, which had the miraculous effect of shutting him up. 'But might it be possible that Robin was not the intended victim, after all? That that champagne glass was meant for someone else?'

'Ooh,' I said. 'That *is* interesting. But is it possible a murderer could screw up twice?'

'Perhaps just the once, the first time. Your friend Robin got the wrong glass.'

'And that's why Karim looked frightened. Karim put the drug in the glass . . .'

'. . . or knew who had done so.'

212

We both looked at each other, me looking upward, of course. Aunt Grace is, after all, on the tall side.

'They'll have to change the name of Long Marsham to St Mary Mead,' I said.

Grace's face moved to laugh, but an alertness came over it instead. 'Quickly now, Jane, let's talk about something else. Elspeth Scrivener is bearing down upon us.'

'I think lamb would be nice,' I declared in an over-bright voice as the Scrivener woman docked beside us like an ancient galleon. I had heard of her. She was a neighbour of Grace's – kindly, but a terrible blabbermouth.

'Now, could this be your niece from Canada, Miss Bee?' Her face, as broad and plain as a pie plate, positively beamed. 'My what a lovely child. It's so delightful to meet you, finally. Jane, isn't it? I think your aunt is perfectly greedy to keep you to herself. You must visit me at my cottage some time soon. I'm told you work at Buckingham Palace. Have you met the Queen? She was here in '77 for her Silver Jubilee. Do you remember, Miss Bee? Such a lovely day it was . . .'

I smiled in an insipid young-niece-from-Canada sort of way as Mrs Scrivener rattled on. I was so grateful for Aunt Grace's good sense. I just knew, without asking, that she would never tell a living soul about what was going on at the Palace, not even if the *Gazette* offered her, well, a good deal more than fifty quid.

'. . . and I can't think why people criticize her hats, I really can't. I think they're quite smart, don't you?'

Grace jumped in before she could release another sentence.

'Very smart, indeed,' she said. 'Now you must excuse us, Mrs Scrivener – Jane is off to the library and I must do some shopping.'

'Oh,' said Mrs Scrivener as I edged away. 'You must come and visit me, Jane. I would so like to hear what is going on at the Palace. It must be so terribly interesting. So many *shocking* things of late, of course. I feel quite sorry for the Queen . . .'

'Mrs Scrivener, my niece is a housemaid.'

'Oh, but still . . . well, goodbye, dear,' she said feebly as I turned and waved, feeling like a coward abandoning my aunt to a chatterbox.

As I walked on, I heard her say: 'Are you buying lamb today, Miss Bee? I'll come in with you . . .'

Poor Aunt Grace. I continued down the high street into Woodside Close and made for the library. It was a low, flat, modern building, part of a new civic centre which included a swimming pool. There was hardly anyone about inside. At the centre desk, bent over a pile of books, was a great thatch of blond hair attached to a stick-insect body.

'Do you have a copy of *Burke's Peerage* or *Debrett's*?' I asked.

A hand pulled the head up. The thatch of hair flopped back and the man under it looked at me blearily. He wasn't much older than me, and he looked extremely hung-over. He burped quietly.

'Pardon me! Yes, *Debrett's*. Red cover. In the nine-hundreds, in reference. Nine-twenty-something. Over there.'

He gestured vaguely towards the reference room in the far corner, burped again, and then a look of alarm came into his eyes. His face lost what little colour it ever might have had, and he darted towards a door behind him and disappeared. As I made my way to the reference section, I could hear the muffled sound of retching. It must have been a good Guy Fawkes party.

It was easy to make out *Debrett's Peerage and Baronetage*. The volume was as red as the Queen's Robe of State and thick enough to anchor a legless chair. It was hard to penetrate the book's organization at first, but finally I found Ulverstone on page 1221 between Viscount Ullswater and Baron Underhill.

'Francis St Aubyn Tukes', it said, '8th Earl; b 24 March 1923; ed Wellesley House, Eton; s 1938 . . .' There was a bit of stuff about the war followed by his 'm in 1949 to Johanna Katherine, da of Sir Rodney Bromley-Walsh of Basingstoke, Hants', then a lot of detail about the coat of arms with such fascinating words as *argent, gules, cinquefoils* and *mullets*, then a listing of his residence: 'Wintertrees, Princes Rd, Ferndown, Dorset'.

Then, a tiny bit further, right under Collateral Branches Living, I found it. 'Robin Bartholomew Tukes is hp to Earldom of Ulverstone,' it said, followed by his address in London, Ontario. And that was it, other than great long paragraphs in tiny print detailing, it appeared, every root, branch, twig or bud that had a connection to the Ulverstone tree.

I felt a keen sense of disappointment. How might I find out who was next in line for the earldom short of contacting the College of Heralds or whoever it was looked into these things? I was just about to close the book, however, when my eye lit on a name in the thick of one of the Collateral Branches Living paragraphs. Wow, I thought, my heart fluttering with sudden excitement.

But I couldn't make any sense of where on the tree the name fitted, and who connected to whom. Was it just a meaningless coincidence?

Aunt Grace had the obvious solution. Stupid me for not thinking of it.

'Why don't you telephone Robin's sister? I'm certain she'll know,' she told me when we joined up and started the walk back to her house. 'Didn't you say she was staying at Brown's Hotel?'

I looked at my watch. It was nearly noon. I might find Katherine in her room before she went out for lunch.

'Okay,' I said, getting excited by the prospect. We quickened our pace.

As Grace prepared a nice lunch of cold chicken and salad, I put in a call to London. Yes, Katherine Tukes was still registered at the hotel, but it took several rings to rouse her. Indeed, she sounded quite cranky, having, she informed me, just been bothered by a certain reporter from a certain tabloid.

Why, she wanted to know once I had recalled to her mind who I was exactly, did I want to know the person next in line for the earldom after Robin? This was a good question on her part, and I had no answer that I could rightly give her other than saying I was asking out of sheer curiosity, which seemed rude, so I hemmed and hawed until, out of annoyance, Katherine told me, adding for good measure that the present Earl of Ulver-stone was just about breathing his last even as we spoke.

Well, you can imagine my wonder when I learned it was the very name that had leaped from *Debrett's*. None other than royal film director Cyril Wentworth-Desborough!

Chapter Fifteen

I left Long Marsham shortly after Sunday lunch, saying my goodbyes to Aunt Grace at the station and promising to telephone her during the week – from a pay phone, of course; they say Buck House phones are tapped! – and let her know if there were any new developments.

Katherine Tukes' revelation about her cousin, or her second cousin, or her first cousin once removed, or however Wentworth-Desborough was attached to the Tukes family tree, had really fired up the synapses in what I'm pleased to call my brain. Here was a guy for whom the whole money-and-title thing must have remained tantalizingly out of reach. English, living in England, W-Dez probably knew the whole situation with his cousin, the present Earl of Ulverstone, or his second cousin, or whatever he was. Knew he was childless, knew that he was dying. And knew that, but for one person, he – Cyril Wentworth-Desborough – would be the next earl.

As Grace and I had gone about our activities on Saturday, driving to nearby Great Missenden, taking a bracing afternoon walk up through the woods and farmland around the Misbourne valley, talking over this new bit of information, I thought over what Neil had

told me earlier about Wentworth-Desborough. At the
time – Neil and I were in a wine-bar in Covent Garden –
I had been only mildly interested in the content of his
chat, asking questions the way you do with a new guy
just to see if there's any real promise to the relationship.
Neil thought he was an arrogant little bastard. So did I.
I'd had a glimpse of it myself.

At any rate, it all made me think. As the train from
Long Marsham to London rattled through the country-
side, I wondered whether film-making wasn't a dicey
proposition. Didn't it take a ton of money, most of
which you had to raise yourself? Doing a film about
Buck House seemed like a sure thing to me, but who
knew these days? These were the nineties, after all.

I was so preoccupied by these thoughts, and others,
that when I stepped off the train at Marylebone and
made my way through a knot of day trippers I walked
right past the newspaper kiosk, glancing at the headlines without taking any of them in. I had nearly made
it down to the Tube when the headline on one of them
finally made its presence known to the appropriate
brain cells. I quickly backtracked.

'QUEEN GAGS GAZETTE!' screamed the headline on the
Gazette.

Of course, you had to buy the awful thing to find out
more, since the amount of text on the front page of the
Gazette made the *Beano* look like Proust.

According to the main story on page three, the
Queen had obtained a writ preventing the *Gazette* from
printing anything contained in a diary that, according
to the writ, had been removed from Buckingham Palace
without Her Majesty's permission, in breach of

copyright. The *Gazette* claimed, in a sort of miffed tone, that it had purchased the aforementioned diary in perfect good faith, and that information contained within had important consequences for the realm and that the Great British Public had a right to know and blah-blah-blah.

So much for Royal Diary Shocker!, I thought. The stupid paper shouldn't have shown its hand in the first place. But, as I stuffed the rag into my bag, I had to admit my curiosity was piqued. Just what was the Shocker thing, anyway? Surely most of what happened in King Edward VII's life would seem fairly tame compared with what was reported about the lives of the modern royals?

Meanwhile, back at the Palace (a line I've always wanted to write), preparations for Tuesday's State Banquet were beginning in earnest. As I made my way past the security sentry boxes, through the Side Entrance, Neil emerged holding what looked like a lamp.

'Where did you get to this weekend?' he said, puffing a little from exertion.

'Visiting my great-aunt in the country.' I made an apologetic face. 'Sorry.'

'You see a lot of the old thing.'

'She's kind of lonely.'

It was an improvisation. He regarded me sceptically. 'Haven't got some other bloke stashed away, I hope.'

'Me? Never.'

A smile stole across his face. He's got nice teeth for an Englishman.

'I've brought something along for you,' he said with a spurious sort of wink.

'The video! Brilliant!'

'Shh,' he cautioned. 'Get yourself up to the Ballroom while I change this piece of equipment. I've got your prezzie tucked away up there. And bring your knapsack.'

I fairly bounded up the stairs and down the Household Corridor to the State Ballroom, which lies at the end of the East Gallery. From the doorway I could see clusters of enormous lights on poles, huge boxes of sound equipment, miles of wiring and the usual filmmaking paraphernalia that had been littering the Palace for weeks. It was all gathered at the end where the Queen normally sits, opposite the wall with the immense organ built into it. The wall sconces were switched on, as were the six great chandeliers, and the inlaid flooring had been covered with a crimson rug that I figured yours truly would probably find listed on her worksheet for hoovering before the day was over.

Part of the horseshoe-shaped mahogany table had been assembled but, probably because they were waiting for the piece of equipment Neil was fetching, everybody was standing around more or less twiddling their thumbs. Cyril Wentworth-Desborough, gripping his walking stick, wore an absurd-looking baseball cap, and was staring down the enormous length of the Ballroom with a look of fierce impatience on his face while everyone else clustered at a distance as though W-Dez were emitting dangerous radiation. In the air I thought I could whiff more than the usual amount of tension that surrounded the crew.

'Why are they setting up today?' I said to Davey Pye, who had appeared in the doorway just a moment after me, clutching a large cloth bag. 'The banquet's not for two days yet.'

'I don't know.' He stretched his neck for a better look. 'Rather odd, actually.'

'They're doing some of it today and tomorrow because Tuesday's time is so tight,' said a voice breezing between us.

It was Neil, bearing the precious bit of equipment that would put the crew back into documentary-making motion.

'I'll be with you in a sec,' he called over his shoulder to me.

'Bloody hell,' Davey muttered. 'I'd better make my exit now or they'll have me up on those tables in my stocking feet setting out the royal plate. *So* undignified.'

I turned to look more closely at Davey. His face had a certain high colour and it wasn't due to a walk in the crisp autumn air.

'Are you trying out at Toodle's again?' I asked him.

'Mmm. What do you think?'

'You're getting a ride there in a car, I hope.'

'Too much?'

'A bit too much mascara, at least for the street. Who is it you're planning to do? Alexis or Krystle?'

'Bette Midler, I'm afraid, darling. I've got the height for those *Dynasty* broads, but I guess I'm just a wee bit too plump.'

'Have you got the boobs in the bag?'

'And a very fetching frock, too,' Davey added brightly. 'Why don't you come with me?'

'Another time.'

'Well, I'd better be off . . .'

'Wait a mo', I said, moving him away from the doorwell. 'I've got a question. Remember Robin's birthday party?'

'Oh, not Robin again.' He looked pained. 'Jane, darling, you're becoming *obsessed*.'

'I am not,' I retorted. 'I just wanted to know something. When Robin dropped his bombshell about getting engaged, and after you all greeted it with stunned silence, who piped up with the idea of a champagne toast?'

'What a strange question. Why do you want to know that?'

'Just because.'

Davey rolled his eyes. 'Well, my dear, if it's so important to you, I think it was Karim. Yes, I'm sure it was Karim. I remember thinking at the time he should be the very last person to call for a toast. And it wasn't very good champagne either. If only we could have tucked into Mother's reserve of Bollinger . . .'

'I thought you were worried you'd be shanghaied into work if you hung around here?'

Neil was heading our way with what looked like one of those nylon recyclable lunch bags and Davey, who was inclined to babble on, needed encouragement to leave. I couldn't risk further conversation.

'Too right,' he said, to my relief. 'And I'm sure you

vant to be alone with this rather scrumptious-looking man.'

'Shoo!'

As Davey moved away down the East Gallery, Neil drew me into a protective niche so we couldn't be seen. He pulled a videotape from his bag.

'Stuff it in your knapsack quickly,' he ordered as he thrust it at me.

'Thanks, Neil. I really do appreciate this.'

'You're up to something, aren't you, Jane? Well, I won't ask. I don't want to know.'

'We could go out this evening,' I proferred, feeling both guilty and grateful and, what the heck, interested in the company of a man who wasn't wearing mascara. 'I know it's Sunday. What about a film? Or would that be a busman's holiday? "Coals to Newcastle"? "Sent to Coventry"? These English expressions confuse me.'

' "Busman's", I think. But give over. I live for film, at least any film but this bleedin' thing.' He nodded, indicating the activity in the room which, from the sound of things, had started up again. 'We didn't get our wage packets on Friday, by the way. I think the bugger's run out of money.'

'You're kidding!' I said.

'It happens.'

'But this is a film about the *Queen*.'

'Queen's *home*, luv. The Queen's hardly in it. I think that's why the Palace agreed to it in the first place. Show the punters they're getting value for their money in the running of a royal residence, not just another documentary showing what fine upstanding folks members of the Royal Family are. Nobody'd believe it these days.'

'But don't you have to have all the money in place first to do these things?'

Neil shrugged.

'Film-making's risky. This isn't a BBC production like those other ones about the Royal Family. I don't now why the high-and-mighty who run this hive put their faith in an independent producer/director like W-Dezzie, but they did. Maybe one of his co-investors has been slow to cough up. There are already rumours of cost over-runs. And, hell, we're working on a Sunday. Double time.'

I was confused. 'Why are you working at all if you haven't been paid?'

'He's promised it at the end of this week, once the filming of the State Banquet is over. With a bonus.' Neil snorted. 'What are we going to do? We have to trust him. Maybe he won't stiff us. We can make life miserable for him, too, if we want. Besides, we're at the point where we just want to get the bleedin' thing wrapped up.'

Fascinating, I thought: Wentworth-Desborough pinched for cash. And I remembered what Neil had told me earlier in the week, about W-Dez having a bit of an argument in the Palace post office with someone with a Canadian accent. Robin now seemed the most likely candidate. Had W-Dez been trying to tap what I now knew to be the family connection between them? Did he, knowing Robin was about to inherit a fortune, ask him to invest and been rebuffed? Or did he need even more money, the sort that would come to him from the earldom that Robin stood to inherit?

'Listen,' Neil said, 'I'd better get back . . .'

'Wait, um . . . what else do you know about W-Dez?'

'Such as?'

'Home life?'

'When he had a home life, you mean. He's recently separated from his wife. But he has two kids. Posh house in Holland Park, bought during the eighties' bubble, of course. Which she's living in. I've told you this before, haven't I?'

'Yeah, I just forgot, that's all. It's sort of interesting, though. Holland Park, eh?' What was it about Holland Park? Oh, yeah. Robin had circled a street in his *A-Z* guide. Abbotsbury Close. It was in Holland Park. 'Anything else?'

'I don't know,' he moaned. 'I've got to go . . .'

'Parents?'

'Father dead. Mother in a nuthouse somewhere. I'll pick you up at the Side Entrance at seven.'

Curious, I thought as I made my way to my room on the top floor: Mother, as Neil so kindly phrased it, in a nuthouse somewhere. Given Cyril's last name, I reasoned, it had to be through his mother that he was a twig on the Tukes family tree. Add this to the fact that Robin's father killed himself, and that Robin himself tended to bouts of depression, it didn't seem like it was exactly mental health week in the House of Tukes. It was kind of tragic, actually.

Still, never one to linger over things gloomy, I pulled the videotape Neil had slipped me out of my knapsack and looked at it as if it were about to impart the secrets of the universe. This was dumb, of course, because all it was was a black plastic box, about as mute as any inanimate object could be.

Oh where, oh where could a video machine be? Especially one I could use in privacy.

There was a VCR in the Staff lounge, but that was out. On Sunday afternoon there would be at least a couple of people lounging about, probably half drunk. The Queen herself undoubtedly had a video machine, but I wouldn't be able to enter her private apartments without practically being arrested. Same with the apartments or offices of members of her family.

There was a machine in the Press Office, though. I had noticed it during my unhappy visit there. Did I dare go down there again and risk getting caught? Well, it was Sunday. The Queen was at Windsor, Sir Julian was probably keeping up appearances with Lady Dench somewhere, and everyone at the Press Office was likely to be away either toasting the momentarily successful stifling of the *Gazette* or resting in the bosom of their families.

Nothing ventured, nothing gained, I thought, making a small withdrawal from my account at the cliché bank. But I had to disguise my purpose somehow, as well as the tape itself. I put my jacket back on to look like I was going out, and tucked the tape inside my pocket.

Of course, wandering about in my jacket in the Privy Purse Corridor looked a bit odd since the servants' exit is on the other side of the building. But to my surprise, no one bothered me. There were few people around, and I was a familiar face. Despite all the talk these days of increased security in the Palace, there's not a lot to show for it.

So before very long I was standing outside the entrance to the Press Office. I gave the handle a little rattle to see if the door was locked – it wasn't – and, after a quick look left and right, I darted inside and shut the door.

Heart pounding, expecting there might be someone in one of the interior offices after all, I called: 'Hello? Anyone home?'

No one was home.

The videotape machine was an old model but, old or new, simple to operate. I don't know why some people, such as my mother, for instance, find them confusing. All you do is pop the tape in, make sure the machine's in VCR mode, switch on the TV, and, as they say in these parts, Bob's your uncle.

Well, I did all that, and *nada*.

I did it again. The TV blinked on, the machine tidily swallowed the tape, the play button lit up, but the only thing on the screen was a football match from somewhere or other. Then I realized the VCR wasn't hooked up to the TV. Silly me.

In a trice, or a nonce, or whatever the word is, I hooked the thing up at the back, fingered the play button and waited for the images to come rolling across the screen.

And they did, after the usual bit of fuzz, minus, thank heaven, the usual stern government warnings about copyright and reproduction. The first part, preceded by the sight of a rather bored individual slapping together one of those clapboard things with electronic numbers blinking on it, was of the Servants' Hall itself, a sort of sweeping shot that took in a number of people already struggling through breakfast and then a bunch of other people lining up at the self-serve. Among them I thought I glimpsed Karim. However, it was dull stuff when you got right down to it.

Then there was some more fuzz, then that clapboard thing again, and then a closer view of the self-serve, through which a couple of people were moving, selecting dishes of cornflakes and those cold, dry pieces of grilled bread the English persist in calling toast, pulling cups of tea from a big silver urn, or pouring coffee from a second urn.

Then, from the left of the screen, there suddenly appeared Robin, dressed in his uniform, holding a tray, his face in profile. Without warning, my eyes brimmed with tears. It was a shock seeing him again, healthy and alive; a double shock seeing him, knowing that within half an hour he would be dead. The routine motions of picking up food and pouring a cup of coffee seemed all the more poignant. He looked around once, just past the camera's eye, as if to check out the seating in the room. It was only a moment, but in that moment there was revealed this perfect expression of alertness, intelligence and even a kind of determination. This was not, I said to myself as I dabbed at my eyes with the cuff of my sweater, the face of a man about to kill himself, least of all kill himself in a bizarre and highly conspicuous way. Indeed, Robin's glance seemed to convey such purpose that I suddenly wondered if it wasn't aimed at someone rather than something.

He moved from the line and then, the camera

following, he walked to a nearby table, joining Angie and Nikki, who seemed to be finishing their breakfast, and Karim, who had evidently just started his. Then I noted something I hadn't seen before: Robin had a newspaper tucked under his arm. Though it was folded, I could see, as he placed it on the table, that it was a copy of *The Times*. He smiled perfunctorily at the others and sat down.

Wentworth-Desborough had insisted to me during our brief encounter at the Side Gate that the sequence was unsatisfactory and, even if he had some ulterior motive for saying so, I could see, rank amateur in film criticism though I was, that he hadn't lied. If the idea had been to get some chirpy sequence with the jolly below-stairs staff tucking into their brekkers, this wasn't it. Robin seemed extremely preoccupied. He was virtually mum. Angie looked like she was trying on several roles at once: film star, happy fiancée, nervous hostess with awkward dinner guests. She glanced at the camera from time to time as if seeking reassurance, which only served to underscore the artificiality of the whole thing. Karim was absolutely rigid, whether with fright or anger it was impossible to tell. The only one approaching conviviality was Nikki. And even she looked strained, probably because she was the only one trying to initiate any conversation. Being around someone who had allegedly tried to commit suicide recently was probably making all of them tentative, too. Finally an exasperated off-camera voice – Wentworth-Desborough's, I assumed – snarled, 'Cut.'

I thought, with disappointment, that this was it. But then, after a bit more fuzz, a new sequence appeared on the screen. It was the four of them again at table, but this time there were new breakfasts in front of Robin and Karim, making it seem as if they had just sat down.

I was immediately alert to one item not present in the first sit-down sequence: a large glass of orange juice gleaming away in front of Robin. My pulse quickened as I watched him lift the glass within the first few seconds of the sequence and take a strong gulp of its contents. Had the two footmen fetched these second breakfasts themselves, I wondered, as I watched Robin lift a forkful of scrambled eggs to his mouth? Or had someone off-screen selected the items and carried them to the table? That meant a new opportunity for poisoning that I hadn't considered before. All along, my mind had been stuck on the coffee. I began to look at Robin's face, searching for clues to budding ill health.

From their demeanour, all four looked as if they had had a talking-to: Angie appeared less flummoxed, Karim less angry (or frightened), and Nikki less gabby. Only Robin seemed the same, but then, as he had had theatrical training, he was probably better able to 'act' naturally. If there was anything unpleasant in the food, it wasn't revealed in his bearing.

They chatted falteringly in an inane sort of way about their work schedules for the day – it was as if they had been assigned a topic, and probably had been – and then Angie said she needed another cuppa and did anyone else want one? 'Yes, please,' they all chorused, which sounded so rehearsed and foolish that I expected to hear the word 'cut' once again to put an end to it all. But the video flowed on, with Nikki and Angie both rising and going off-screen to seek more hot refreshment. Unhappily, however, the camera failed to follow them. Instead, it remained on the boys who were left stranded, looking faintly uncomfortable, rerouting the desultory conversation slightly to the subject of their duties for valeting the RamaLamaDingDong when he arrived the following week. Gosh, this really was a yawn, cinematically speaking.

A short time later Angie and Nikki returned, each laden with two cups of liquid. Here, my attention sharpened. I was hoping for an indicator, something to show that this was the fatal juncture: an expression of distaste after a sip, perhaps, or a remark about the awfulness of the coffee that morning, or a creeping pallor. It was Angela who handed the cup to Robin, who was attentive with the milk jug. She watched him meditatively, disinterestedly, while Nikki and Karim carried on a conversation. But I was no longer listening. I was filled with horror. Angela, all blonde and high cheekbones, seemed suddenly to me like some wicked ice queen coolly attending the elimination of an enemy.

Oh, my imagination was running away with me – surely it was!

But Robin was quick. He finished the orange juice, then gulped down the whitened coffee. He grabbed the newspaper and rose from the table, saying impatiently that he had to go.

Startled looks greeted him. He was evidently not supposed to do this. But then he was gone. The others looked to the camera. A voice shouted testily, 'Cut!'

Chapter Sixteen

Early Monday morning I found myself in the Belgian Suite, dusting this and polishing that. My mind was not really on my work. The Belgian Suite, which is on the ground floor of the Palace looking south-west over the gardens, is the place where all heads of state stay when they make official visits to London. It was to be occupied by the RamaLama the very next day and had to be positively gleaming or, so Mrs Harbottle intimated to us, heads would roll, and they wouldn't be crowned heads.

I was in the Spanish Room, the smallest of the three main rooms in the Belgian Suite, pondering for the umpteenth time what I had witnessed on the videotape the day before. Or had I witnessed anything, really? Who would be foolish enough to poison somebody when there was a film camera about?

Someone desperate, I thought, eyeballing the Sèvres clock to make sure it was put back exactly in the middle of the mantelpiece. Someone willing to take the risk. Someone who figured Robin would probably bolt through his breakfast because he had something important to do, such as seek an immediate audience with the Queen. Or someone whose access to the film would allow him to destroy it quickly if it became necessary to do so. Or some of the above. Or all of the above.

That second breakfast, that glass of orange juice. Had Robin fetched it himself? Or had it been brought to him? What about that second cup of coffee? Angela had placed it in front of him. Recalling the look on her face still filled me with disquiet. But surely she, of all people, had nothing to gain by Robin's death? At least, as far as I knew. In fact, didn't she have everything to lose? Then there was Karim, who had so much to gain. But he seemed to be absolved simply because he was sitting there the whole time. Unless he had happened to fetch Robin's second breakfast as well as his own.

What about the others? Wentworth-Desborough had been there directing the action. Even Sir Julian had been there, 'conferring' with W-Dez about the film's progress.

'Hmm,' I murmured to myself as I knelt on the floor and started the thankless task of pulling the books from a series of shelves and dusting their tops. My mind seemed to be going in circles. What I needed was to hear somebody tell me about that breakfast sequence – fill in the gaps, so to speak. I had asked Neil, but he said he hadn't been paying any attention. He had been too busy at the time fiddling with some piece of equipment. Karim wouldn't speak to me. Nikki only got back to the Palace on Sunday night after I was asleep and she didn't get to Servants' Hall for breakfast in the morning until I had left. Besides which, she was skivvying in another part of the Palace today. Of course, Sir Julian wouldn't presume to chat to me about such matters, nor was it likely that W-Dezzie would.

But, I thought in an *aha!* sort of way, Angie was working in another part of the Belgian Suite, in the Eighteenth-Century Room, which is the main room of the apartment. I could hear the hoover whining away. I really didn't want to talk to her, though. I was still bothered by her odd look in the film sequence. On the other hand, she was available. So, when the noise of the hoover stopped a few minutes later, I dumped the books and took the opportunity. Nothing v, nothing g.

When I entered the Eighteenth-Century Room Angie was bent well over, examining something in the Axminster, holding on to the hoover with one hand for support, giving me a superb view of the bum that had won the heart – or more likely some other body part – of Sir Julian Dench.

'Oof, you scared me!' she exclaimed, rising and turning to me with an irritated expression when I called her name.

'What are you staring at?' I asked, intrigued.

'There's something stuck on the rug.'

'Chewing gum, probably.' I came around and dabbed at the dry, encrusted wad with my shoe. 'Yup, chewing gum. Haven't you come across it before?'

'No,' she replied defensively, 'have you?'

'Constantly. I'm surprised you haven't. Haven't you seen The Harbottle's directive? We're supposed to use a kind of fixative to make it hard if it's still gooey and then chip at it with a blunt knife, then hoover the bits. This looks like it's been here a while, though. And what's this?' I bent closer and felt with my fingers. 'It looks like shards of glass. Jeez.'

'What kind of a nutter would leave gum on one of these pricey rugs?'

'A question that has vexed greater minds than yours.'

I don't think Angie heard me. She continued to focus on the gum, tapping at it herself with her shoe.

'What are we supposed to use again? I don't know how Mrs Harbottle can expect us to do everything,' she said peevishly.

'Never mind, I'll get the stuff and do it,' I said, thereby defeating my own attempt to lure Angie on to a topic of greater importance than cleaning muck off rugs.

Fortunately, something else was on Angie's mind which helped to defeat my defeat – two negatives making a positive, so to speak. As I turned to make for the Marble Hall, the corridor that goes past the Bow Room and the Queen's Cinema towards the kitchens, she called out.

'Wait, Jane. There's something I've been wanting to tell you, since we were at the pub and all last week.'

She paused. She was looking contrite in a phoney sort of way. Practically simpering.

'You know how I said Robin and I had slept together last Tuesday morning, the morning of his . . .?'

I nodded solemnly.

'Well, we didn't. Sleep together, that is.'

It didn't take a genius to figure out why she was telling me this. Sir Julian had warned her that I was being a little snoop and so she was covering her ass. Putting herself too much around Robin that morning was like advertising that she might have had access to a certain death-inducing drug.

'Oh, yeah?' I said, shrugging.

'I just thought you should know.'

My indifferent response was clearly giving her a case of the miffs.

'Okay, that's fine, Angie. Thanks for telling me.'

I thought I sounded blithe, but I guess it came off sounding a bit sarcastic. Her simper hardened abruptly.

'Well, sod off, then,' she snapped, and yanked the hoover as if she were about to start it up again.

'Nice talk, Angie.'

'You don't believe me!'

'I believe you! I just don't care whether you slept with Robin last Tuesday. Or any Tuesday, for that matter.'

I had come to believe that Robin hadn't slept at all that night, the last night of his life. He had stayed up reading, or worrying, or both.

'Then why are you skulking around, asking everybody questions?' she demanded petulantly.

'Oh, yeah? And who told you I've been "skulking around"?'

'I've got eyes in my head. You're poking about where you've got no right. You think Robin was done in, don't you?'

'As it happens, I do.'

What was the point in denying it now?

'Nobody else thinks so,' Angie argued stubbornly. 'The Royalty Squad here aren't bothered. If you stir things up, Jane, you're just going to get someone into trouble.'

'The murderer, I hope.'

'No, I mean . . . well, never mind. Just you leave me out of it.' Her tone was fierce.

'I would have thought you would be concerned, Angie. You were engaged to him, after all.'

'That's all over . . .'

'. . . not to mention, of course, that he was heir to an earldom and was due to come into a whole lot of money.'

Her face fell. A guardedness crept into her eyes. 'How do you know that?'

'His sister told me. She was here last week. It was Robin's inheritance that made you get tested to find out the sex of the child, wasn't it?'

She looked steamed. 'So what if it was? It was important to Robin. It's males what inherit in this system, you know. Not females.'

'So Robin really cared about this title stuff, about making sure he would have a son who would get it after him?'

'Yes,' she said fiercely, 'he did.'

Could it be? Was it possible Davey Pye's conjectures about Prince Hal were true? Had Robin turned from rebel to upper-crust wannabe in so quick a fashion?

'And it was really a boy, was it? They don't usually give those tests to women as young as we are.'

'Are you saying I'm lying?'

'No.'

How did I know? Angie put up a convincing front. But she would have to have gone through some man-oeuvring to get a doctor to agree to such a test. Young, healthy women with no family history of genetic dis-order were discouraged from having amniocentesis

238

because of the slight risk involved. At least that's what Jennifer, sister of mine and future doctor, once told me.

Apparently satisfied that she had silenced me, Angie reached again for the hoover. But before she could switch it on, I grabbed it and pulled it away.

'Watch it, you,' she snarled, grabbing it back.

'I want to ask you something first,' I grunted, pulling at the machine. 'About last Tuesday, about the filming—'

'What of it?'

She moved her hands to her hips as I successfully wrested the handle away again. I asked, 'Who brought Robin his food?'

'He did.' She eyed me as if I were stupid. 'It's self-serve.'

'No, I mean the second time. Who brought it? Or did he get his own?'

'You weren't there. How do you know any of this? And why are you so bloody bothered?'

It suddenly hit her what I was on about.

'I'll swing for you, I will!' she said, raising her voice. 'If you think I put some . . . poison, some drug or other, in his food . . .'

I edged back. She almost looked as if she were about to come at me, fists flailing.

'I didn't say you did!' I said determinedly, keeping my eye on her and preparing to fight. 'I just want to hear someone else tell it. I said I thought he was murdered, and I meant it. Now somehow, somewhere, someone stuck something into his food or his drink that morning. It had to have happened. I don't believe this suicide crap for one minute.'

Angie's eyes flickered at my sudden burst of temper.

'Well, it bloody well wasn't me!' she exclaimed.

'Prove it.'

'I didn't touch his food!'

'Where did that second breakfast come from?'

'Somebody brought it. We all stayed seated after the director shouted, "Cut." Who else have you asked about this? Didn't they tell you the same?'

'I asked Neil, one of the guys with the crew. But he wasn't paying that much attention. Now, don't you remember who brought it?'

There was a stubborn set to her face, but there was also illumination in her eyes and a hint of anxiety.

'It was Wentworth-Desborough himself,' she replied stonily, staring past me as if the scene were being re-enacted in front of her eyes. 'Yes, I'm sure it was. He put the plate in front of Robin. And a glass of juice.'

'But do you think he put the food together himself? Poured the juice?'

Angie's little reverie stopped abruptly. So did her lately found patience.

'How do I know?' she snapped. 'I wasn't everywhere in the room.'

'You got up later to get coffee. You brought Robin back a cup. You handed it to him.'

'How do you *know* all this?'

'Neil saw it,' I lied.

'Well, I didn't . . . hand him the cup, that is.'

'You did too!'

'Well, I handed it to him, yes,' she said savagely. 'But I didn't pour it.'

'That makes a lot of sense.'

'Don't get sarky with me, Jane Bee. I took the coffee

to Robin because he was seated next to me. I drink tea. I poured two cups of tea, one for me and one for bloody Karim.'

'Then who poured the coffee?'

'Nikki, of course. She went up to the self-serve with me.'

'Nikki?'

'Yeah, Nikki. Didn't your friend Neil tell you? She was pouring coffee, one for herself and one for Robin. She gave me the one for Robin and I gave her one of the teas to take to Karim. So there you go.' She rolled her eyes extravagantly. 'Now do you see how barmy all this is? And give me back that machine!'

I absently released the handle of the hoover. I had been thrust into perplexity. Nikki? The coffee, then, couldn't be the means by which Robin had been fatally poisoned. But Wentworth-Desborough serving the second breakfast and the juice? It seemed so menial a thing for a man like him to do, a task strictly for the lackeys. On the other hand, I knew from Neil that W-Dez was apt to have little temper tantrums when he would shove aside an offending employee and do the work himself to illustrate how the thing should be done. Had he deliberately worked himself up over the breakfast scene so he would have an opportunity to doctor a glass of orange juice? This was a man, I now knew, who might well be in some kind of financial crisis. And a man, for all I knew, who was greedy for the prestige of an ancient title. Robin had announced his marriage to a woman who was, to all intents and purposes, carrying his child, a child who would rob W-Dez of the earldom forever. If he was desperate enough to kill Robin for an inheritance, he would have had to do it before marriage made Robin's child legitimate.

Of course, that didn't really explain the first 'suicide attempt' – the one following Robin's birthday party. Wentworth-Desborough hadn't been there. Or at least no one I talked to remembered him being there. Or so I thought. Was I wrong?

Angie had switched the hoover back on while I was standing there pondering these possibilities. After a few swipes across the Axminster she shut it off again and glared at me irritably.

'Well? Are you going to get that whatever-it-is to take this gum out, or not?'

Angie was charming. She was the sort of person who figured that besting you in an argument gave her leave to boss you around.

'I'm going now,' I told her, with matching irritability. I was happy to get away from her anyway.

As I left via the Marble Hall I noted Humphrey Cranston striding toward me, loping along on his stick-insect legs the way he did. Normally a Page of the Backstairs, being among the somewhat higher orders, wouldn't acknowledge one of the lower orders such as yours truly in a public corridor with a bunch of other nobs filtering through. So I expected him to pass by with little more than a frosty glance, despite my visits to the Queen that he might be the only person other than HM to know about. However, just as we were about to pass each other he flashed his eyes at me, put four fingers across his chest, and looked up at the ceiling.

How strange, I thought, as I headed for the fixative. And then I realized it was a signal in a kind of code. Four fingers. Four o'clock. The ceiling? Above us was the Picture Gallery off which was the White Drawing Room, which was over the Belgian Suite. *Meet the Queen at four o'clock in the White Drawing Room*. It was like a game of Cluedo but with a royal twist. And without the lethal weapon, of course.

I got the fixative and a butter knife from the house-maids' pantry and was passing the kitchens when Cyril Wentworth-Desborough burst through the door. He nearly knocked me over. The expression on his face told me it was my fault for having had the gall to stroll down a corridor just when he felt like crashing into it. The director was evidently angry about something, and I could guess, if he was filming in the kitchens, that it was probably the Royal Chef, a hugely fat and astonishingly temperamental person, who was responsible.

'Sorry,' said W-Dez irritably, glaring at me. Above his black turtleneck sweater his face was pulsing like a nuclear beetroot.

'No problem,' I replied brightly. I picked up his walking stick, which had clattered to the marble floor, and handed it to him, practically batting my eyelashes as I did so. I figured this was an opportunity.

'I understand you're a relative of Robin Tukes,' I ventured cheerily as he snatched the stick from my hand ungraciously and turned to leave. 'A cousin, or something.'

This certainly caught him short. He stopped dead in his tracks.

'Who are *you*?' he demanded, turning back.

It was like being addressed by the Caterpillar in *Alice in Wonderland*. Only instead of a languid, sleepy, after-a-quiet-toke-on-the-hookah-type voice, the tone was savage and cross.

'Jane Bee, sir.'

'Weren't you the girl bothering me last week about the film? Well, Miss Bee, buzz off.'

And he turned again.

'I also understand the Earl Of Ulverstone is about to . . . go west, so to speak,' I said loudly to his retreating back.

He spun around. The air snapped as he slapped his walking stick against his open hand. 'Out with it, girl. What do you want?'

'Nothing,' I replied disingenuously. 'I just thought it was interesting that you and Robin were related, that's all.'

'And that he was heir presumptive to the title, which I'm sure you must also know. And that, now that he's dead, I'm to have it. Is this what's interesting you, Miss Bee?'

'Well, yes,' I said. I actually hadn't expected him to be so forthright.

'Then what of it?' He leaned towards me. His eyeballs were inflamed. His breath wasn't so great, either.

'I just wondered about your relationship, that's all.' I took a half-step back.

'Our *relationship*?' He began to beat a tattoo against his palm. 'What appalling American jargon. We didn't have a *relationship*. He was less than half my age, essentially a foreigner, a queer, flippant about this country's

244

heritage – and his own – and utterly undeserving of his inheritance. We had nothing in common.'

'But he was family.'

'He was a second cousin. His father and my mother were cousins. The link is tenuous and made more so by that enormous body of water called the Atlantic Ocean.'

'But you had some things in common. I mean, Robin was interested in acting, in the theatre and such. And you're in films. I thought maybe you would have helped him along . . .'

'As I said, we had nothing in common.'

'Did he get in touch with you when he first came to England?' I recalled the circling of W-Dez's Holland Park street in Robin's *A-Z* guide.

'He showed up on my doorstep. I sent him packing. I'm extremely busy. I don't have time for long-lost relatives and I certainly don't have time for you, either.'

'But you used him in this film,' I insisted before he could turn again to go.

The soft drumming of his open hand continued. Between clenched teeth he said: 'This is a documentary about the workings of Buckingham Palace. He was only a footman, one tiny part of it – quite replaceable, in fact.'

'You could have chosen another footman for that below-stairs breakfast sequence you shot last week.'

'Robin is – was – photogenic.' Wentworth-Desborough scowled as if it bothered him to say it. 'Quite handsome, in fact. That's why he was chosen. Handsome people attract audiences. Those are the dictates of the medium. Robin couldn't act worth a damn, but it mattered little in this case.'

Gosh, this guy was distasteful. He could be

intimidating – a walking stick had nastier functions than aid or affectation – but I decided to try a little intimidation of my own.

'If you and Robin had no relationship, then why were you having such an *intense* conversation with him in the Palace post office a couple of weeks ago?'

Wentworth-Desborough's jaw started to hang on its hinges.

'I also hear you're a little tight for money these days,' I pressed on. 'Weren't looking for some new investors, were you, by any chance? Even from remote second cousins who happened to be about to inherit fortunes?'

The drumming stick stopped in mid-beat. W-D looked so astonished and red-faced that the poor man practically started giggling.

'How dare you, you silly, stupid little girl! How dare you talk to me like that!'

'Free speech.'

And this time I was the one who turned. And left him standing there.

Just before four o'clock, having spent the rest of the morning tidying the Belgian Suite, including removing the gum from the Axminster, and the early afternoon doing bathrooms (yuck) in a more remote part of the Palace, I found myself once again in the good old reliable White Drawing Room. I was still on a kind of high. Having scored one against the terribly self-important Cyril Wentworth-Desborough was what had done it. I felt I was making some headway, somehow.

Only a feeling, mind, but it seemed like I was at last groping my way to a solution.

Now, I thought, as I came across yet another wad of gum on the carpet, if only I could catch whoever it was who was doing this. None of the acres of carpet in the huge Palace belonged to me, but when you're cleaning it five days a week you start to take what you might call a proprietorial interest. Besides, removing the stuff was a beast! I had spent part of the morning doing it, and didn't feel like devoting another minute to it in the afternoon.

So, when the pier-glass and mantel swung back once again, I guiltily left the offending bit of rubbery goo (it was fairly fresh) and didn't mention it to Her Majesty. She, I figured, had enough on her mind, with the State Visit beginning tomorrow.

'Your Majesty?' I said when I stepped into the Royal Closet. 'Ma'am?'

'In here, Jane,' came the familiarly squeaky, yet somewhat muffled, voice.

The Queen was through the next set of doors, in the Audience Room.

'Ma'am?' I said, poking my head through, wondering who had opened the fireplace and doors. Humphrey, probably.

'It's all right, Jane. I think we'll talk in here.'

The Queen rose from a desk as she spoke, took off a pair of bifocals and stepped around a pile of snoozing corgis. From the contents of the desk it looked as though she had been writing a letter. She was wearing a pale yellow dress that was tied in a bow at the neck. No pearls. It must have been an at-home day.

'Do sit down.' She indicated a pair of couches on either side of a small fireplace in which a fire was blazing nicely. By Buck House standards, the Audience Room is quite cosy. There's busy flocked wallpaper on the walls like in so many homes in England, the furniture has a lived-in look and the portraits don't look big enough to swallow you. Lamps were switched on against the gathering gloom of the autumn afternoon, and, as I curtsied and made my way to one of the couches, I noticed something on a small table that just about added up to the ultimate in cosiness.

'Tea?' said Her Majesty as she sat on the couch opposite me, near the table.

'Wow.'

I must have looked slightly stunned, because the Queen was looking at me quizzically while she held the milk jug expectantly over the first of two china cups.

'Oh, yes, thank you, Ma'am,' I said, recovering slightly. 'Milk and two sugars.'

'Are you ill, Jane?'

'No, Ma'am. It's just . . . well, it's just . . . it's The Dream.'

'The dream?' the Queen echoed as she poured the milk and measured two level spoonfuls of sugar into my cup.

'The Dream. The one millions people are said to have had. You know, where they have tea with the Queen. With you, Ma'am.'

'Oh, *that* dream. Yes, I have heard of that. Odd . . .' She handed me my cup.

'I've had the same dream. Indeed, I have it rather often.'

'Really? But, I mean, the Queen, you, Ma'am, having a dream about having tea with, well, you, it's . . .' I stammered to a stop.

'No, no. That would be peculiar, wouldn't it? No. In my dream, Jane, people are taking tea with me. Do you watch *Coronation Street* at all? In my dreams, I often find myself in Emily Bishop's sitting room, discussing the most unusual things. Cucumber sandwich?'

Coronation Street? Emily Bishop? I barely managed to reach for the sandwich and thank her.

'Have you had The Dream?' she inquired politely.

'Yes, actually.' And I told her its contents.

'I see,' she said. 'I gather they tend to express a degree of anxiety.' She studied me for a moment, then smiled. 'The most common one, I'm told, is of people finding themselves naked in front of one. Funny old world, as one of my prime ministers once said.'

'It's never happened to me. The nude dream, I mean.'

'Good for you,' she said briskly. 'Now, did you have a pleasant weekend?'

'Yes, Ma'am,' I replied, grateful for the change in the conversation. I was beginning to feel I was in the middle of a dream myself. 'I went to Long Marsham to stay with my great-aunt. And while I was there I visited the library and looked up the Earl of Ulverstone in *Debrett's*.'

'Oh, good. And did you find anything?'

'Actually, it wasn't much help, Ma'am.'

'I thought it mightn't be,' Her Majesty said. 'It even had a mistaken entry about one, once. Got the year wrong for the Collar of the Order of the White Rose of Finland. It was 1961, not 1960. But go on.'

'Well, it did list Robin as heir presumptive and it did contain another familiar name, but I couldn't figure out if it was meaningful,' I replied, taking a sip. The tea was hot and sweet, just the thing on a damp afternoon in a damp palace. 'So I phoned his sister, who's staying at a hotel here in London, and found out who was the next in line. You'll never believe it, Ma'am – it's Cyril Wentworth-Desborough!'

The Queen's face registered a certain blankness, as though the name were unfamiliar.

'The film director, Ma'am. *Your* film director.'

'Ah,' she said. Mild surprise registered on her face. 'How very odd. Another sandwich?'

'Thank you.'

The Queen regarded the plate thoughtfully – or was it regretfully? – but didn't take a second one herself. She's said to be always watching her waistline.

'And how very interesting, as well,' Her Majesty continued, settling back on the couch with her teacup. 'If we presume for one moment that Mr Wentworth-Desborough is our murderer, then he would have been under some urgency. Robin's marriage to – what is her name again? Angela? – would legitimize his child and, if it were a boy . . .'

'It is a boy, Ma'am. Angie had a test done.'

'Indeed? Well, there you go. The child would displace Mr Wentworth-Desborough in succession. But only if a marriage took place. With Robin dead, the earldom now passes legitimately to Wentworth-Desborough.'

'He's in need of money, too, Ma'am. At least that's what I've been told.'

And I related what Neil had told me about not being paid and about W-Dez's other possible financial short-comings.

'Really!' the Queen said in an unamused fashion when I had finished. 'One has received not a whit of intelligence on this matter. I was given to understand Wentworth-Desborough had an excellent reputation in the film world. I even have some recollection of him passing tea out during the filming of *Royal Family* twenty-five years ago.'

'The need strengthens his motive, don't you think, Ma'am? And he had the opportunity, too.'

I described the 'breakfast scene' I had seen on video.

'But what about the first instance?' Her Majesty asked. 'The evening when one first . . . *encountered* Robin Tukes in a less than sober state. Was Wentworth-Desborough filming in the vicinity at that time?'

'No, Ma'am, I don't think so. I had a date with a member of the film crew that evening, so if he wasn't there, that means they weren't filming. Still, Mr Went-worth-Desborough might have gone to Robin's surprise party on his own . . . I have to admit,' I added sheep-ishly, 'that I've never thought to ask. I just assumed he wouldn't be there.'

'Then you should ask,' Her Majesty said in a consti-tutional-right-to-encourage sort of way.

'Yes, Ma'am,' I replied.

'Well, then,' she said, changing the subject slightly. 'I, too, did some poking about over the weekend. I asked my husband about his earlier references to the present Earl of Ulverstone. He was quite pleased that I did. It gave him an opportunity to rag one at one's expense.'

She took a sip of her tea. 'Being Queen is no insurance against a provoking sort of husband,' she continued, not unhappily.

Marriages have always seemed to me to be a test of wits – that's what my parents' was like – so I didn't take her complaint too seriously.

'As I told you last week, my husband did have an opportunity to look at my great-grandfather's diary . . .'

'And you stopped the *Gazette* from printing it, too! Brilliant, Ma'am! Sorry to interrupt.'

'Yes, the *Gazette* won't be printing excerpts from the diary. They will be making a financial contribution to charity, and they will be co-operating in the investigation of the diary's theft, but,' she said, the look of satisfaction leaving her face, 'there is something contained in the diary over which I am afraid one is powerless to prevent press speculation.' She paused, then added, 'And it concerns the Earl of Ulverstone. Not the present earl, but his great-grandfather.'

The Queen paused and pursed her lips, emphasizing the little frown lines.

'The Earl of Ulverstone's name appears in King Edward's diary in circumstances that are, well, most unpleasant. The diary, you see, is for the years 1887 to 1889—'

The Queen broke off. 'You do know the succession from Queen Victoria, do you?' she asked.

'Yes, I think so,' I replied, puzzling at the sudden need for a history quiz. 'Edward VII, George V, Edward VIII, George VI and then you, Ma'am.'

'Yes, good. Now George V, my grandfather, was the *second* son of Edward VII. George was the Duke of York

252

and it wasn't thought that he would come to the throne because he had an elder brother who was Albert Victor, the Duke of Clarence. Are you following?'

'Yes, Ma'am, I think so,' I said. 'Didn't the Duke of Clarence die young, or something?'

Why did I know this? I wondered. Though I read my grandmother's royalty books when I was at her place in Charlottetown I wasn't a big reader of British history, yet it was all starting to sound strangely familiar.

'Quite right,' the Queen continued. 'The Duke of Clarence did die young, in 1892. He was only twenty-eight years old. Influenza, I believe, was the cause.'

While I was finding all this family history from the cynosure of the said family fascinating, I was beginning to feel that HM was straying a bit. Cut to the chase, Ma'am, I wanted to say, but of course that would have been rude. There are some things you just can't say to the Queen.

'Now,' she said after another sip of tea, 'there have been some very, very unsavoury things said about the Duke of Clarence over the years. I remember an American writer in the 1970s – not long after one's Silver Jubilee year – who insisted quite publicly that one release the files. "What files?" I said to my Private Secretary at the time. There were no files, of course. It's all quite unfair, but one is largely powerless to stop these rumours.'

'What was the rumour?' I prompted Her Majesty.

'The rumour,' she replied with little enthusiasm, 'was that the Duke of Clarence – Eddy, as he was known – was Jack the Ripper.'

Of course, Prince Eddy! That's why the story

sounded familiar. It was the nickname I needed to make it click. When I had taken the Ripper walking tour in Whitechapel, Prince Eddy's name was mentioned as one of the possible suspects. And I had read about him in Robin's book about the Ripper, the book in which I had found the business card for Cholmondeley & Featherstonehaugh.

'He wasn't, was he? The Ripper, that is.'

I still wasn't quite sure where the Queen was leading with all this.

'Of course he wasn't,' Her Majesty replied frostily.

I sank into my seat. At that moment, one of the corgis chose to fart.

'Ma'am,' I said hastily, leaping into this embarrassing breach though HM looked unruffled, 'isn't the stuff about Eddy . . . the Duke of Clarence being Jack the Ripper just something made up recently?'

'No, unfortunately.' She frowned as she replaced her teacup. 'It was whispered in my great-great-grandmother's day. And this brings me back to King Edward's diary. The King – or the Prince of Wales as he was then – was sufficiently concerned about these rumours concerning his son that he initiated his own private investigation. According to the diary, or I should say according to my husband, who looked at the diary, my great-grandfather was completely satisfied that Eddy had no involvement in these horrible murders. However, he recorded the name of someone his investigators had strong reason to believe was the Ripper . . .'

Click went a switch in my head.

'Oh, surely not . . .' I said.

'Yes, I'm afraid so – the Earl of Ulverstone.'

Like dice, things began to tumble around in my mind: Robin was reading a book about the Ripper on the morning of his death. This meant Robin knew about his ancestor. But how did he know? Did the rumour run in his own family? Or, more likely, did he learn about it through the royal diary? He couldn't have stolen it himself, I was sure of it. That meant someone else had told him of its damaging contents. But only three people that I knew of had actually had the diary in their possession before it disappeared into the hands of the *Gazette*: the Queen, her husband ... and Sir Julian Dench! Did *he* tell Robin?

I was so absorbed in my thoughts that it took me a minute to realize the Queen was still talking.

'I'm sorry, Ma'am,' I interrupted. 'My mind just ... I mean, wow, it's incredible.'

'Yes, isn't it? As I was saying, the Earl was apparently an acquaintance of the Duke of Clarence. They were about the same age, and had been at Trinity College together and, I understand, were part of the same circle.'

'But why ...?'

'More tea?'

'Yes, thank you, Ma'am. But why,' I repeated as she took my cup, 'wasn't it reported?'

'I really couldn't say,' Her Majesty replied as she poured milk into my cup. 'I can't excuse my great-grandfather's judgement, but we must remember, Jane, it was a different era. I assume he wished to protect his son. Any attention brought to a friend of the Duke of Clarence over these horrible murders would inevitably reflect on the Duke himself. And he was next in line to the throne, after his father. 'Also – ' a tiny smile puckered the edges of the Queen's lips as she handed me my cup – 'my great-grandfather lived in considerable trepidation of his formidable mother, Queen Victoria. I'm sure the idea of keeping bad news at bay from her played no small part in his mind.'

'Will this hit the papers, do you think, Ma'am? About the Earl of Ulverstone being Jack the Ripper?'

'I'm rather surprised it hasn't already. One's injunction prevented the *Evening Gazette* from quoting King Edward's journal or from naming it as the source. But there's no reason why they couldn't find someone else to name the Earl of Ulverstone and then write a story about it. They're probably having trouble finding a suitable academic or someone else with credentials. Most respectable people don't wish to have their names in that publication. I only wish there were a way one could keep one's name out.'

'When it does come out,' I said, 'I'll bet Cyril Wentworth-Desborough may think a lot less of inheriting the title.'

'When it comes out,' the Queen laughed, 'it will probably finish off the present Earl! Oh, dear, that wasn't very nice. Still, I'm very, very glad now that my father sent him packing from Court.'

'Do you know what became of the fifth Earl?' I asked.

'Only a little,' she replied. 'One had an opportunity to do some investigating of one's own. He was born in 1865, married rather late, in '95 I believe, had one son who would be the grandfather of the present Earl, and died in 1906. Curiously, he appears to have died by his own hand.'

What an ill-starred family. Robin's father a suicide, Wentworth-Desborough's mother in an asylum. And then there were Robin's depressions. There seemed to be a thread of mental illness winding its grim way down the generations, although what the fifth Earl did, if he did it, seems well beyond the realm of mere mental illness. I shuddered at the memory of the five women whose grotesque murders rocked London in 1888.

'There's this book that's come out recently suggesting the Ripper was some Liverpool businessman,' I said, hoping that the Earl of Ulverstone thing mightn't be true.

'It's quite possible, I'm sure,' Her Majesty replied. 'My great-grandfather's investigators may have been mistaken. Although I understand this Liverpool businessman theory is being discredited.'

'Still, Ma'am, Robin must have believed it . . . about his ancestor, that is.'

'You think he knew the contents of the diary, then.'

'Well . . .' I hesitated. I thought about the Jack the Ripper book in Robin's room. 'I'm sure he must have known. The question is: how did he know?'

'I'm not sure in any case that this quite explains why the young man wished to see one,' Her Majesty demurred.

'No, I suppose it doesn't . . .' I was thinking furiously. 'Ma'am,' I said impulsively, 'besides yourself and His Royal Highness, there is only one other person who had his hands on the diary. Is that right?'

'Yes,' she replied, her mouth set disapprovingly. 'My

Private Secretary had it last. As I said before, as he is also the Keeper of the Royal Archives, I had asked Sir Julian to read and evaluate its contents in case it contained something important that needed to be conveyed to my government before I had the diary destroyed.'

'And then it ended up at the *Gazette.*'

'Sir Julian is as baffled by this as I am.'

Or he claims to be, I thought.

I must have been chewing my bottom lip in consternation, because the Queen said to me suddenly: 'Jane, you look distressed.'

I was. Something had occurred to me. It was Nikki's story about Angie, the one about her great-grandfather being the illegitimate son of Edward VII. Nikki thought it was a load of old cobblers, but I didn't doubt for a moment that Angie firmly believed it to be true. And then this scenario: one day her lover comes along and tells her he has a long-lost diary belonging to her supposed royal forebear. What could be more intriguing to a woman with Angie's restless ambitions?

And yet I didn't fancy telling the Queen about Angie Cheatle and Sir Julian. After all, it was still only hearsay. And who knew what the consequences might be? Still, if it led to the solving of Robin's murder, it was worth it. So I took an invigorating swig of tea and said: 'I think, Ma'am, there might be someone else in the Palace who had their hands on that diary.'

And I explained. As I did so, Her Majesty's face became more and more severe. 'I see,' she said coldly when I had finished. I couldn't determine if she already knew or didn't know, whether she disapproved of my telling her or whether she disapproved of *what* I had told her.

'I'm sorry, Ma'am,' I said, for I felt a terrible need to apologize.

'Don't be.' But she said nothing more for a moment, continuing only to sip her tea thoughtfully. One of the corgis had waddled over and was regarding her expectantly. She put the cup down, patted the dog's head and said: 'This means, then, do you think, that this housemaid – Angela? – sold the diary to the *Gazette*?'

'Well . . .'

'She was, after all, engaged to be married to a young man with, as it turns out, considerable prospects, prospects of which she was aware all along.'

'Yes, that's true,' I said, somewhat deflated. 'But maybe,' I continued, brightening, 'she couldn't resist the idea of some quick and easy money?'

'She would put her . . . association with Sir Julian at risk.'

'Perhaps she didn't care, Ma'am. Sir Julian was probably giving her the push. Maybe she did it out of revenge. How much, if you don't mind my asking, did the *Gazette* pay for the diary?'

'About twenty-five thousand pounds, I believe.'

'Really! That's just the amount that Karim needed to get his sister out of hock, or whatever you might call it.'

'But the diary disappeared, I believe, in August at the latest,' the Queen said.

'Oh, right.' I followed her train of thought. Karim could probably have used £25,000 – who couldn't! – but there was no pressing need for such a sum until he received the letter from his sister in October.

'And twenty-five thousand pounds, from what one has been told, is not a great sum of money in the realm of film-making,' the Queen continued.

'True enough, Ma'am. And besides, Wentworth-Desborough's money problems are relatively recent, as far as I know.'

'And it's hard to imagine that the man would risk his reputation.'

'Still, Ma'am, it is twenty-five thousand pounds. Someone could use that kind of money.'

'Angela Cheatle?'

'If she killed Robin because he knew about the stolen diary it would be like killing the goose that laid the golden eggs though, wouldn't it?'

'Or someone else?'

'Sir Julian?'

'Officially my Private Secretary was the last to see the diary.'

'Still . . .' I said.

'Hmmm,' we chorused.

'It's all rather a puzzle, isn't it?' Her Majesty said. 'It's like the jigsaw in the next room. There are just a few pieces missing. Get those, Jane, and the whole picture, I'm sure, will shortly become quite clear.'

Chapter Seventeen

It was well after five o'clock when I left the Audience Room. The Queen and I tried fitting different bits into our puzzle but nothing quite worked, although I felt, and I'm sure she felt, too, that we were getting oh so close. There was something niggling at my brain, something I had surely overlooked, something I had somehow neglected to credit. I could feel it in my bones.

Just before I rose to leave, a moment after the Queen reached down and touched her handbag to signal that the interview was at an end, there was a tap on the door.

The Queen murmured, 'I had asked not to be disturbed.'

The door opened and Sir Julian came in carrying a Red Box.

'Sorry to disturb you, Ma'am,' he said, 'but this just arrived from the Foreign Office.'

'Thank you, Julian.'

The Queen's back was to her Private Secretary, but I got a full view of him as he passed by the couch on the way to HM's desk. He regarded me nastily.

The Queen favoured him with a tight smile as he turned and bowed from the neck.

'Is there anything else, Julian?'

'No, Ma'am.'

'Then we'll see you tomorrow morning. A busy day ahead of us.'

'Yes, Ma'am.'

'Goodnight, Julian.'

'Goodnight, Ma'am.'

The door closed. Her Majesty frowned.

'What nonsense,' she said. 'The Foreign Office rarely sends dispatches to me at this time of day.'

'I'll bet he wanted to see who you were talking to.'

'Yes, probably.'

And so I told the Queen about my unpleasant little chat with Sir Julian in his office on Friday. 'I think people are starting to wonder about me,' I added, understating the case. 'Especially when I start asking all these uncomfortable kinds of questions. I even had someone from the *Evening Gazette* hounding me on the Underground.' I described my encounter with Andrew Macgreevy.

'You must be very careful, Jane,' Her Majesty warned as she rose from the couch. 'Yes, very careful.'

She studied my face as I placed my teacup on the table and likewise rose. Concern was etched in the familiar lines of her familiar face, and yet it was a concern quite different from what people see in her public face, the one that says nice things to pensioners in old folk's homes.

'You must tell me immediately if anything happens,' she said, going to her desk.

'But . . .'

'Yes, I know. It will be difficult, but you must try.'

'Yes, Ma'am.' I curtsied, about to depart back through the Royal Closet to the White Drawing Room. Good heavens, I thought, this sounds ominous.

'Ma'am,' I said, and I don't know why this popped into my head but it did. 'Has there ever been a murder before in Buckingham Palace?'

'How very odd you should ask,' the Queen replied, removing a small box of dog biscuits from a drawer in her desk and sending the pile of hitherto dozing corgis into a noisy dither. 'I was just thinking of that . . . now, shush, darlings, here.'

She sat and began to feed each dog a biscuit.

'Yes,' she continued, 'the story is that there was a murder here in my grandfather's reign. I think it was in his Silver Jubilee year, 1935. It was kept very quiet at the time, rather the way this one is being kept quiet. But I don't believe my grandfather was ever told. He lived less than another year. However, my grandmother, Queen Mary, learned of it somehow and she told me long afterwards. I'm afraid I'm not quite sure now which room it was said to have occurred in, and I don't remember much about the circumstances either.'

'Do you remember who the victim was?'

The Queen dusted her fingers, then clasped her hands in her lap.

'Yes, I do remember that,' she said, regarding me solemnly as I hovered by the door to the Royal Closet.

'Who?'

'It was a housemaid, Jane.'

*

Well, it wasn't exactly a cheery note on which to depart the Presence, but depart I did, peering into the Picture Gallery from the White Drawing Room to see whether Sir Julian was hanging around waiting to bawl me out. He wasn't fortunately. And neither was anyone else, since it was nearly dinner time.

Stuffed as I was with royal tea, I didn't feel like any dinner myself. I was on a sugar high, and so I bounced myself up to the attic floor to my room to consider what to do next. The stuff about Jack the Ripper had really amazed me. The first thing I did when I closed the door was take the Ripper book from the pile where I had dropped it the day Katherine Tukes visited the Palace on her grim errand. I immediately start to reread bits of it.

I supposed most people know a little about Jack the Ripper, this crazed killer who absolutely terrorized the East End for a brief period in the late summer over a hundred years ago. He's been the subject of books and plays and films and, of course, endless speculation. His five known victims were prostitutes, women driven largely by poverty to sell themselves in what must have been the stinking, awful streets and tenements of the very worst part of nineteenth-century London, White-chapel.

Even though Whitechapel today is an odd mixture of old and new (the East End bore the brunt of London's Second World War bombs), you can still feel the creep-iness when you walk around at night there. Anyway, that's how I'd felt when I took the Ripper walking tour, sort of chilled and horrified. Of course the tour guide, a Canadian doing a Cockney imitation, didn't refrain from putting in all the grisly details as we went from the spooky arched entry at cobbled George Yard, where Martha Tabram's butchered body was found, to the shabby Ten Bells public house, where Annie Chapman was seen shortly before she was killed. They were the same details I reread and reimagined as I perused the Ripper book in my room that night. Jack eviscerated his victims, disembowelled them, ripped them from belly to throat. It was like something out of a Stephen King novel, only worse: it really happened.

To be the direct descendant of someone like that would be appalling. Every family has a skeleton in its closet somewhere, but few have the unlucky experience of witnessing that skeleton come dancing out so spectacularly. And that's what would happen if King Edward VII's diary fell from private hands. Was this the real basis of Robin's connection to the diary? The Queen's interest in keeping her great-grandfather's diary out of the public domain had to do with her famous sense of duty. But Robin's interest looked to be even greater: preventing embarrassment and shame and humiliation and speculation and so on. To himself? To his family?

He knew, he must have known. The book sitting on my lap was the very one he had been reading only hours before his death. But the question remained: *how* did he know?

I had heard Angie passing down the corridor to her room a little earlier. You get to know the sound of people's treads, and Angie's in flat shoes has a kind of determined galumph to it that is greatly at odds with her leggy slimness. You would have thought a woman

with her ambitions would have cultivated a more graceful way of propelling her lower limbs. Anyway I decided
there wasn't going to be a better time to investigate the
case of Angie and the King's Missing Diary, so I hopped
off my bed and beetled down the corridor to her room.

'What do *you* want,' she said ungraciously when I
knocked and entered. It wasn't a question. She had
changed from her uniform to a dress and was examining
herself in a cheval glass, an extravagant item she had
hauled into her room at her own expense over Mrs
Harbottle's acid objections that such things were not
done.

'Angie,' I said, closing the door behind me, 'if I said
"Jack the Ripper" to you, what would you think?'

Her eyes in the mirror rolled heavenward. 'Well, I
don't know. What a daft question.'

'Seriously. Jack the Ripper. Mean anything to you?'

'What are you on about?'

'Ripper, Ange.'

'Some bloke who sliced up a lot of women last
century. Somewhere in the East End, wasn't it? Is this a
quiz? What are you doing, scouting for *Mastermind*?'

She opened a tube of lip gloss and began applying it
to her lower lip. She seemed unaffected by my question. Interesting, I thought.

'Well . . .?' she said impatiently.

I waited a little while to add to the effect of my next
question. Angie's reflection in the mirror glared at me.

'So,' I said finally, 'I guess you didn't read the diary,
then.'

Her hand stopped suddenly in its sweep of her
upper lip.

'What diary?'

'King Edward VII's.'

'I don't know what you're talking about,' she said sharply.

'A diary belonging to King Edward VII was found some time after the fire at Windsor. The Queen passed it to her Private Secretary. Somehow it ended up at the offices of the *Gazette*. Somewhere along the line there was a theft.'

Under her blusher Angie's face had lost a degree of colour. She replaced the top of her lip gloss with studied control.

'What's any of this got to do with me?' She turned her face away, replacing the make-up among a midden of similar objects on a nearby bureau.

'Two things,' I replied. 'You believe you're descended from King Edward. And you're Sir Julian Dench's lover.'

There was a moment's silence.

'Shit!' she said bitterly, and then turned to face me, her complexion now burning. 'Sod you, Jane Bee. Why don't you mind your own damn business?'

I said nothing. There was nothing to say.

'Oh, Jesus, I'm sorry,' she continued, suddenly placating in the same breath as if the implications of public knowledge had just hit her with full force. 'Look, you won't . . . Oh, hell!'

She plunked herself down on the edge of the bed, caught somewhere between anger and resignation. I remained standing.

She heaved a sigh. 'How do you know . . . about Julian?' she said.

'Deductive reasoning.'

'What?'

'I put two and two together.' This was a lie. I had what you might call 'informed sources', but I thought 'deductive reasoning' sounded better. 'I know about the missing diary. I know you think King Edward fathered your great-grandfather out of wedlock—'

'That little bitch Nikki told you, I suppose.'

'—and I was pretty sure Robin wasn't the father of your child.'

'He might be!' she said defiantly.

I let this pass.

'What happened with the diary, Angie?'

'I didn't steal it! I don't know how it ended up at the *Gazette.*'

'But you had it? Where? Here?'

'I . . . well, sort of borrowed it from Julian when we were at his flat. I just wanted to see, you know . . . I thought, maybe, there would be a mention of my—'

Angie regarded me with suspicion. Tenacious old Ange, she doesn't let much really set her back. 'How the hell do *you* know about the diary, anyway?'

Good question. I could hardly tell her the Queen told me. On the other hand . . .

'The Queen told me,' I replied.

'Oh, piss off. If you're not going to be serious . . . oh, shit, does security know?'

'I don't know.'

'Look, I only had that damned diary for *one day*. I barely had a chance to look through it! I came back here and the sodding thing had vanished.'

'When was this?'

'I don't know. Late July, early August. Before we went to Balmoral.'

'Did Sir Julian actually *lend* it to you?'

'Well, no, not exactly. I spotted it on the desk in his study when I was leaving his flat early one morning. I saw the Prince of Wales' feathers and the 'E', and when I opened it I saw it was a journal of some sort, so I stuffed it in my bag. It was an impulse. I was going to return it. I was going to tell Julian. And then it was gone.'

'Did Sir Julian ask you about it?'

'Finally, yes. We were at Balmoral. The thing was supposed to have been packed, or the Queen wanted it, or something. Anyway, he asked if I had seen it.'

'And?'

'I lied. I think he wanted me to. I mean, he didn't want to have to involve me because, of course, it would involve him. So, I guess he's sort of been trying to put Her Majesty off, make excuses . . . shit, shit, *shit!*'

'Do you have any idea who took it?'

'No! And how could I try and find out without everybody knowing? I just hoped it would all go away. And then the bloody newspapers started in . . .'

'Royal Diary Shocker. Or do you mean the adverts?'

'What adverts?'

'Oh, nothing. Did Robin know you'd taken the diary?'

'Of course he didn't. I only had it for a bleedin' *day*!' Her eyes narrowed. 'What's this got to do with Robin?'

Was she fibbing? Had Robin seen her at some earlier time with the diary, unaware of its origin or significance, and then, only later, with the help of the newspaper advertisement the Queen had placed,

269

grasped what he had seen? And wanted to do something about it? But that still didn't explain his knowing the contents.

'I don't know. Nothing, probably,' I replied reluctantly, turning to go.

'Wait a minute, Jane. What are you going to do?'

'Wash my hair.'

'No, what you going to *do*?'

'Angie, you know what the Palace is like. Secrets aren't easily kept around here.'

'Can't you keep this one? Please, Jane.'

She actually seemed vulnerable for once.

I said reluctantly, 'It's sort of out – at least the bit about Sir Julian and you. Someone told me. It really wasn't just two and two.'

'Oh, hell. Who?'

'Can't say.'

'Thanks a bloody lot. Christ!'

'Sorry, Ange. Really.'

Well, I did feel sorry for her, in a way. I guess she thought she had been getting ahead in the world, the only way she knew how, which is a pretty old-fashioned way for a woman, if you think about it: through a powerful man, or a man who would be powerful thanks to money and title. Well, one relationship died, literally. And I wasn't about to lay odds on the other settling into anything permanent.

She was regarding me with an expression of disgust and distrust. 'Jane, you still think someone did him in, don't you?'

I shrugged, moving to open the door.

'And what's the Ripper got to do with any of this?'

'Just something in the diary.'

'How do you know what's in the bloody diary? It disappeared months ago.'

'Two and two, Ange. Two and two.' I nipped out of the door.

But before it closed, I heard her shout: 'Oh, go to hell!'

Angie's not really *that* vulnerable, in the long run.

Tuesday morning dawned, dawning before dawn for some of us in the lower orders. I had had one of those extraordinarily odd dreaming sleeps in which you seem to awaken from one dream only to find yourself emerging into another, like a psychic version of those Russian dolls that open up only to reveal another doll inside. In my dream I passed through a succession of rooms, much the way one passes through rooms in the Palace, one opening on to the next. Each room I awoke into seemed brighter and simpler than the one before, from the first dark and damp Gothic chamber, through an encrusted Baroque vestibule, to a dazzlingly white space almost glowing in intensity. Anxiety faded with each succeeding room because, I realized with dream logic, there was less and less that needed cleaning. In the final room, as at the centre of a hive, was none other than the Queen, as a solemn young woman on the day of her coronation, in a pure white dress, under St Edward's crown, sceptre in one hand and in the other, not the orb, but a squiggly bit of card, a piece of jigsaw puzzle. I woke late in a kind of physical torpor, but my mind seemed to be curiously clarified. It was as though in the dream I had come to see something, to know something, that now, in my waking state, was eluding me, but only just.

One thing this strange winnowing experience had isolated for me was Aunt Grace's remark about intended victims. Karim, Davey said, had proposed the champagne toast at Robin's birthday party. Karim, Nikki said, had looked quite peculiar when that toast was drunk. Was it because he was watching a murder take place, one that he had planned? Or was it something else?

The atmosphere in the Palace was charged that morning. It was the beginning of the State Visit, the culmination of so much work on the part of so many people, and everyone seemed to be moving at a quicker pace, or at least a pace quicker for them. My schedule had me delegated by mid-morning to do some last-minute hoovering and a whip round with my duster in the 1844 Room, which is stuck (in as much as the huge State Rooms of Buck House can be said to be 'stuck') between the Belgian Suite, where the RamaLama would be residing for three days, and the Bow Room, where there was to be a luncheon with the Queen, members of her family and a bunch of other people.

When I shut the hoover off I could hear muffled activity next door in the Bow Room. The dining table, having been set up the day before in front of the curving window with its magnificent view of the gardens, was in the process of being set with the usual linens dating from Queen Victoria's day and the kind of china and glassware that would make your own best stuff look like Woolworth's. Davey Pye, it occurred to me, might be the best person to give me some more detail about the champagne birthday toast, and there was a good chance he might be helping in the Bow Room. But when I opened the heavy connecting door and looked in, there was no Davey to be seen.

Damn, I thought. It wasn't going to be easy slipping off on this day of all days. On such days there was to be no deviation from schedule, no slip-ups, no casualness, lest certain members of the Household – especially the formidable Mrs Harbottle – catch you like a deer in their headlights and run you down.

'Have you seen David Pye around anywhere?' I stopped a gloved Freddie the under-butler in his concentrated placing of dinner plates at measured distances from each other and from the table edge. I could feel Graham Dowse, the Palace Steward, glowering at me.

Freddie frowned. 'Hmmm,' he said. 'I did see him earlier in State livery, so like as not he's doing carriage duty.'

'Hell, I wonder if the carriage has left for Victoria Station?'

'Dunno.'

'Don't you have other duties?' Mr Dowse inquired frigidly.

Wan smile from me. I returned to the 1844 Room and ran a cloth distractedly around the 'Negress Head' clock, a sort of awful thing with eyelids that open and close to display the hours and minutes of the day and which, in my opinion, deserves relegating to some basement somewhere.

Would the carriage have left for Victoria Station? I knew the Queen would leave by car for Victoria just after noon to greet her guest. Only the return to Buckingham Palace was by carriage, accompanied by the Household Cavalry and the whole pomp and ceremony bit.

I looked at my watch. Nearly ten o'clock. Did I dare shirk my duties and dart down Buckingham Palace Road to the Royal Mews, which housed the stables and all the carriages, coaches and cars? I dared. A few minutes later, after dashing out of the Side Entrance and jack-knifing my way as best I could through the crowds on the narrow street, I arrived at the gates of the Mews. And there, under the Doric archway with its weathercock-surmounted clocktower, was Davey, all scarlet and gold braid, holding with a fully extended arm the bridle of one of a pair of magnificent bay horses. Both he and the horse seemed to be looking askance at each other.

'I really don't care at all for the beasts,' he said after I whistled at him to come over and endured his response, a coquettish wiggle of the hips.

'I don't think they like you either.'

'Shouldn't you be hoovering Mother's rugs? Or couldn't you resist the sunshine?'

In fact, I had barely noticed the weather. After days of endless drizzle, the skies had cleared. The sun was shining as hard as November sun could in London.

'I've got a question.'

'Ask away.'

'About Robin's birthday party.'

'You really are obsessed.'

'But you're so good at noticing things, Davey. Now, the champagne toast – Karim's idea.'

'I said so the other day, yes.'

'Did Karim actually hand the glasses of champagne to Robin and Angie?'

'Cups, my dear.'

'Cups?'

'You know the state of things in the staff lounge. It's all chipped china and never enough glasses. So it was cups. I remember quite distinctly. They were some awful old cheap ones from Mother's wedding, I think. Or perhaps the coronation. Anyway, ancient. And yes, Karim did hand the cups to them. Good thing he picked cups with Mother and Father on them. Chuck and Di or Andy and Fergie cups would have been rather bad luck, don't you think? On the other hand, perhaps it *was* bad luck. When—'

A voice shouting across the quadrangle interrupted us. 'Pye! Hop it!'

'Oh, I guess we're off. Like my gear? Weighs a ton.'

'Was there anything else? Anything unusual?'

'I was just going to say. Karim handed them the wrong cups. Well, I thought so. And I said so. It offended my sense of symmetry, or proportion, or something like that, to have Angie drinking from the Philip cup and Robin from Mother's.'

'I would have figured anything less would have offended your sense of irony.'

'How droll you are, Jane.'

'*Pye!*'

'Tch! Dear! Must go, lovely.'

'So Robin and Angie switched cups.'

'Yes.'

Then his eyes widened dramatically. 'Oh, you don't

think, do you . . .? Goodness! It never occurred to me that—'

'PYE!'

Even the horses started.

Davey scowled. 'He's going to have my sweet guts for garters.' He adjusted his black velvet riding cap and turned to leave.

'One quick other thing, Davey – was W-Dezzie there that night?'

'Yes, briefly.'

'Before or after the toast?'

'Um, let's see. Just before. Must go. Back one-ish, Jane, if you need to talk . . .'

'That's all right,' I replied, my suspicions confirmed and my heart sunk low. 'I've got what I need.'

Or near enough. But I had to talk to Karim, unhappy a task as I knew it was going be. As I watched the State Landau roll out into Buckingham Palace Road, I noted that at least the footman accompanying Davey was not Karim. They never seemed to use him in processions anyway. Probably because he didn't quite 'match', skin-tone-wise, in the fussy and prejudiced mind of the Travelling Yeoman who organized the footmen's schedules.

I got back to the 1844 Room in double time, only to find La Harbottle having a fit. I was reduced to my junior high school excuse for getting out of volleyball: cramps. Ascending eyebrows and a my-eyes-glaze-over expression told me Harbottle wasn't buying, but all she did was reiterate in jaded tones her famed heads-will-roll speech if I didn't stick to the schedule, and then left me to finish up. Which I did, wondering all the while how I was going to collar Karim without, as Harbottle would consider it, *ruining* the entire State Visit. That's if I could find him.

Next on the schedule was the real donkey work, changing beds and tidying some of the private rooms on the top floor. Dead boring, believe me, but at least there was less traffic about and you could do a little of what I think of as creative malingering. This, of course, was our floor, us housemaids and footmen. And it occurred to me that at some point Karim might pop up to his own room to change into some version of livery suitable for serving the luncheon.

So I'd do a bed, then I'd tear down to the west wing to the footmen's rooms to see if anyone was about, then I'd go back and do a bed, then back to the west wing, and so on until, finally, with the morning nearly over, I heard a rustle behind Karim's door. Without thinking I barged in. I had half a second to admire Karim's naked backside before he spun around, his scarlet tailcoat clasped to his chest.

'Do you mind!' he exclaimed.

'Oh, sorry.'

Though I had been approaching this interview with some anxiety, now that I was here I couldn't help giggling. The split in the back of the tailcoat had revealed yet another critical part of his anatomy. Grim-faced, Karim lowered it the necessary inches.

'Now, if only Wentworth-Desborough had been around to capture this real-life moment backstage at Buck House . . .'

'I'm dressing,' he snapped. 'What do you want?'

'Do you change underwear every time you change livery?'

'Go away.'

I couldn't put it off.

'Okay, I've got something serious I want to talk about,' I said, feeling a wave of uneasiness crash over me. 'Do you want me to turn around while you . . .?'

But Karim clutched the tailcoat tighter and fell back on to the bed.

'You're going to go on about Robin, aren't you?' he muttered resignedly.

I nodded.

'Can't you just let me dress?'

'You tried to poison Angela, didn't you?' I ignored the special pleading in his voice.

Karim groaned.

'It was at the birthday party,' I continued, newly confident. The only way was to be quick.

'You proposed the toast and then you poured the champagne into cups that were easy to identify: one with the Queen on it, and one with Prince Philip. But you didn't count on silly old Davey fussing that each of them drink from the . . . *gender-appropriate* cup, did you? You put the drug in the Prince Philip cup and gave it to Angie. At Davey's insistence she handed it to Robin.'

Karim was silent. He had slumped over his crumpled tailcoat, his head in his hands.

'And then you looked on as Robin drained the cup.'

Behind his hands, Karim began to sob quietly. So damn haughty and defensive before, now he seemed to have broken down. I felt awkward.

'Look,' I said, 'I mean, maybe . . .'

'No,' he said hoarsely, looking up, his eyes red-rimmed. 'No . . . no maybe. Oh, God.'

'But why?'

'I don't know! I lost my head. When Robin told me he was going to announce an engagement I just . . .' His voice degenerated into sniffles.

Poisoning someone with drugs sounded pretty cold-blooded to me, and I said so.

'I didn't want to kill her, Jane. I just . . . wanted to scare her. Or something. I thought maybe she'd go away. I thought of scaring her in other ways, afterwards. Anything . . .'

'So you went to Robin's room, where you knew he had a prescription for Zolinane and – what? – stole a handful from the bottle?'

'Yes,' he croaked.

'Was the bottle full? Half-empty? Quarter-empty?'

'Nearly full.'

'Didn't you think Robin would notice? Didn't you think that when Angie got sick – or died . . .? And what about the baby! I mean, what do you know about dosage? Didn't you think that Robin would have been the first one under suspicion?'

'I didn't think. I didn't think.'

'You idiot!'

'I didn't think,' he repeated wretchedly, wiping his eyes with the sleeve of his livery. Then, realizing what he had done, he tried to wipe away the damp spot.

My mind was racing ahead.

'And then, when you finally screwed up the courage to see him on the Sunday, you told him the whole story and Robin, kind Robin, let you off the hook by concocting this suicide story.'

'Well . . . no.'

'What?'

'The suicide story was already about.'

'That's right, it was,' I said, startled at my own stupidity. 'It was about, wasn't it? On the Friday. But who told you?'

'I don't remember. I don't.'

And I couldn't remember who told me, either. When I sat down with Nikki and Davey that lunchtime, it just seemed to have been in the air.

'Try.'

'I can't. I was too upset to think straight that day,' he said miserably.

'Yes, I suppose you were.' For more than one reason. I thought of him looking stunned when I ran into him at the Side Entrance as I was on my way to see my aunt.

'He must have liked you a lot,' I said, 'to go along with this suicide story. And the thing is,' I muttered half to myself, 'everybody believed it, everybody went for it.'

'What?' Karim looked suddenly evasive, wet-eyed though he was.

'The suicide story. Nobody questioned it. Okay, he had bouts of depression, and he became withdrawn at Balmoral and so on, but, for heaven's sake, that doesn't mean . . .'

'He still might have, the second time.'

'Oh, don't be ridiculous!'

'Well . . .' His voice was strangled. 'He *was* . . . HIV-positive. Maybe he felt—'

'Get real!' I interrupted. 'Robin was murdered, and

you know it! Otherwise you wouldn't have come up to his room so fast the morning he died. You weren't looking for any stupid jumper. You were looking for that letter from your sister. There were two people who stood to benefit financially by Robin's death, particularly if he died before marrying, and you were one of them. You thought that if anyone started to ask questions, fingers would end up pointing in your direction.'

He regarded me sullenly.

'It's still a good motive, Karim. Don't you think? All that money, and you wanting to get out of here and start your own business?'

He dropped his eyes and rubbed again at the damp spot on his livery.

'It makes me wonder why you didn't say anything, you know. You could have. He was your friend, your very good friend. And you were ready to let his memory be stained by this suicide thing. It just makes me wonder.'

He flinched, as though each of my words was a blow. I didn't care. I was disgusted with him. I turned to leave.

'Oh, dry your tears, Karim,' I said. 'Her Majesty's got guests coming.'

'What are you going to do?' he asked in a choked voice.

A fierce anger seized me. 'I don't know!' I shouted, and slammed the door behind me.

It was nearly noon. I was in a state of agitation. Karim was such a prick. And I wasn't confident he couldn't have murdered Robin, or maybe done it in concert with

W-Dez. Both certainly had a lot to gain. I was storming off in the direction of my own room when suddenly I felt the absence of something. In my darting between the attic floor bedrooms and Karim's room, I hadn't realized I had left my duster in the 1844 Room.

Yikes, I thought. The Harbottle would have a foaming fit if the Queen led her guests into the room, only to see a lump of dusty cloth perched on top of the Negress Head clock because that's where I'd left it.

I raced down the stairs to the ground floor, hoping to get to the 1844 Room before there were any inspections. The Palace seemed oddly quiet, a calm before the storm of the State Visit. I skirted the Grand Entrance, hopped up the few stairs to the Marble Hall and was in 1844 in a trice. And there was the cloth, as predicted, like a great dirty cloud over the face of the Negress Head. I whipped it off and stuffed it into the pocket of my uniform. It had been a close call.

I just stood there for a moment and enjoyed the relief of it all. Then I wondered what I was going to do next. I had this crazy sense of urgency, but I couldn't focus on anything. So, half absent-mindedly, I headed next door to the Bow Room to preoccupy myself with a look at the table in its readiness for the luncheon.

It was odd. As I opened the connecting door, I had this sudden feeling of doing something I shouldn't be doing, as though I were about to violate the purity of a room whose rejuvenated charm should be witnessed first by the Queen and her guests. Nevertheless, I stole in and stood for a moment in the shadow of a column to take in the brilliance of the setting. Sunlight poured through the bow windows with a vigour that had not been seen in London for weeks. The white linen shone and the Minton dinner service and exquisite glassware gleamed. Small arrangements of flowers seemed to drink in the light. To be sure it was not the splendour of the State Ballroom, where the State Banquet was to take place later that evening, but it was decidedly lovely and serene. My earlier disquiet seemed to evaporate.

Until, that is, I heard a faint rustle. Startled, and at first unable to locate the source, I edged back into the column's shadow. The linen billowed at the edge and I noted a flaw in the arrangement that had escaped my eye before: just the slightest misalignment in the chairs, an utterly unforgivable sin in the art of royal table setting. Suddenly the chair moved even further out of alignment, as if self-propelled, hitting the adjacent chair with a delicate cracking noise. Before I could catch my breath a figure began to emerge from under the table, slowly, cautiously, like a reluctant baby coming into the world. But this was no newborn. It was someone very familiar. Alarmed and uncertain, I receded further into the shadows. I watched as the figure rose, realigned the chair, studied the table setting for a moment and then turned to leave. Not this way! my mind cried out in a response that seemed irrational. But I counted myself lucky. Egress was through the 1855 Room, opposite.

My heart was racing and my mind in turmoil. What was going on? A strangely familiar odour had wafted its way towards me in those first moments, an over-sweet, artificial, almost sickly perfume. Chewing gum. Of course! And then it seemed as if the sunshine brightening the room had burst through into my mind, clarifying

C. C. BENISON

with its searching light. Sun-spun, the missing bits of the jigsaw puzzle twirled and finally fell into place. I knew now who. And, yes, even a glimmer of why.

I must have been rooted there for some minutes, playing and replaying certain events of the past eleven days in my mind. What had once been obscure or incidental now seemed so clear, so essential. How could I have missed these things? How could I have been so stupid? And the last thing to rush through my brain were the Queen's very own warning words spoken only the day before: *'You must tell me immediately if anything happens.'*

But how?

With a pounding heart I passed back through the 1844 Room into the Marble Hall. A clutch of people were gathered at the end of the corridor by the Queen's Entrance. I moved towards them as quickly as I could without seeming like I was fleeing a forest fire. They were the film guys, and among them was Neil. I was never so glad to see someone familiar.

'Has the Queen gone to Victoria?' I shouted.

'You look like you're about to *join* Victoria in Buck-House-in-the-Sky. You all right?'

'Yes,' I gasped, out of breath more from shock than exercise. 'Has she gone to Victoria? Tell me.'

'Yeah, she just left . . .'

'Oh, God . . .!'

'What's the matter?'

'Nothing.'

'Wait . . .' he called as I turned and raced back down the corridor.

'It's nothing,' I shouted back over my shoulder.

But where was I going? What was I to do? Should I tell the police? Security? But where were they? Most of them were bound to be with the Queen herself or at Victoria, waiting for her and the visiting King. I found myself at the security kiosk at the Side Entrance but the bobby was on his portable phone. He glanced at me uninterestedly and kept talking. '*You must tell me immediately,*' she had said. '*You must tell me.*'

'*Me.*'

I had to try. What other opportunities were there? In less than an hour she would be riding back to the Palace in the State Landau with the RamaLama in front of thousands of people. Then she would be surrounded by high-ranking members of the Household and important guests through official presentations and then lunch. After that, for all I knew, there was an afternoon of ceremonial functions before the State Banquet in the evening. And then it might all be too late.

So, for the second time that day, I raced out into Buckingham Palace Road, this time with Victoria Station my destination, this time with more urgency. I was still in my white uniform and my black flats. I must have looked like a shop girl who had lost her mind as I sliced through the happy crowds gathering for a glimpse of Her Majesty on a nice day. As I passed the Queen's Gallery, then the Royal Mews, I fretted about how I was going to get near the Queen. The security! The crowds! If I didn't get killed trying to get her, could I speak to her without attracting attention? What words could I use without raising undue alarm?

And then it hit me. Flowers. People always gave flowers to the Queen when she went on one of her walkabouts. I could slip a note among the blooms and hand the bouquet to her. If she saw me among the crowds, she would know something was up. She would know what to do. And I remembered there was a new flower shop further down the road, just past Eaton Lane.

But I had no money! I had run out of the Palace without a penny in my pocket. Oh, God! I couldn't stop and beg. There were hardly flowers along the roadside to tear up and present as my own, and I knew the flowers in the windowboxes of the nearby Shakespeare Tavern had died long since. And then, across Lower Grosvenor Place, I saw a busker, no doubt encouraged in his trade by the good weather and the extra crowds. He looked small and thin, but he also looked encumbered with a guitar strapped around his shoulder and a harmonica wired in front of his mouth. I could just make out the notes of some creaky folk tune, the sort of Bob Dylan thing my mother liked. I couldn't believe what I was about to do.

As I went past him, in one fell and graceful swoop I reached into his open guitar case and snatched a single five-pound note weighted down with a couple of fifty-pence coins. The coins rattled and the music stopped.

'*Hey!*'

'I'll pay you back,' I shouted. 'Really!'

And I was gone. No one came charging after me. If anyone other than the busker noticed I had just committed my first major theft, no one cared.

A few moments later I was in Victoria Flowers, clutching the five quid, almost hopping like I needed to pee while a willowy man about my age finished with another customer.

'Oh, hurry up, hurry up,' I muttered.

The other customer, an elderly woman in clothes that matched in hue from hat to shoes, received her change. She stared at me frostily as she turned to leave the shop.

'How may I help you, madam?' the man said smoothly.

'I need some flowers.'

'Well, we have some lovely—'

'Doesn't matter. I've got five pounds. Give me five pounds worth of anything . . . and nothing wired,' I added, remembering having read somewhere that the Queen doesn't like receiving wired bouquets for fear of being cut.

'Um, well, how about tulips, daisies, a little baby's breath. They're very nice for—'

'Fine, fine.' I scrabbled at the rack of cards. 'That's five pounds *including* VAT,' I babbled, grabbing a pen from the counter.

Keep calm, Jane, I said to myself. Gather your thoughts. There wasn't much room on the tiny card, and I couldn't very well stuff a big one among the blooms, so I had to be concise. On the card, as firmly as my trembling hand would let me, I wrote a single name and a single warning.

'There,' said the man, admiring his handiwork. It didn't look like much to me; I'd forgotten how expensive flowers are. 'That will be five pounds, twenty-one pence.'

'I said I had only five pounds!' I shrieked.

C. C. BENISON

'Well, this pink dahlia looked so nice, I thought . . .'

'Bugger the dahlia. Take it out.'

His mouth formed a little moue of distaste.

'Very well, then.' He removed the flower, then wrapped the flowers in a cone of green paper. 'That will be four pounds, seventy-two . . .'

'Thanks.'

'Your change,' he said disdainfully.

'Keep it. I'm stinking rich.'

'Bloody American,' he muttered as I pulled open the door.

'CANADIAN!' I roared back.

That felt good. Cathartic, I guess is the word. I continued down Buckingham Palace Road at a brisk trot, feeling more sure of myself, crossed at Victoria Street, turned left at the Grosvenor Hotel, and, as the rumble of cannons sounded in the distance, hurried past the Tourist Information Centre, bursting into the bright bubble of Victoria Station. The place is, of course, huge and noisy, and at first I didn't know where the Queen might be, but a crowd of non-commuter types surging to my left suggested Platforms One and Two might be where to find her. From that direction, too, I could hear a military band starting up some tune or other. I pushed my way through – being small helps in such circumstances – and popped up at a temporary barrier that had been erected along the terrazzo floor from the ticket wicket at Platform Two to the great arched formal entrance to Victoria. Outside I could glimpse the State Landau and the horses and Davey.

'This isn't a walkabout, miss.' A policeman eyed my flowers and then me, pityingly.

'Lovely blooms,' enthused a tall, gap-toothed woman beside me as if she felt obliged to defend my foolishness. 'What does he know, anyway,' she added, bending down in a cloud of perfume to whisper in my ear as the policeman moved down the line.

'Where is the Queen?' I asked. 'I can't see her.'

'Look, there she is now.' The woman nodded down Platform Two. There the Queen, dressed in a soft apple-green coat and a beige hat with a tuft of green feathers, came into view accompanied by a thin, sallow man in a white uniform and an explosion of medals – the Rama-Lama, presumably. Following her were the Duke of Edinburgh and a short, rotund woman in a bright pink coat, presumably Mrs RamaLama. Following *them* was a bunch of other people in various robes or morning dress.

'Ma'am!' I said in a loudish voice as HM got nearer, feeling slightly foolish because everyone else in the crowd was being rather reserved.

'My goodness,' exclaimed the woman next to me.

Miraculously, the familiarity of my voice must have registered, for the Queen, without missing a step, moved towards the crowd. Startled expressions appeared on the faces of her officials, slightly confused looks on those of her guests. Suddenly it was a walka-bout and cameras across the way broke into a shrill chorus, echoed by a kind of groan of pleasure from the people pressed around me. A few feet away, I could hear Her Majesty asking a young mother about the baby she was holding and then an elderly man wearing a poppy a question about the War. Finally, she came to me, her face set in its familiar public mask of kindly interest. But her intensely blue eyes bore into mine.

'And from where have you come today?' she said.

'From Canada originally, Your Majesty,' I replied, dipping into a curtsey and handing her the flowers.

'Such a long way. And are you staying long in London?'

'I'm working here, Ma'am. At a shop called, um, Stems. It's near *Down*ing Street.'

'How very interesting.' The Queen smiled, and, as I smiled back, I could tell that two fingers of a gloved hand were dipping ever so cautiously into the bouquet.

'Good luck to you,' Her Majesty said.

She passed down the line, but I could tell from the way she was clenching the thumb of her right hand that she had retrieved my card. She was nimble enough to be a magician. My bouquet passed to a lady-in-waiting.

The woman next to me was still gasping either at my audaciousness or by being so near the Presence, but I didn't linger. Other members of the official party, unhappily, had joined in this impromptu walkabout, none more confused-looking than the RamaLama, who, I presume, wasn't fluent in English or in walkabout. I squeezed my way back out of the crowd, an enormous sense of something awful having been lifted from my shoulders. People streamed at cross purposes, some heading for their train, some for the Underground. My attention shifted from navigating the horde to a clutch of protesters under police observation sullenly holding signs calling for an end to monarchy.

And that's when I walked right into Andrew Mac-greevy.

Chapter Eighteen

I arrived at the Throne Room, as per instruction from Humphrey Cranston, just before 4.30 that afternoon. It had been a little over three hours since the episode at Victoria Station, and I had been on tenterhooks ever since. With the State Banquet nigh, the Palace was running like clockwork for once – which is to say, all the Staff were sober. However, there was something else. There was this buzz, this intense undercurrent, and it wasn't just the occasion. Unbeknownst to me and others in the lower orders lost in the late morning rush, the *Evening Gazette* had splashed a significant story on the front page of its early edition in the usual bold black type:

World Exclusive
WE'VE GOT
THE *REAL*
RIPPER!

And off to the left side was a related story under the headline in reverse white type on black:

RIPPER HEIR IN
MYSTERY PALACE DEATH

It was Andrew Macgreevy who pointed it out to me, although 'pointed out' would be too nice a way of putting it. I more or less crashed into him and he, after picking me off his front, smugly unfurled a copy of the offending rag with an enlarged nineteenth-century black-and-white photograph of a face which bore an uncanny resemblance to Robin's covering much of the front page.

'You get about, don't you, *Stella*?' he said with mock good cheer as I scanned the headline with a sinking heart. 'One day it's the Queen's solicitor. The next you're handing tulips to Her Maj. Don't you see enough of her at BP? And here you are at Victoria on an autumn day and you're not even wearing a coat.'

'I gave it to Oxfam,' I retorted, not feeling awfully clever at that moment.

'I've never seen the Queen do an impromptu walkabout. Have a nice chat?'

'Oh, usual. Price of fish and chips.'

His smarmy smile didn't falter. 'Here, then,' he said, shoving his paper into my hands, 'you can wrap your cod supper in this. You've read it, I presume. Or have you not?'

'I think they're calling your train, Mr Macgreevy.'

'I do believe you haven't, Stella! Well, do take a moment to peruse it. You'll be extremely interested, I'm sure.'

'I doubt it.'

'We'll meet again,' he shouted above the growing din as I quickly moved away.

In hell, I thought savagely. But as I left Victoria Station and trudged back up Buckingham Palace Road, I couldn't help passing my eyes over the trashy prose that covered most of pages two and three in a number of connected 'world-copyrighted' stories. As the Queen had more or less predicted, a tame academic and a gaggle of rent-a-Ripperologists had proclaimed, without any overt reference to King Edward VII's diary, the verity of the fifth Earl of Ulverstone as the real Ripper, easily recasting the clues supporting one or other of the various traditional suspects in the rogues' gallery. Of course, there was enough allusion to assure any regular *Gazette* reader that crucial evidence also lay in a certain royal diary, excerpts of which could not be legally printed.

As for Robin, the bulk of the newspaper drivel was innuendo, of course, but inside, a skeleton of truth rattled. It had the *who, what, when* and *how* of his death correct. But the *where* in Buckingham Palace he had died was left out – a significant detail in my estimation – and, of course, the *why* – the real *why*. Interestingly, the article didn't speculate on such things as depression, and its author didn't seem to know about the HIV-positive thing – the sort of stuff that might lead to suicide. Instead, the article linked Robin's death to the fifth Earl of Ulverstone being Jack the Ripper, as if the knowledge was just so overwhelming that Robin had no alternative but to kill himself. Pretty melodramatic, I thought, but it's the kind of twaddle that sells newspapers.

Then there was a story about the present Earl of Ulverstone, featuring mostly autobiographical details interspersed with comments from various village yobbos indicating they had 'always thought there was something funny' about the Earl. And, naturally, the story highlighted the fact that the Earl had been at Court and that he had once been considered a possible match for King George VI's elder daughter and that he had left Court under 'mysterious circumstances'.

'DID THE KING KNOW?' another headline shouted. And then the final one: 'SUICIDE OR ???', in which the writer speculated about the unusual veil of secrecy about Robin's demise, the possible removal of the body in a laundry van, the no-comment from the Palace, and the exceptional reticence of 'other sources' (i.e., the below-stairs moles, the family in Canada, Scotland Yard and the Coroner of the Household).

Trash.

The Throne Room was hushed as a church and cold as a cathedral when I entered. Several of the velvet-covered gold chairs with the funny animal feet, which normally stand at the perimeter of the room, were grouped in a semi-circle in front of the fireplace. I was drawn there immediately. The room was in partial shadow, the windows overlooking the interior court gathering little light in the late afternoon, but someone had lit the candelabara on the mantel and they cast a warm amber glow across the Aubusson carpet. The electric heater – just like the one in my old Earl's Court bedsit – was switched on, too, and its orange bars made a fitful attempt to warm the volumes of chill air. I sidled between two of the chairs, put the backs of my legs towards the heat and looked around.

Only to be nearly shucked out of my skin by a figure

sitting on the throne. For a second, in the dim light, I thought it might be you-know-who: the only person actually entitled to sit there. But it wasn't. The figure was seated with elbows on knees, head in hand as though engaged in contemplation of one's shoes. The glint of red hair was my clue: it was Nikki.

'What are you *doing*!' I shouted across the shadowy room, compelled to say something. 'That's the *throne* for heaven's sake!'

'I'm trying it out,' came the voice.

'What if the Queen catches you?'

'Now, how is she going to do that? She's got this banquet to bother about. And what are you doing here anyway?'

'Same as you, I guess. There was . . . a note in my box.'

'Oh? The Harbottle gave me the word. What's it about?'

'Dunno.'

'I thought maybe she was in a fury about the cleaning. Odd place to meet. This throne's not very comfy, you'll be pleased to know. Oh, who's this now . . .?'

The mirrored doors opened tentatively and Karim slipped into the room, dressed in his full scarlet livery decorated in gold braid. He looked dead handsome and intensely worried, regarding me with unhappy surprise when his eyes caught me in my pose by the fireplace.

I shrugged as if I didn't know what was going on, though of course I did. After her luncheon in the Bow Room and wishing her guests well on their standard afternoon tour of Westminster Abbey, St James's Palace and Clarence House for tea with the Queen Mother, the Queen and I had rendezvoused once again in the Royal Closet. As she placed the final jigsaw pieces in the sky surrounding Charles II – the jigsaw manufacturer had sent her the missing bits post-haste – we went over the final pieces in another puzzle. It had been, contradictorily, both a cheerless and gratifying discussion. And things weren't over yet.

'I thought this was going to be about cleaning,' came the voice from the throne.

Karim spun around. 'Who's that?' he demanded in a strangled voice.

'Nikki,' I replied. 'She's pretending she's the Queen.'

'Who sent you here?' Nikki called.

'The Travelling Yeoman. I thought it was going to be about tonight's—'

The door opened again and Angie appeared. 'Bloody hell,' she muttered as soon as she spotted Karim. 'What's this?'

'An investiture, Ange,' said the throne. 'You've going to become the Duchess of Skivvy.'

Angie looked to the dais, back to Karim, and then me. She scowled and turned away. 'Well, I'm not having any of this . . . ooph!'

She crashed into Cyril.

'. . . and I'm *supposed* to be directing a *film*. Ow! Get off me, woman. What the hell is this . . . Julian? Julian!'

Sir Julian brought up the rear. He looked on reprovingly as Angie peeled herself off Cyril and then glared at the rest of us. Silence fell over the room. The Private Secretary's presence seemed to bring a new and unsettling dimension to our little gathering. I could see the alarm in Karim's eyes as he stared into my own. Angie straightened her uniform with brisk, irritable motions.

'What on *earth* is this all about?' Cyril demanded peevishly, hands on hips.

But Julian had caught sight of Nikki.

'Get off that throne,' he snapped. 'Now!'

We all looked towards the unmoving figure under the burgundy canopy.

'Yes,' came a high voice in tones that would freeze the Thames in a heatwave, 'get off my throne.'

Nikki shot off the rose-pink damask as though stung by bees. The rest of them, clustered by the door, began to bob foolishly amid murmurs of 'Your Majesty,' jostling each other as they tried to clear a path.

The Queen was not amused. At least, she didn't look amused. Somebody told me once that HM wasn't keen on confrontation, but if she wasn't, you could have fooled me. Maybe in the wake of her horrible year she had gone into a take-charge-of-one's-life mode, reading Anthony Robbins's *Unlimited Power* or some other self-help guide late in bed. Her mouth had a set to it that made her lips look like she had swallowed them. Even from where I stood I could see that her blue eyes were chips of ice.

'Sit down, all of you,' she commanded quietly. 'You, as well, Julian,' she added when her Private Secretary seemed to hesitate.

I had half-hoped the Queen would arrive in full State Banquet gear – sash and ribbons and jewels and tiara, the stuff that puts the majesty in Majesty – but she had changed from the outfit she had worn to meet the RamaLama into one of her serviceable shirtwaist jobbies, this one printed with tiny blue, purple, black and white shapes that looked like a mosaic. Formal dressing was to come later, I presumed, after she had inspected the State Ballroom with the Master of the Household and, of course, after what was about to ensue.

I took the chair stage right of the fireplace. Nikki sat beside me. Karim faced the fireplace dead on with Angie beside him, while Cyril, without intending to, came between Angie and Julian, the latter taking the last chair directly opposite me. Her Majesty remained standing – monarch standing, subjects sitting isn't the usual order of things, but then these were unusual circumstances. Everyone shifted uncomfortably, shooting curious glances at one another. There was a tension in the air you could have sliced with one of those oh-so-English fish knives.

The Queen stood at the mantelpiece, the ever-present handbag having been relegated to a nearby chair. A corgi or two disported themselves at her feet. She cleared her throat.

'A week ago today,' she began in a formal way that reminded me of her Christmas broadcasts, 'Robin Tukes, a footman, was found dead – not in his room, as some of you may believe, but in the corridor just outside my apartments. Some of you, too, may not be aware of this, but it was I who found him.' She glanced at me. 'It was not,' she added drily, 'a pleasant experience.' She nudged a corgi indulgently with her foot and continued. 'I was given immediate assurance that the death was a suicide. It struck me at the time that this was a conclusion made in almost unseemly haste, but

298

at that time I had no other information that might suggest a different point of view. I was told the young man was prone to bouts of intense depression and, I later learned, that he was quite ill, or at least likely to become quite ill – he was HIV-positive.'

Angie gasped. Both W-Dez and Sir Julian looked disapproving.

'Yes,' Her Majesty said to Angie, 'but I really don't think you need worry . . . Now,' she continued briskly, 'put together, these facts make a most convincing case for suicide. It seemed to me at the time that it was rather peculiar to take one's life in such a fashion, in a Palace corridor, near one's apartments, but I was persuaded that the young man was prone to a certain theatricality. It was also suggested that he had some reason to want to embarrass me, or call my attention to his death in a pointed way, as some sort of "statement". It wouldn't have been the first time someone wished to get one's attention by making a spectacle of himself.' She sighed softly. 'Nevertheless, shortly thereafter I was presented with another point of view.'

Sir Julian tore his eyes from the Queen and let them rest on me. I met his gaze and felt just the tiniest tickle of triumph when he looked away first.

'Robin Tukes, it was suggested, was not suicidal,' Her Majesty continued while several other pairs of eyes moved in my direction. 'His depression was intermittent and controllable. He was interested in theatre but he was not "theatrical". But, most important, he was not out in the corridor making a spectacle of his death. He was, quite simply, trying to see me.'

'But surely, Ma'am, he would have seen you many times in the Palace,' Cyril interjected.

'When I say "see", Mr Wentworth-Desborough, I mean, "talk to",' the Queen said with a hint of exasperation. 'Robin Tukes wished to meet one privately. This, of course, is highly unusual. It is also particularly significant that he wished to do so outside the usual channels. Why did he wish to do so? We'll get to that in a moment.

'Now . . .' The Queen paused as if to gather her thoughts. The candelabrum flame above spun gold from her silver hair while the pearly glow from the windows opposite, the only other light in the room, sharpened her expression of gravity. 'It became evident to me that Robin Tukes did not die by his own hand. He was, to put it plainly, murdered.'

'Nonsense!' Sir Julian boomed as shock at the word 'murder' crackled between us like electricity along a downed line. Everyone began to fidget. I suddenly felt Nikki's tension as she shifted uncomfortably in her chair.

The Queen gave Sir Julian a glacial stare.

'Of course,' HM continued calmly, 'why would anyone want to murder so young a man? There seemed to be no apparent motive. Yet within an hour of his death one person had gone to his room seeking something that would distance himself from suspicion – a letter.'

Karim kept his head bowed through this, as though he found Her Majesty's shoes (a sensible pair of black pumps) absolutely gripping. I couldn't see the expression on his face, but his hands clutched the arms of the chair in a way that made the cat's heads adorning each end look like they were being strangled.

'The letter was a plea from a family member for money, twenty-five thousand pounds, which the letter's recipient didn't possess. But he alone of Robin's friends knew that Robin was due to inherit a considerable sum of money on his twenty-first birthday, a sum that was also intended to finance a business venture that he and Robin had planned. Robin had also recently made a will, which seems over-cautious for so young a man, but indeed not so in the light of his unfortunate diagnosis. The beneficiary named in the will is Karim Agarwal.'

The Queen scrutinized Karim, who had frozen in position, his chin gathered in the starched white ruffle around his neck.

'Ma'am,' he said, addressing the buttons on his livery in a half-whisper, 'I didn't know about any will.'

'So you say. And yet, not only did you have business ambitions that required money, you were very angry with Robin, angry over an attachment he appeared to have made with one of my housemaids. So angry, in fact, that you placed a dangerous quantity of a certain drug in a cup from which Robin drank.'

Karim began to shake. 'But, Ma'am . . .' he said weakly.

'Yes, I know, you intended the cup for Angela. Or at least, that is your story.'

Angela recoiled from Karim in shock and then, in a sudden blaze, oblivious to the Queen's presence, lunged forward in her chair and began to slap him about the side of his head, cursing colourfully. Karim put one hand up half-heartedly to ward off the blows. His eyes were squeezed shut as if he didn't want to believe what was happening. Her Majesty sighed.

'Stop that at once!' Sir Julian commanded.

'The little bleeder,' Angie spat out, clasping one hand in the other as though each were a separate instrument that needed restraining. 'God, sorry, Ma'am,' she gulped, realizing that her language and behaviour were not those of any aristo-wannabe.

'Someone else stood to benefit financially from Robin's death,' Her Majesty continued, disregarding Angie. 'Indeed, there was more at stake than money. As we all know from the *Gazette* this morning, Robin Tukes was heir presumptive to an earldom and all that that entails. I am told by sources more reliable than the *Gazette* that the present Earl is gravely ill and that, since he is childless, Robin would very shortly have inherited the title of Earl of Ulverstone.

'Now, Robin was about to have a direct heir of his own, or so one is led to believe – a son who would be the legitimate heir upon his marriage and who would succeed to the title and the fortune even if his father were dead and the infant were only a day old. But if the father were to die *before* his marriage, any child conceived would have no claims on the title. It would pass to someone else. In this case, it would pass to someone who didn't believe Robin deserved the title at all: his second cousin, Cyril Wentworth-Desborough.'

As Her Majesty spoke, Cyril's face turned scarlet with suppressed emotion – whether anger, embarrassment or indignation, it was hard to tell. He could hardly have one of his little directorial tantrums in front of the sovereign.

'With respect, Ma'am,' he sputtered, his mouth opening and closing in fishy fashion, 'I had nothing to do with this . . . murder, this death, I mean. I . . . really, I must get back to my film . . .'

'. . . which,' Her Majesty interrupted smoothly, 'I understand is having some financial difficulties. You possess a motive, Mr Wentworth-Desborough. You've wanted nothing to do with your cousin, Robin Tukes. You've always disapproved of him, but that didn't deter you, in the first instance, from seeking funds from him after you heard that some members of my Staff were planning a surprise twenty-first birthday for him. You correctly surmised he would come into a sum of money on that day, as you once did on your twenty-first birthday. You confronted him in the post office and appealed to him on, one presumes, grounds of consanguinity. But he quite rightly refused to lend you money. You had hardly been friendly to him . . .'

'But . . .'

'. . . and when that didn't work, you thought about the other inheritance. You were angry . . .'

'Your Majesty . . . Ma'am, this is . . . outrageous!'

The Queen regarded him frostily. 'And you had opportunity,' she continued. 'Indeed, you *all* had opportunity. Robin's room was quite accessible. Anyone could have gone in and found the drug . . . yes, even you, Julian,' she added, raising a finger as her Private Secretary opened his mouth to interrupt. 'I am reliably told you were in Servants' Hall during last Tuesday's filming. Not your usual whereabouts, is it?'

'Ma'am, I was merely satisfying myself as to the

film's progress. Its purpose, of course, is to present Your Majesty in a most positive way.'

'Quite.'

The Queen had an 'I-will-not-be-flannelled' look on her face.

'Julian, I am aware of your relationship with one of the young women in this room. It is not something I can condone. One cannot have around one senior advisers – a most senior adviser in your case – who is behaving in a way that may cause scandal.'

'Ma'am, your own family . . .'

'*Silence!*'

I had never heard the Queen thunder. I could never have imagined it. She doesn't seem the type, or to have the voice. She always seemed so controlled. But thunder she did, and all of us leaped in our seats when she did so. Even the corgis were roused from their slumber. It was a glimpse, I thought, of what absolute monarchy must have been like. Or what the Balmoral breakfast table must have been like the day the tabs revealed who was sucking the Duchess of York's toes.

'*My family is not part of this discussion.*'

To be so insolent, Sir Julian must have known his days were numbered. But he looked neither apologetic nor embarrassed, merely faintly surprised at Her Majesty's rare burst of Hanoverian spleen.

The Queen quickly recovered her composure. 'You believed you had been discreet. But your interest had begun to wane. You were looking forward to Balmoral being what I understand is called a "cooling-off period". Am I correct?'

'As you say, Ma'am,' Sir Julian replied evenly.

'Lady Dench accompanied you. And then you found that Angela was one of two housemaids brought to Balmoral from London. This was unhappy news. Balmoral has a different atmosphere. It is smaller. It would be difficult to be discreet. You had to disentangle yourself from this affair lest it reach my ears, as it might very well have in such circumstances.' The Queen paused and then added: 'You may be a fool, Julian, but you are not a complete fool. You knew Angela was attracted to you in good measure for your title, your money and your power, advantages which she covets, perhaps feels she deserves . . . I am told,' she went on, now addressing a pouting Angela, 'that you believe we are somehow related.'

Angie shot both Nikki and me a glance of indignation and then responded feebly: 'It was a story my Gran told me, Ma'am.'

'I see.'

The Queen folded her arms in front of her. She had been standing for some time but seemed untired. Training, I suppose. Standing is one of the things members of the Royal Family do well.

'Please do correct me if I'm wrong, Julian, but at some time earlier, before Balmoral, you told Angela about Robin Tukes. You had read my great-grandfather's diary and the name Tukes had seemed familiar to you. You went to *Debrett's* and found that a young man you knew only as a footman in Buckingham Palace was heir to a great title. I'm certain you made inquiries and learned that the present Earl was both elderly and ill. In telling Angela all this in confidence – all of it except for the unpleasant part about the Ripper – you planted a

notion, hoping perhaps that if she saw another opportunity within her orbit she might seize upon it. What
ensued must have been both surprising and gratifying.
She and Robin became engaged to be married. One is
inclined to view this as all rather convenient.'

We waited for a response from Angie and Sir Julian.
The latter kept his counsel, merely raising an eyebrow
at Angie, who was staring at him intently.

'You tried to manipulate me, you bas—'

'Angela!' Julian barked. 'Need I remind you that you
are in the presence of Her Majesty?'

Angie swallowed her words and turned back to the
Queen. 'Ma'am,' she said contritely, 'I didn't plan it, not
really. I knew about the title, but I thought he was
supposed to be, you know . . . I mean, he and Karim
here . . .' She regarded Karim distastefully and muttered, 'At any rate, it was all Robin's idea.'

'He sought you out?'

'Well, no.' Angie squirmed in her chair. 'It just sort of
happened. You see, Julian told me it was all off. We
were, I mean. Right before the Ghillies' Ball, too, Ma'am,
and I guess I had already had a bit much to drink at the
dance, so I left and went out walking. Next thing I'm in
the Dee. Robin fished me out.'

'Dead romantic!' Nikki spoke for the first time. 'Did
you fall in accidentally or deliberately?'

Angie looked at her sharply and then turned to the
Queen as if for guidance. The Queen remained silent.

'It was an accident,' Angie finally replied with indignation. 'I didn't plan to jump into that bloody freezing
river, if that's what you're on about. I was legless. I could
have drowned!'

'Lucky old you, Robin being at the ready,' Nikki threw in aggressively.

'I didn't know he was there!'

'Robin Tukes fished you out...' the Queen prompted.

'Robin fished me out and ... well, he had been brooding about something of his own. I mean, he wasn't at the Ball. Anyway, he helped me back to my room. I was wet and miserable and felt sick. Nobody was about – you were all in the Ballroom. So I told him everything. I didn't care what happened. I didn't owe you silence, Julian,' she exploded, giving an angry shake of her blonde hair. 'I would have gone to the press at that point. I still might!'

I noted the Queen's foot tapping lightly on the carpet, a sure sign that she was more than vexed, although she continued to regard Angie evenly. 'That would not be wise,' HM said in tones that brooked no nonsense.

Angie pursed her lips and shrank back in her chair.

'Robin offered you a solution to your problems, I believe,' the Queen continued.

'Yes, Ma'am,' Angie replied. 'He offered to marry me and claim the child as his own.'

'Which you leaped on,' Nikki cut in again.

'Which I did not,' Angie denied hotly. 'I said I had to think about it.'

'Oh, yeah? And didn't you wonder *why* he would want to do something like that?'

'I don't have to answer *your* questions!' She appealed to the Queen for support. 'Ma'am ...?'

'The question is well taken.'

Angie sighed and replied grudgingly: 'He said he wanted to get his life straightened out. And he told me about the title and everything. Of course, I already knew . . .'

'And you couldn't resist,' Nikki needled her.

'I wasn't about to raise a kid on a footman's pay! Of course, it was . . . attractive. Why wouldn't it be? But I'm saying I didn't go for it straightaway. The idea was a bit peculiar, him being gay and all. But the more I thought about it . . .' She raised her shoulders and then let them drop. 'I thought, why not?'

'He wanted to prevent me from inheriting,' Cyril muttered darkly.

'He didn't say anything about that. He never even told me you two were related. He did ask me later whether I knew if it was a boy or a girl, though. I said I could get a test done . . .'

'And did you?' the Queen asked.

'Well, no, Ma'am. I didn't fancy the idea. I told him it was a boy because . . . I thought that's what he wanted to hear, being about to inherit, and males being the ones who get the title.'

'Maybe what he really wanted was to make sure the baby was going to be healthy,' I interjected. 'I mean, I think maybe it was important because it wasn't his baby – biologically speaking, that is.'

'Yes, perhaps,' the Queen said, taking my cue. 'Undoubtedly, all of you have read the *Evening Gazette* by now and know the speculation about a disturbing connection between the Earl of Ulverstone and Jack the Ripper. I believe Robin already knew of this connection. One may conjecture that in a frightening way it illuminated for him a strain of mental imbalance that seems to run in his family. That may be why he was interested in Angela having a test, although I believe it is mistaken to assume that such tests can indicate mental imbalance . . . some congenital mental defects, perhaps, but not imbalance. Nevertheless, Angela was attractive as a marriage partner. Unhappy news had quickly made Robin a much more serious young man—'

'And so, by getting the title and having a male heir he would be able to make amends to his sister and mother in Canada,' I said brightly, picking up the thread. 'At the same time he would be able to break the biological chain that, for him, was kind of creepy . . .'

'Yes, quite possibly.' The Queen looked at me reprovingly for interrupting her. 'Of course, the question remains: how did Robin know in advance what all of Britain knows today? There is only one way. Julian?'

'Ma'am?' he replied evenly as all eyes shifted in his direction.

'You told Robin about certain entries in King Edward's diary.'

'Ma'am, I told him an old diary had come to light that suggested a disagreeable connection between his ancestor and the Ripper. But I made no reference to King Edward. I wished to ensure, in passing on such information, that nothing could cause distress to Your Majesty.'

'Yes, I'm sure,' the Queen replied drily. 'Nevertheless, Robin needn't have received this information at all. There was no benefit.'

'I disagree, Ma'am.'

'Perhaps you are right: but it is you who indeed

benefited. The arrangement between Robin and Angela had, almost miraculously, resolved your dilemma. But one difficulty remained: Robin knew the truth of your relationship with Angela. And such knowledge was a potential threat to someone in your position as my Private Secretary. You needed to balance the scales and you knew something that would possibly do it. One might speculate that you told the young man there was considerable pressure to release this diary to the public, but that you, as Keeper of the Royal Archives, could ensure it remained sealed for a very long time. Robin would have had no reason not to believe you, and he would have taken the point, I'm sure.'

Sir Julian merely raised his eyebrows in acknowledgement.

'And then,' the Queen reasoned, 'not long after my family returned to London, Robin made an attempt – not once but twice – to see me privately. The first attempt, as we now know, was frustrated by Karim. But the circumstances of that evening, Robin's condition, and one's unfortunate encounter with him, soon become well known among Staff and Household. That is quite significant given the very few witnesses, but I'll return to that presently.

'As we noted earlier, Robin sought a private audience. This is not something that members of Staff normally seek, but it is not impossible. However, to do so he would have had to make a formal request which would necessitate scrutiny by my Private Secretary. That he felt compelled to circumvent protocol is highly significant.

'For you, Julian, the very disagreeable idea arose

that Robin intended simply to tell me about your activities. Perhaps he had had a change of heart about an impending marriage that was more an arrangement than a love-match. It was sufficiently worrying to cause you to go to Servants' Hall early in the morning well before your regular appointment with me.'

I could see Sir Julian's jaw muscles rippling as he strained to keep his indignation under control. But he stayed mute.

'But one wonders why Robin would wish to inform on someone? I am led to believe that he was not the sort of person who would inform on another, or break a bargain. Indeed, he seems to have been quite an honourable young man.' She shook her head. 'No, it all comes back to my great-grandfather's diary, the sole source of information connecting the Ulverstones to Jack the Ripper.'

'But, Ma'am,' Sir Julian insisted, 'I did not tell Robin that the diary had belonged to King Edward.'

'No,' the Queen said patiently, 'I'm quite sure what you say is true.' Her Majesty's eyes travelled over the faces in front of her. 'As some of you are aware, the diary of which I am speaking, which belonged to my great-grandfather, King Edward VII, and came to light after the fire at Windsor, subsequently went missing. Despite resistance from some quarters I determined to retrieve the diary, which I believed had been stolen, through a newspaper advertisement worded in a way that would be meaningful only to those who had the diary in their possession. I wanted no publicity. The journal is my family's private property. And it was the King's express wish that his diaries be destroyed. It was my intention to follow his wishes.

'Robin, I have good reason to believe,' she went on, 'not only read this advertisement, but was one of the few able to comprehend its meaning. You may also have feared, Julian, that Robin was intent on seeing me because he felt you had betrayed your promise to keep the source of unpleasant information about his family private.'

Sir Julian gave the barest possible nod of assent.

'That was incorrect. There was only one way someone would be able to make sense of this advertisement.' The Queen paused significantly. *'And that is if he or she had actually seen the diary.* It is quite distinctive-looking, crimson leather, with the Prince of Wales' feathers and an embossed "E", with a gold clasp. Robin deciphered the clues because he had seen the diary.'

The Queen let the last words sink in, then continued: 'That is why he was intent on talking with me.' Once again she allowed her eyes to travel over our faces. 'It's really extremely simple. He had seen a distinctive-looking book in the hands of someone in this room, and only later, much later, when he read the advertisement, did he understand what it was he had seen, and understand that this was the "diary" to which Julian had alluded. I'm sure, Julian, he must have felt that you had deceived him in some way.'

'Ma'am, if he felt something was amiss he should have gone to the proper authorities.'

But Robin was kind, I thought sorrowfully. He had been kind to Angie by providing a way out of her dilemma. He had been kind to Karim with his promise of financial help. He had been too kind. When he had realized the game Sir Julian was playing, he should have gone to the authorities. I glanced up at the Queen and realized she had been looking at me. Some understanding passed between us.

'Robin,' she stated, addressing Julian, 'resisted that course because he wished to protect someone.'

A silence fell over the Throne Room. It was broken only by minute pops as specks of dust collided with the bars of the electric fire. I couldn't help gripping the lions-head arms of my chair. I knew what was to come: it filled me with both sadness and dread.

'Robin knew the circumstances of your father's death, did he not, Nikki?'

'Yes, Ma'am,' Nikki replied. There was the slightest surprise in her voice.

'It was a circumstance you shared, each of you losing your father in a cruel way at the beginning of adolescence. One might imagine that he had a special sympathy for you. And when he understood that you were caught up in something unlawful, he decided he needed to protect you.'

Nikki's face flushed suddenly. 'He could have kept quiet about it,' she said with feeling. 'It was none of his business.'

'Not entirely. Robin was quite concerned about the possible effects on his family if the diary reached the public, it was true. But he was more concerned about you. By talking to me, he was hoping I would intervene so that you would be spared the punishment that a court of law would surely mete out. Perhaps he sensed a trap – that the advertisement had been placed not only to retrieve the diary but to uncover the thief as well. He was not far wrong.'

All eyes regarded Nikki speculatively.

'So it was you who took the diary,' Angie said wonderingly. 'What were you doing in my room?'

'As if you don't come into mine! I was looking at myself in your cheval-bloody-glass, if you must know.'

'But I stuffed that diary in a drawer.'

'It was a new pair of jeans. I thought I'd try it with one of your belts.'

Nikki's streak of defiance did not falter, not even in the presence of the Queen. But I could feel that she was taut as a wound spring.

'Well, you had no business,' Angie said huffily.

'That's hardly the point, Angela,' Sir Julian interjected.

The Queen gave them both a severe look. 'Your father's death was an accident,' she continued, returning to Nikki.

'It was no accident. There are no accidents.'

'The inquest was conclusive.'

Nikki snorted. 'You stupid bloody careless people can twist anything you want in your favour.'

It was a day for *lèse-majesté*. Everybody was shocked into silence. Nothing in the sovereign's face, however, revealed that she was affronted. Imperturbably, she said: 'My family has always felt very involved with the people on the Sandringham estate, and one has always felt very much that one has a responsibility towards them. In the case of your mother and you and your brother, everything was done that could be done. It was your mother who chose to leave the estate. I was sorry that she did so. I understand that life became more difficult.'

'Too right, it did.' Nikki's tone was harsh.

'When you subsequently sought employment in my service, the application came to me personally. A member of my Household recognized the name. Although you had got yourself into trouble I was pleased to recommend your employment, hoping that it would be of help to you. Now I know you had another purpose.'

But Nikki had turned her attention to me. Anger seemed to flare in her like a flame.

'You and she have been in this together,' she snarled.

'Jane has been most helpful,' the Queen said before I could reply. 'Now, I want you to pay attention.'

Nikki raised her head to meet Her Majesty's gaze with almost grim determination.

'Robin saw you with King Edward's diary,' the Queen told her.

Nikki blinked, then turned to look round the circle of faces now regarding her with amazement and outrage. Lastly, she turned back to me. Rancour blackened her face, but uncertainty flickered somewhere behind her eyes.

'Yeah,' she said at last. And it came out like a sigh. 'But I didn't know about it. Not until later, after he had read that ad and shown it to me.'

'At his birthday party?' I asked.

'Yeah,' she replied sullenly. 'At his birthday party. He said the description reminded him of a book he saw me hand over at the McDonald's behind Victoria Station.' She paused and spat out: 'I told that idiot not to take it out of the bag, but two seconds after I left that's just what he did.'

'Who did?' I said.

'Just somebody. None of your business. None of anyone's business! Robin was there. He had been at a table behind a big plant pot. I didn't know he was there.'

'And he overheard you talking.'

'Maybe. What he told me was he had got up to take his tray to the bin – this was after I had left – and as he stood up he saw my . . . friend take the thing out of the bag. He got a good look at the cover. But he didn't think anything much about it, until later, when he read the ad . . .'

'And made a connection to what he had been told by Sir Julian.'

'I suppose. He didn't tell me that bit.'

'I don't understand,' Angie interjected, frowning. 'Does this mean you . . . *poisoned* Robin just because of this silly diary business? I don't get it.'

'That's because you're thick as two planks,' Nikki snapped, as Karim sank back in his seat to avoid further possible blows.

'I think you'll find that Nikki Claypole is not the average young woman of her generation,' the Queen interjected quietly. 'At least one hopes she isn't. No, the diary was stolen to serve a particular political cause. Isn't that right, Nikki?'

Nikki twisted in her seat but didn't answer.

'And it was an unexpected threat to that cause, the threat of exposure, that prompted her to do what she did. You see,' the Queen told us, 'Nikki was quick to see that the private diary of a king might attract someone with money – money that could be used to further something she apparently believes in quite devotedly. I don't think I'm far wrong in guessing that her theft also ingratiated her with those others who share her cause. And there was a bonus, too, when the *Gazette* turned out to be the final purchaser – the publicity would have been quite embarrassing to one and to one's family.'

Her Majesty's eyes swept her audience as she made her announcement: 'I don't believe I shall be contradicted when I tell you that Nikki Claypole is a member of something called the English Republican Army.'

There was a collective intake of breath. Everyone regarded Nikki with varying degrees of astonishment.

'The cause has not been taken too seriously, I'm afraid. You can tell from the name that its members have attempted to model themselves on a certain other terrorist group, and though they've claimed credit for some recent acts of terrorism in London, their claims have been met largely with scorn. My information has been – or, rather, had been – that the ERA was a small and disorganized alliance of unemployed youth and disaffected intellectuals, and that although one's position in life makes one a potential target of unhappy people with a republican point of view one needn't worry. Well, of course I didn't worry. If I did worry about such things, I wouldn't be able to do my job. However, something happened earlier today that has caused me to change my mind.'

Here the Queen looked very grim indeed. Frown lines formed around her eyes and mouth like crushed parchment. The air crackled with anticipation. I knew of course what she was going to say, but I still felt this awful sense of foreboding.

'For the last few weeks there has been, I am told, a virtual epidemic of chewing gum on the carpets in the State Rooms. At first it seemed as though it were some extraordinary form of carelessness. One occasionally has guests, for instance, who are a little unfamiliar with our forms of etiquette. I also wondered, Mr Wentworth-Desborough, if some members of your film crew were less than mindful of where they were.'

'Ma'am, I . . .'

'No, I know it wasn't your people. It was happening too often. Someone deliberately wanted to spoil the carpets, or make a nuisance of themselves in some way. There was intent. It was the motive for such actions that remained obscure, although one could hardly imagine there was peril involved. Yes, Julian, peril,' she added with a hint of impatience as her Private Secretary regarded her with disbelief.

'Yesterday, glass shards were found in the gum. That should have been a clue that this was becoming more than a prank, but the details of the incident travelled no further than our Housekeeper, who decided in view of the impending State Banquet that other things were more urgent. She kept an eye out this morning to satisfy herself that there was nothing unpleasant on the carpets in the room that my guests and I would be in, but she didn't think to look under the luncheon table in the Bow Room.'

At this point Her Majesty had turned the full force of her countenance on Nikki, regarding her with a kind of strange detachment that was practically cold-blooded. Nikki did not meet her gaze. Instead, her eyes darted towards the door to the Picture Gallery, her hands gripping the carved heads on the arms of the chair so tightly that her knuckles had turned to hard white knobs. Electricity seemed to pour from her, almost thrilling in its intensity.

Suddenly, there was a loud crack. Nikki rose with such speed that the heavy chair overturned, splintering the ancient wood along its gilded back. She raced towards the Green Drawing Room, grabbed the ornamental knob on the door and rattled it fiercely. The door was locked. Sir Julian sprang from his seat, but the rest of us were too surprised to do anything. Only the Queen, whose expression I caught as I jerked my head towards the end of the room, regarded the performance with studied indifference. She raised a cautioning hand to Sir Julian. In the subdued light of the Throne Room, I saw Nikki's shadowed face in the mirrored surface of the door. It had crumpled into a mask of fear and frustration. I felt awful at that moment – awful for her and because of her.

'What would it have been next time?' the Queen inquired as Nikki edged towards a couch under an eighteenth-century portrait of the Duchess of Brunswick.

There was no reply. Instead, with renewed energy Nikki raced to the set of doors to the Picture Gallery, seized the knobs and, this time, with expectation flickering across her face, pulled the weight towards her. A shaft of the Picture Gallery's radiant light surged into the room and with it two uniformed officers, who grasped Nikki firmly by the arms and lifted her like a recalcitrant child from our shocked sight. There was a short, sharp scream, the sound of struggle and cursing, and then silence as unseen hands closed the doors and the semi-gloom enfolded us once more.

We who were sitting sat, to say the least, stunned. Even I, who knew what was to pass, felt strangely chastened by the transformation of someone whom I had counted as a friend into a thrashing fury. The Queen appeared to be absorbed in her own thoughts, imperturbable as usual. It was Julian, who had remained standing, alert, who broke the silence.

'Ma'am? Next time?'

Her Majesty lifted her eyebrows. '*This time* it was tear gas. She had encased a vial of tear gas in the chewing gum.'

'Oh my God,' Cyril intoned over the murmurs of the others. 'Did it . . .?'

'No, it was caught in time.'

The Queen gave me the slightest, most imperceptible of smiles. Everyone, for a moment, seemed lost in his or her own thoughts.

Finally Karim said in a mournful voice: 'It was because of me, wasn't it?'

'No, not really, Karim,' I told him. 'But you gave her an idea. Robin had already confronted her that day with his knowledge about the diary. And then she saw this . . . *look* on your face during the champagne toast for Robin and Angie's engagement. She knew immediately there was something terribly wrong. So when Robin looked at his watch and then departed so abruptly, she followed him. I suppose just to see what would happen at that point. Then she realized where he was headed. It must have happened very quickly. Her Majesty would have just stepped off the lift a moment after Robin got to the Page's Vestibule to wait. Nikki would have been in the shadows of the Ante Room and witnessed . . . well . . .' I looked hesitantly at the Queen.

'Witnessed the accident,' she said. 'It's common knowledge, Jane.'

'Yes, of course, Ma'am. Anyway, it was Nikki who spread the story around. And it was Nikki who started the suicide rumour. It's easy to start a rumour. All you have to say is that someone else told you and then embellish at will. Of course,' I added darkly, 'it was a rumour that suited a number of other people.'

Those seated regarded me with various expressions of antipathy.

'Nikki quickly made plans,' I continued. 'She knew Robin would try to speak with Her Majesty again. She had found the drug easily enough in Robin's bedroom, ground it up and waited for an opportunity. It came in Servants' Hall that Tuesday morning.'

'It was an awful risk,' Cyril muttered. He was looking at me with what I was pleased to think was something approaching respect.

'Maybe. But she had done the groundwork. No one would be too surprised if someone who had tried to commit suicide once tried it again. Angie gave me the clue.'

'I *told* you she poured Robin's coffee.'

'I know. I know. I guess my mind couldn't accept the idea. The motive was missing. And what's worse, she had nearly blown it days earlier, and still I missed it. The story was that Robin had died in his room. Only a few people actually knew he had died outside Her Majesty's own apartments, and they all had reasons to keep quiet. Last Wednesday night, one day after the murder, Nikki let it slip that she knew the truth about where Robin had died. At the time, I just thought that the word had got out. But as time went on – and I only realized this today – no one else seemed to bring it up. It should have been a point of interest, the way it was the first time.'

'But Nikki didn't follow Robin,' Karim protested. 'She didn't know where he was going. She was in Servants' Hall with us.'

'But she knew what his intentions were. She saw he had a copy of *The Times* with him. She knew Her Majesty's morning routine. From that, she could infer Robin's destination. Let me ask you something: after Robin left so suddenly that morning, after you had finished eating, who gathered up the dirty plates and cups and put the tray in the tray rack?'

Angie and Karim looked at each other.

'Nikki,' they said simultaneously.

'And the evidence had gone through the dishwasher before anyone had time to think it important.'

Silence shrouded us once more. The Throne Room had become quite dark, and the faces of the others were now elusive moons reflecting the flickering flames of the candelabra. I couldn't help thinking of the lethal coffee cup moving in merry cartoon fashion along some conveyor belt towards scalding water and oblivion.

Suddenly there was a tap on the doors to the Picture Gallery. Before anybody could respond, a figure came into the room, scarlet and gold livery gleaming in the burst of light.

'Goodness!' said a voice. 'Wherever's the switch? Oh, here it is,' he answered himself as his hand pulled at a panel cleverly hidden in the ornamental door frame.

The five chandeliers overhead suddenly blazed like forests of diamonds.

'Eeek!'

It was Davey Pye. He clutched at the lacework around his neck and gaped at us goggle-eyed while we squinted in his direction.

'Why are you . . .?'

And then he noticed the Queen and bowed hastily from the neck.

'Oh! Your Majesty! I . . . You . . .'

'Yes, David. I shall be along in a few moments. You may tell the Master of the Household I am ready to inspect the table. You may go.'

Davey hesitated and cast his eyes over us all once again in amazement, lingering on me.

'Ah . . .'

It was rather nice to see him speechless for once.

'You may go,' the Queen repeated kindly.

'Ma'am,' Davey responded, recovering slightly. He bowed and left the room, his feet well before his face, which cast me a last look of keen inquisitiveness before it passed through.

The Queen reached for her handbag and crooked it over her arm. It was a reassuring gesture, a return to normality more than an indication that our peculiar audience was over. The corgis scrambled to their feet attentively.

'Thank you for coming,' she said in her speechifying voice. 'And now I believe my husband and I have a dinner engagement.'

Epilogue

Of course, Nikki Claypole was put on trial. She pleaded guilty, which was a bit of a surprise at first. She *was* guilty, of course, but I thought she might plead not guilty and would use the trial as a political platform. She was sentenced to life imprisonment, the requisite punishment, but the judge made a recommendation that she serve a minimum of fifteen years, implying the possibility of parole. All this suggested one thing: that a deal had been done. A guilty plea and the enticement of parole, in exchange for the naming of names. The English Republican Army seemed to vanish after that.

The trial was held late the following February, starting on a day that awoke to something rare in London, a blizzard that seemed to paralyse the capital. I easily outdistanced the cars creeping along Buckingham Palace Road as I made my way on foot to Victoria Station, and when I came up from the Tube at St Paul's the air had turned white, a swirling, exhilarating mass that made me briefly homesick for the great crashing snowfalls that would bury Charlottetown overnight and leave you snowbound, temporarily released from the burdens of work or school.

I wish I could say I saw Nikki and witnessed the

proceedings at the Old Bailey, but I didn't. The weather did not deter the press, no surprise, but neither did it discourage a gaggle of trial groupies, an eccentric-looking lot who had already bagged the few seats available to the general public. That left me out in the cold, so to speak. It was disappointing. I had promised Her Majesty a report.

As I approached the snow-shrouded Newgate Street entrance, a certain individual emerged from the phantoms as if he knew to expect me. It was Andrew Macgreevy from the *Evening Gazette*, his hair glistening with beads of meltwater and flakes of snow, his expression both wary and amused. My unwillingness to blab – for on several occasions after Nikki's arrest he had attempted to get me to contribute to another of their 'exclusives' – had brought me a new-found respect, I thought. Or at least I had become a more interesting challenge. Our conversation that morning, however, was fitful. Perhaps it was the weather. Perhaps Macgreevy hadn't had a decent breakfast. He suspected all kinds of things, I knew; but he had been no more successful at uncovering a new angle than had any of his more seasoned colleagues at the other newspapers.

I needn't go into detail about the newspaper coverage – the clippings from those days are included with this account, and if they're not there's always the library. Suffice to say, the press had only the bare bones: a murderer desperate to safeguard her role in a republican plot. They never learned of the other intrigue. They never learned of the unpleasantness under the Bow Room lunch table. And, of course, they never learned of the Queen's role (or mine) in the detection. No one involved, no one seated before the fireplace in the Throne Room that day, had a strong reason to get cosy with the press.

Sir Julian Dench resigned his post some safe time after the event so that no one would draw the wrong conclusions. Parliament and press were all hot and bothered about Palace security (again!) during this period, but the Private Secretary's position and his resignation was not thought to be connected to the issue. The Queen was happily rid of him, though. Disposing of him was probably more than half her motive for involving herself in the investigation in the first place. But Sir Julian seemed unharmed by the episode. From time to time I see his name in the papers. He dabbles. And he's still married, at least in name.

Angie left the Palace and had her baby, a girl, which she named – get this – Beatrice Eugenie. I ran into her once coming out of Victoria Station with the baby, which I wish I could say looked the spitting image of Sir Julian, but which looked more like Margaret Thatcher must have looked as an infant, all mad eyes and disagreeable frown. It turned out that her grandmother was quite forgiving about the baby and Angie's lack of marital status, which just reaffirms for me the notion that grandparents behave much differently to their grandchildren than they did to their own children. She was living with her Gran at the time but was in transit. She was mysterious about where. And she looked smashing, turned out in an awfully pricey-looking frock for a Tuesday afternoon in summer, which made me suspect that some money had been withdrawn at some point from Sir Julian's bank account. I never saw her again after that.

Karim I see from time to time, although I think he's never too pleased to see me. With the bequest he received from Robin he set up the shop he claimed he and Robin had planned. It sells all kinds of interesting knick-knacks and gew-gaws and books to do with the theatre. Since it's in Covent Garden, it occasionally falls into my itinerary. Karim only extends me a few words, however, before finding some reason to disappear into the back. It's his sister Meena I talk to. Karim did manage to extract her from the clutches of her suitor after all. I'm not sure what she knows, but she never lets on. And neither do I.

Cyril Wentworth-Desborough found the money and finished his film, *Housesluts and Footpigs* or *The Queen's House*, as it was finally titled, paying homage to the name given to the Duke of Buckingham's residence when King George III bought it for his wife, Queen Charlotte, in 1762. In Canada the documentary was shown on CBC, and I got a flurry of transatlantic phone calls afterwards from friends and relatives. There was one long shot of me pushing a hoover down the Picture Gallery, with the narrator blathering on about what a housemaid's duties are and what our schedules are like and so on. My father was greatly amused by the time I had to get up in the morning. I gather from Neil, whom I still see from time to time, that Cyril's next film project is the House of Lords. This is no surprise, since he is now a member. The Earl of Ulverstone finally went west, on Christmas Day as it happened, and W-Dez got the title. He's also spending time and money trying to prove that the Ulverstones have no connection to Jack the Ripper. He's quite heated about it. A book is in the works. Ripperology continues.

The Tukeses, Katherine and her mother, shut themselves off completely from the whole affair. There were no interviews or quotes in any of the papers; I noted only one picture, a small shot of the two women on an inside page of one of the broadsheets. They were leaving a memorial service in London, Ontario, Katherine looking fiercely at the camera while tugging at the arm of a frail-looking woman, presumably her mother.

Davey Pye remains at the Palace, as do I, and though he was witness to our final gathering he has never, nor would he, as he puts it, betray Mother.

Mother, of course – that is to say, the Queen – is still doing the queen thing: signing legislation, opening Parliament, entertaining Heads of State, putting up with the Prime Minister on Tuesday evenings, travelling about seeing and being seen, advising, encouraging and warning. She even had another opportunity to advise, encourage and warn me. A little over a year later, in the winter, something happened at Sandringham, her country home in Norfolk. We had another adventure. But that's for another writing-up, another day.

And, by the way, that busker I swiped £5 from to buy the Queen some flowers: I was changing trains at Tottenham Court Road one day in the summer and there he was, strumming away on his guitar at the bottom of an escalator. I took a fiver from my bag, bent down and dropped it in his open case. He didn't even look up.